CRAMPTON HODNET

Barbara Pym

WINDSOR
PARAGON

First published 1985
by Macmillan
This Large Print edition published 2012
by AudioGO Ltd
by arrangement with
Little, Brown Book Group

Hardcover   ISBN: 978 1 4458 2829 9
Softcover   ISBN: 978 1 4458 2830 5

British Library Cataloguing in Publication Data available

Printed and bound in Great Britain by
MPG Books Group Limited

INTRODUCTION

Crampton Hodnet is a novel with a most intriguing and unusual title. One's first reaction upon seeing it is to think: 'What on earth can this be about?' Anyone English would suspect straight away that it must be about a picturesque village in one of the rural counties—such a name is on a par with Piddletrenthide, Thornham Parva or Blisworth. The village turns out to be entirely invented, an improvised lie on the part of a clergyman in the novel, who does not want people to know where he has really been. Incidentally, Hodnet is a village in Shropshire, the county in which Pym was born, and Crampton was her middle name.

It may seem strange that a novelist should write a perfectly good novel and then never get round to having it published. Writers often sit on their work like this, however, and it can happen that a book goes through several drafts over a period of twenty years or more. If you feel that it is not quite right, or could be improved, or has missed the tide, it is natural to withhold it and think of reworking it later. Pym seems to have felt that *Crampton Hodnet* had missed the tide.

She began to write it shortly after the outbreak of the Second World War, and had finished it by April 1940. However, she obtained war work in the censor's office in Bristol, and then fled a very painful passion by joining the WRNS, a job that took her to Naples in 1944, where one of the naval officers of her acquaintance became material for the character of Rocky Napier in *Excellent Women*. *Crampton Hodnet* has nothing to do with the war or with the way that the world had suddenly changed, and it must have seemed to Pym to have become an irrelevance. She might have thought of it as juvenilia, or an apprentice-piece. After the war she worked at the International African Institute in London, and edited the journal *Africa*, thus moving her even further away from the little world she had created in her unpublished novel.

Time and taste move on, and nothing travels in the same direction for very long. In retrospect it seems clear that *Crampton Hodnet* sits comfortably beside the six novels that constitute Pym's early career in writing, and that the fact that it seemed dated when first written is no longer relevant seventy years later. The book has not in fact dated. The distance given by time has shifted the perspectives so that what seemed beside the point in 1944 now fits in where it had seemed not to, like a new building erected in an established garden that only looks exactly right many years later.

It is frequently said of Pym that her novels seem slight and even trivial, but actually are not. They are often about genteel people living in straitened circumstances, and there are plenty of Anglican clergy. *Crampton Hodnet* is very specifically set in north Oxford, and the novel will have particular resonance with people who know it, who will immediately be familiar with Magdalen Bridge or the Bodleian Library.

Crampton Hodnet is rescued from obscurity by the fact that it is about characters who immediately become real, and are very human indeed. At least three of them feel that their lives are going nowhere. One is resigned; she is the only one with much common sense or acuity, but she has a lowly opinion of herself, and finds it terribly disillusioning, but also rather entertaining, that an Anglican clergyman can turn out to be a liar. This clergyman wonders whether or not he should settle for second or third best. A don elopes with a student who really does turn out to be 'a cold fish' rather than a last, fabulous, incandescent passion. There are two outrageously camp gay characters who adore spreading scandal and causing trouble; the writing about them is perfectly comic. There is a woman in middle age who no longer gives a damn about either her husband or the metaphysical poets that fired her in youth, and another who sees herself as a kind of *grande patronne*, who really knows what's what and what should be done. What particularly strikes this reader is the sense of stifled and unrequited passion, the unspecific yearnings on the part of people who know that their lives could have been, or still could be, so much more interesting and meaningful. One character does not have the resources or the energy or the courage to do anything about it—perhaps because she is actually quite content as she is. Our eloper does do something grand and ambitious, but it doesn't work out, and he seems fairly relieved after all. His partner in crime, who thinks she has been in love, turns out to be pathetically frightened of what being in love leads to. A third character unexpectedly falls in love, and is exalted in a way that only falling in love can achieve. The characters are pathetic and ridiculous, each in their own way, but Pym's mockery of them is entirely affectionate and her psychology is astute. Her humour is barbed, but sympathetic and ironic, the humour of someone English who sees how peculiar the English are, in particular the English of the unspectacular middle class, who are rather like Oxford, in which 'Everything went on just the same . . . from year to year. It was only the people who might be different. The pattern never varied.'

Crampton Hodnet is a novel with one happy ending and some not-with-a-bang-but-a-whimpers. The reader might be disappointed by these outcomes were it not that the characters themselves seem very satisfied with them, and it is just possible that Miss Morrow might find happiness and satisfaction in the fictional meta-life hereafter, possibly with the curate who replaces Mr Latimer in Miss Doggett's household, and that Anthea will find another Simon, Freddie or Patrick with whom to fall in love. Fortunately the reader's pleasure lies not in the outcomes, but in the reading. The book is crammed with witty aperçus that make me wonder whether Pym had been a fan of Oscar Wilde in her youth. The difference is that Wilde's humour is pointedly outrageous, and Pym's is more subtle and truthful.

I remember English people who were just like these characters, and I still come across them. They are the kind of people who keep the village halls running, volunteer to manage the village shop, work one morning a week in a charity shop, and arrange for someone mildly famous to open the fete. We should always assume that they are full of yearnings and longings, because they almost certainly are. The people might be different, but the pattern never varies.

I think that Pym fell out of fashion for a very long time because new literary tastes developed that seemed to leave her behind. The likes of Kingsley

Amis came along; there were Angry Young Men; the French existentialists were transforming the way that intellectuals perceived the world; there were those who wanted to write about the difficult lives of working class people. Attention shifted away because a new snobbery developed that assumed that genteel people were not real people who led real lives worth exploring, that they were somehow less completely human than others. In particular, tastes became very metropolitan. There was more verbal violence, and humour slowly became more cruel. Characters didn't take muddy walks any more, or worry about whether or not to take the last biscuit, or buy kettles and lampshades from Woolworth's.

As is well known, later in her career Pym found new recognition thanks to support from such writers as Philip Larkin, David Cecil and John Betjeman; Larkin, especially, had massive prestige and was reverently listened to. Pym published her beautiful novels *Quartet in Autumn* and *The Sweet Dove Died*. Her old or unpublished novels were put out by Macmillan, and she enjoyed just two vindicatory years of success before cancer took her away in 1980, when she was in her mid-sixties.

Crampton Hodnet was not published until 1985, but it received instant recognition that might have surprised Pym herself. For the Pym admirer, it was like having a Christmas hamper left in the porch on Boxing Day and finding that it was from a long lost friend who had not forgotten what they liked. I devoured it in the course of two long railway journeys, and when I had finished it I found myself thinking, 'Oh damn,' in a wistful tone of thought. I held it in my hands with a distinct sense of annoyance that the pleasure of reading it had come to an end and, just as you should when you finish a good read, I happily went through it again, trying to find all the best passages—such as Mr Latimer's proposal.

When thinking of a writer's place in the canon, it is sometimes pertinent to ask who the competition is. With some genres, such as fantasy or crime, it is very obvious. With literary fiction you can ask whether someone is in the same arena as Tolstoy or Austen, Cervantes or George Eliot, and so on. If a writer is sufficiently individual, one will not be able to make such assignations, and that is the sign that a writer is not just 'literary', but special. I believe this to be the case with Pym, who is not really like anyone else and did not try to be. She had her very own way of doing things, her own preoccupations which she tackled from different directions, and a voice that is identifiably Pymesque.

That she stuck to her guns all through her wilderness years shows great doggedness and faith in the face of what must have been a terrible period of disappointment, discouragement and self-doubt. A good writer keeps an eye on the world all the time, even when not writing, storing ideas and manuscripts away for later use, even if that 'later' turns out to be many years ahead and there is an intervening desert to cross.

In the case of *Crampton Hodnet*, a whole book got stored away, but now here it is, back in the light after its first publication in 1985, an entertainment that is funny, poignant, observant, and truthful.

Louis de Bernières
2012

NOTE

Barbara Pym began *Crampton Hodnet* just after the outbreak of war in 1939. In spite of wartime tasks, housework and evacuees, it progressed steadily:

18 *Nov.* 1939: Did about 8 pages of my novel. It grows very slowly and is rather funny I think.
22 *Dec.* 1939: Determined to finish my N. Oxford novel and send it on the rounds.

In January 1940 she wrote to her friend Robert Liddell:

I am now getting into shape the novel I have been writing during this last year. It is about North Oxford and has some bits as good as anything I ever did. Mr Latimer's proposal, old Mrs Killigrew, Dr Fremantle, Master of Randolph College, Mr Cleveland's elopement and its unfortunate end . . . I am sure all these might be a comfort to somebody.

The novel was completed and sent to Robert Liddell in April. But before she could send it 'on the rounds' she became more deeply involved in war work and the novel was laid aside.

After the war she looked at it again and made some revisions and alterations, but it seemed to her to be too dated to be publishable. Instead, she concentrated on revising the more timeless *Some Tame Gazelle*, and the manuscript of *Crampton Hodnet* remained among her other unpublished works. Now, for readers in 1985, the period quality adds an extra dimension to the novel.

Crampton Hodnet is one of Barbara's earliest completed novels, and in it she was still feeling her way as a writer. Occasional over-writing and over-emphasis led to repetition, which, in preparing the manuscript for press, I have tried to eliminate. I was greatly helped by Barbara's own emendations (made in the 1950s) and by some notes she made about this novel in her pocket-diary for 1939.

Faithful readers of the novels will welcome the first incarnation of Miss Doggett and Jessie Morrow. It is interesting to see how, in *Jane and Prudence,* she redraws them from a more ironic and more subtle point of view. And it is not impossible that the young Barbara Bird of *Crampton Hodnet* might have grown into the brusque novelist of the later work.

Barbara herself lit upon the exact word to describe this book. It is more purely funny than any of her later novels. So far, everyone who has read the manuscript has laughed out loud—even in the Bodleian Library.

Hazel Holt
London, 1985

SUNDAY TEA PARTY

It was a wet Sunday afternoon in North Oxford at the beginning of October. The laurel bushes which bordered the path leading to Leamington Lodge, Banbury Road, were dripping with rain. A few sodden chrysanthemums, dahlias and zinnias drooped in the flower-beds on the lawn. The house had been built in the sixties of the last century, of yellowish brick, with a gabled roof and narrow Gothic windows set in frames of ornamental stonework. A long red and blue stained-glass window looked onto a landing halfway up the pitch-pine staircase, and there were panels of the same glass let into the front door, giving an ecclesiastical effect, so that, except for a glimpse of unlikely lace curtains, the house might have been a theological college. It seemed very quiet now at twenty past three, and upstairs in her big front bedroom Miss Maude Doggett was having her usual rest. There was still half an hour before her heavy step would be heard on the stairs and her loud, firm voice calling to her companion, Miss Morrow.

It was cold this afternoon, but there would not be a fire in the dining-room until the first of November. A vase of coloured teasels filled the emptiness of the fireplace over which Miss Morrow crouched, listening to the wireless. It was a programme of gramophone records from Radio Luxembourg, and Miss Morrow's hand was on the switch, ready to fade out this unsuitable noise should the familiar step and voice be heard before their time.

Jessie Morrow was a thin, used-up-looking woman in her middle thirties. She had been Miss Doggett's companion for five years and knew that she was better off than many of her kind, because she had a very comfortable home and one did at least meet interesting people in Oxford. Undergraduates came every week to Miss Doggett's Sunday afternoon tea parties, and her nephew, Francis Cleveland, who lived only a few houses away, was a Fellow of Randolph College and a University Lecturer in English Literature.

Miss Morrow, in spite of her misleading appearance, was a woman of definite personality, who was able to look upon herself and her surroundings with detachment. This afternoon, however, she was feeling a little depressed. She shivered and pulled her shapeless grey cardigan round her thin body. She looked out of the window at the dripping monkey-puzzle tree, whose spiky branches effectively kept out any sun there might be. Then, turning back to the wireless, she advanced the volume control so that the music filled the dark North Oxford dining-room and seemed to bring to it some of the warmth and sinful brightness of a continental Sunday. *There's magic in the air* said a smooth, lingering voice against a background of rich, indefinite music. Miss Morrow knew this one. It was chocolates, a programme for Lovers. And then suddenly it went scratchy, and she remembered that it was not really a gay continental Sunday she was listening to but a tired, bored young man sitting in a studio somewhere between Belgium and Germany, putting on innumerable gramophone records to advertise all the many products that thoughtful people had invented to help you to attract your man or get your washing done in half the time.

If I had any strength of character, thought Miss Morrow, I should be able to take a wet Sunday afternoon in North Oxford with no fire to sit by in my stride. I might even take a pleasure in its gloominess and curiously Gothic quality. But such pleasures are only for the very sophisticated who can look on them from a distance without being swamped by them every day of their lives. There were one or two young men who enjoyed Miss Doggett's tea parties and found delight and comfort in the Victorian splendour of her drawing-room, but Miss Morrow did not pretend to be anything more than a woman past her first youth, resigned to the fact that her life was probably never going to be more exciting than it was now. With a sudden twist of her hand she turned off the music. It was degrading to think that she could not take a quiet pride in her resignation and leave it at that. In less than half an hour the undergraduates would begin to arrive, filling the hall with their dripping mackintoshes and umbrellas.

Miss Morrow went quickly upstairs to her large, cold bedroom and put on her dark green marocain dress. The mirror was in an unflattering light. She saw only too clearly her thin neck and small, undistinguished features, her faded blond hair done in a severe knot. There was no time to put powder or a touch of colour on her cheeks for Miss Doggett was already calling her.

'Miss Morrow! Miss Morrow!' she called, her voice rising to a shrill note. 'Where are the buns from Boffin's? Florence says she can't find them. You ought to see to these things. Where did you put them?'

'In the sideboard, in a tin,' shouted Miss Morrow, struggling with the hooks of her dress.

'Which tin?'

'The Balmoral tin.'

'*What?* I can't hear you. Why don't you come down?'

Miss Morrow rushed out of her room looking rather dishevelled. 'I mean the tin with the picture of Balmoral on it,' she explained.

'Oh, here they are, madam,' said Florence. 'I'm sorry, I didn't look in here.'

'Well, hurry up! The young men will be arriving soon,' said Miss Doggett. She was a large, formidable woman of seventy with thick grey hair. She wore a purple woollen dress and many gold chains round her neck. Her chief work in life was interfering in other people's business and imposing her strong personality upon those who were weaker than herself. She pushed past Miss Morrow, who was hovering in the doorway, and entered the drawing-room.

'The fire has been lit for half an hour,' she said, glancing swiftly round the room to see that everything was as she liked it. 'It ought to be quite warm now, but in any case young people don't feel the cold. Nor would older ones if they wore sensible underclothes,' she added in a deliberate tone.

Miss Morrow understood the implication. It concerned a cotton vest which had been found among the laundry four years ago. It had been claimed by Miss Morrow.

'There is no warmth in cotton,' continued Miss

Doggett. 'We would hardly *expect* to find warmth in cotton.'

Miss Morrow felt the reassuring tickle of her woollen underwear and turned away to hide a smile.

The big, cold drawing-room, with its Victorian mahogany furniture and air of mustiness which the struggling fire did nothing to dispel, waited to receive the young people. Miss Doggett moved heavily about the room, arranging chairs and putting out the photographs of Italian churches, the dry-looking engravings of Bavarian lakes and the autographed copy of *In Memoriam* which Lord Tennyson had given to her father, in case any of the young men should be interested in Art.

The bell rang. There was a pause, then the sound of the front door opening and a scuffling in the hall.

Florence announced Mr Cherry and Mr Bompas.

Mr Cherry came, or rather stumbled, into the room. Mr Bompas, with a whispered 'You go first', had pushed him too hard.

'Ah, the first arrivals,' said Miss Doggett, making them feel that they had come too early. 'Your aunt is a very great friend of mine,' she added, turning to Mr Bompas.

'Oh, yes?' said Mr Bompas vaguely. He had a great many aunts and was trying to think which one could have been responsible for this invitation. He was short and thick-set, with fair, bristly hair. He was expected to get his Blue for football. Mr Cherry was thin and mousy with spectacles. He was a thoughtful young man, quite intelligent, but very shy.

Miss Doggett now turned to him. 'Canon Oke wrote to me about *you*,' she said ominously.

5

'Canon Oke?' Mr Cherry waited uncertainly. What was the vicar of his home parish likely to write about him? he wondered. He believed that it could hardly be anything to his discredit.

Miss Doggett paused and said in an impressive tone, 'He told me you were a Bolshevik.'

Mr Cherry was as startled as the others at hearing this violent word, and he was as conscious of its incongruity as applied to himself as he imagined they were. 'I'm a Socialist,' he said shyly. 'I suppose he meant that.'

'Socialist may have been the word he used,' said Miss Doggett, 'but I really see no difference between the two.'

'Oh, yes?' How silly that one couldn't think of a more powerful reply! 'Of course I'm a Socialist!' he ought to have said passionately. 'How can any decent and reasonably intelligent person be anything else?' But he lacked the courage to say this in a North Oxford drawing-room, when they hadn't even started tea.

'What, you a Socialist?' said Mr Bompas. 'Surely you don't go to the Labour Club?'

Mr Cherry, feeling all eyes on him, sat twisting his hands confusedly.

'I think it's so nice to have all these clubs,' said Miss Morrow pleasantly. 'You must find them a great comfort.'

'Comfort?' said Miss Doggett. 'Whatever should young men of nineteen and twenty be wanting with comfort?'

'Well, of course they don't need it in the same way that we do, but surely there is no person alive who doesn't need it in some way,' said Miss Morrow, hurrying over the words as if they might give offence.

'You certainly don't need it when you're dead,' said Mr Bompas cheerfully.

'No, I don't think so,' said Miss Morrow in a dreamy tone. 'I think I should certainly need no comfort if I could know that I should be at rest in my marble vault.'

'I think it is extremely unlikely that you will be buried in a marble vault, Miss Morrow,' observed Miss Doggett in a dry tone.

At that moment Florence opened the door and announced three more guests. First came two beautiful young men, one dark and the other fair. The dark one was carrying a small cactus in a pot.

'Oh, Miss Doggett,' they said, giving the impression of speaking in unison, 'how *wonderful* of you to ask us again! It gives us such *Stimmung* to come here. We've brought you a little present.'

'Oh, Michael and Gabriel, how kind of you!' Miss Doggett stood with the cactus in her hands, looking for somewhere to put it. 'Perhaps you would kindly put it on that little table, Mr Bompas,' she said, handing it to him.

Mr Bompas stood up, awkwardly holding the cactus. As far as he could see, the room was full of little tables, and the tables themselves were covered with china ornaments, photographs in silver frames, shells from Polynesia and carved African relics. Not one of them had room for the little cactus. Was he then to be burdened with it all through the afternoon? he thought with rising indignation and a disgusted look at the young men who had brought it. At last, taking care that nobody saw him, he placed it on the floor between himself and Mr Cherry and sat down again. 'Mind you don't tread on it,' he whispered urgently.

'You must meet each other,' said Miss Doggett. 'Of course Michael and Gabriel are *quite* at home here,' she added, smiling. 'They are in their second year. Whom have you brought with you?' she asked, noticing for the first time another young man, who was still standing in the doorway.

'Oh, we didn't *bring* him,' said Michael. 'He just happened to be coming in through the gate at the same time. But we gave him some words of cheer. Gabriel quoted Wordsworth to him.'

'Yes, I quoted Wordsworth,' said Gabriel, in a satisfied tone.

'Ah, you must be Mr Wyatt,' said Miss Doggett triumphantly. 'Now we can have tea.'

The five young men were now arranged round the room.

Where but in a North Oxford drawing-room would one find such a curiously ill-assorted company? thought Miss Morrow. The only people who seemed really at ease were Michael and Gabriel, but then they were old Etonians, and Miss Morrow was naïve enough to imagine that old Etonians were quite at ease anywhere. They sat giggling at some private joke, while the others made an attempt to start a general conversation.

Mr Wyatt, a dark, serious-looking young man who was reading Theology, asked if anyone had seen the play at the Playhouse that week.

Nobody had.

'I hope that doesn't mean that we shall have nothing to talk about,' said Miss Morrow gravely.

'Now, Gabriel, you like Russian tea, don't you?' said Miss Doggett.

'Yes, he thinks he is a character out of Chekhov,'

8

said Michael. 'He looks perfectly *lovely* in his Russian shirt. He nearly wore it this afternoon, but we thought it wasn't *quite* the thing for North Oxford and we can't *bear* to strike a discordant note, can we, Gabriel?'

'But isn't there something Chekhovian about North Oxford?' said Mr Wyatt unexpectedly. 'I always feel that there is.'

'Yes,' said Miss Morrow, 'but I don't think you feel it when you live here. You lose your sense of perspective when you get too close, and the charm goes.' She said these last words rather hurriedly, hoping that Miss Doggett had not understood their implication.

But Miss Doggett was talking about shirts. 'I think it is just as well to dress conventionally,' she said, 'otherwise I don't know where we should be. I suppose Mr Cherry would be appearing in a *red* shirt.'

'Oh, really? *Do* tell us why.' Michael and Gabriel turned to the unfortunate Mr Cherry, whose face had turned as red as the shirt he might have worn had he not put on his most conventional blue-and-white-striped one.

'I suppose Miss Doggett means because I'm a Socialist,' he said, in a muffled voice.

'*Oh.*' Michael and Gabriel were obviously disappointed at this dull explanation. They were not interested in politics.

'You have nothing to eat, Mr Cherry,' said Miss Morrow, passing him two plates.

He hastily took a chocolate biscuit and then regretted it. When your hands were hot with nervousness, the chocolate came off every time you picked up the biscuit to take a bite. He ought

9

to have thought of that before, but he had been so grateful to Miss Morrow for offering him something that he had eagerly seized the nearest thing. So often at tea parties you had to wait ages before anyone noticed your empty plate, and when your tea had been finished in nervous little sips there was nothing to do but hope and gaze bravely into space.

Mr Cherry surreptitiously wiped his chocolaty fingers on his clean white handkerchief. He wasn't really at ease with people like this, he told himself defensively. He couldn't be expected to have much in common with this old woman and her companion, those two giggling pansies on the sofa, that hearty Bompas or even with Wyatt, the theological student. He wouldn't come here again. Next time he would have a previous engagement.

'Now, Michael, what are you laughing at?' asked Miss Doggett indulgently.

'He wants to see the engravings of the Bavarian lakes,' said Gabriel, 'but he's too shy to ask.'

'I shall be glad to show them to you,' said Miss Doggett. She turned to the others. 'Michael and Gabriel are really interested in *Art*,' she said impressively. 'One so seldom finds that nowadays. I don't mean that hideous stuff *you* call Art,' she said suddenly to Mr Bompas. 'Not those pictures that might just as well hang upside down.'

Mr Bompas, whose pictures, being school groups and photographs of actresses, were of the sort that must of necessity hang right way up, had nothing to say to this.

Miss Doggett sat down between Michael and Gabriel and opened the portfolio of engravings.

The others began some sort of a conversation

10

with Miss Morrow, but it was a poor thing which soon flagged, and eventually the three of them stood up to go.

'But you can't go yet,' said Miss Doggett. 'I've hardly spoken to you.'

'I'm afraid I really must,' said Mr Wyatt. 'We have chapel at six.'

'And Mr Cherry and Mr Bompas, you have chapel too?'

For one fatal second they hesitated and were lost.

'I want to talk to you about your aunt,' said Miss Doggett to Mr Bompas. 'And, Mr Cherry, I think you need some advice from an older person.'

Michael let out a snort of laughter and received a sharp kick on the ankle from Gabriel's elegant suède shoe.

Miss Doggett cleared her throat and said impressively, 'I always think it such a pity when I see young people up here wasting their time in doing something which can only bring disgrace upon their families. All this Socialism and Bolshevism, for instance. If you take my advice, Mr Cherry, you'll have nothing to do with it.'

'I don't see how it can bring disgrace on my family,' said Mr Cherry, with sudden boldness.

'Do you think your mother would like to see you speaking in Hyde Park?' demanded Miss Doggett.

'My mother is dead,' said Mr Cherry, feeling that he had scored a point. 'I was brought up by an aunt.' He smiled. He rather liked the idea of himself speaking in Hyde Park.

'Oh, I see.' Either a natural pity for a motherless boy, or a feeling that bringing disgrace on an aunt was not quite the same thing, stopped Miss Doggett

11

from pursuing the subject any further. 'Join the Conservative Club, if you like,' she said, in a more kindly tone, 'or even the Liberal Club. I am by no means one of those narrow-minded people who condemn *all* forms of political activity.'

'Oh, Miss Doggett, is it *really* so late?' said Michael and Gabriel suddenly. 'How terrible of us to have stayed so long! We were so *engrossed* in dear Lord Tennyson's signature.'

'Yes, it must be nearly half past six,' said Miss Doggett, glancing at the marble clock on the mantelpiece. 'I'm afraid I must send you away now. We are going out to supper at my nephew's house.' The Clevelands would not be having supper before half past seven at the earliest, but Miss Doggett always liked to be there a good three quarters of an hour before that time, so that she could catch the last of the Sunday afternoon guests. It was sometimes interesting to see who stayed longest.

Mr Cherry and Mr Bompas stood up eagerly. Then, to his horror, Mr Bompas heard a crack and felt something scrunch under his foot. It was the little cactus he had told Mr Cherry to be careful about. With elaborate concentration he moved the crushed mass of flower-pot, earth and plant with his foot, until it was hidden behind a footstool embroidered with pansies. The others were so much absorbed in their leave-taking that they did not notice his rather curious movements, as if he were practising dribbling a football.

'I'm afraid we've monopolised you,' said Michael and Gabriel. 'We'll be *really* unselfish and not come to tea again till next term.'

'Oh, Mr Bompas, I meant to have a long talk with you about your aunt,' said Miss Doggett. 'You

12

must come again.'

And so, with many protests and mumbled speeches of thanks from Mr Cherry and Mr Bompas, who seemed to be having a race to see who could get out of the room first, the party broke up.

Miss Doggett followed them out into the hall, but Miss Morrow stayed to put the chairs back into their proper places. First of all she removed the crushed cactus from behind the footstool. It could easily be repotted. She was full of admiration for the skill which Mr Bompas had shown in dealing with the situation. She hadn't believed him capable of it. Perhaps the future held something more for *him* than sitting in a room somewhere in Luxembourg, putting on gramophone records. She really believed that he might go farther than that, and the discovery made her glad and filled her with hope even for herself, so that she walked upstairs humming one of the tunes she had heard earlier in the afternoon.

2

THE CLEVELANDS

At the exact moment when Miss Doggett was walking up the drive to her nephew's house, Anthea Cleveland, his daughter, was being kissed in the library. The light was on and the curtains were not drawn. And so Miss Doggett was able to see Anthea in the arms of Simon Beddoes, who was telling her that although he had not known of her existence

13

before he entered the Clevelands' drawing-room that afternoon, he had fallen desperately in love with her.

He had stayed on talking after the other guests had gone and, pretending an interest in some of her father's seventeenth-century first editions, had contrived that Anthea should show him the library.

Anthea had often been kissed by undergraduates before; indeed, she was the chief reason why the sort of young men who generally avoided North Oxford tea parties would condescend to accept an invitation from the Clevelands. She was a tall, slender girl, with golden hair curling onto her shoulders and a gentle, pretty face, not too intelligent but just right for one whose only occupation in life so far had been to fall in love and be fallen in love with. She was wearing a rather sophisticated peasant dress of blue wool, embroidered with little flowers. Simon liked that. He often went to Kitzbühel for the winter sports.

'Now you're angry with me,' he said in a pleading voice. They usually were at first. 'Please don't be angry,' he said again, with attractive shyness.

He was dark and thin, just a little taller than she was. He had a young, lively face and charming manners. Was it necessary to go through the tedious comedy of being angry? Anthea supposed that she ought to show some kind of disapproval, because it was the first time they had met, and they were standing in a lighted, uncurtained window where anyone might see them. Perhaps, after all, she ought to explain this to him. At least she ought to try. 'Simon,' she began, 'I'm not *angry* . . .'

'You're not angry! *Darling* Anthea.' He kissed her again with even greater confidence. 'You're so sweet.'

'I don't want to be ungracious,' said Anthea at last, 'but we've got people coming to supper, and I must help to get things ready.' She gently pushed him out into the hall.

'But when can I see you again?' he asked urgently. 'I *must* see you tomorrow. I'll call in the morning. Good-bye, darling. I shall think of you every moment till tomorrow,' he called, as he went out of the front door.

It is to be hoped that he has no essay to write, thought Miss Doggett drily, as she came into the hall from the cloakroom, where she had been taking off her coat. She found Anthea gazing thoughtfully at a vase of dahlias which stood on the oak chest.

'Doing the flowers, Anthea?' she said brightly. It was time she found a suitable husband, she thought. It was bad for her to be hanging round Oxford with men too young for her.

'Oh, do go into the drawing-room, Aunt Maude,' said Anthea. 'Father and Mother are there. Haven't you brought Miss Morrow with you?'

'She is coming later. I believe the vicar and his wife are expected, aren't they? They will be able to tell us about the new curate.'

'Yes, I expect they'll be late. Mrs Wardell is so hopelessly unpunctual.' Anthea shepherded her great-aunt into the drawing-room, where the rest of the family were eating up the remains of tea.

Francis Cleveland stood with his back to the fireplace, holding a slice of fruit-cake in his hand. The crumbs dropped onto the carpet as he waved his hand about to illustrate what he was saying. He was a tall, distinguished-looking man in the

15

early fifties, with a thin, sensitive face and dark hair streaked with grey. Young women flocked to his lectures on the seventeenth century. It was a delight for them to hear him read Donne in his rather affected voice, or to smile—not laugh—at his subtle jokes, exactly the same jokes, had they but known it, that had delighted generations of admiring young women. Francis Cleveland was a fortunate man with a comfortable, easy occupation, some private means and nothing to do but give the same lectures and tutorials he had given for the past twenty-five years. When he had any leisure he worked at his book. This was a study of his ancestor, John Cleveland, the poet. He had started it twenty-eight years ago as a thesis for a post-graduate degree. It was not yet finished, and there seemed no prospect that it ever would be.

Margaret Cleveland, who had at one time helped and encouraged her husband with his work, had now left him to do it alone, because she feared that with her help it might quite easily be finished before one of them died, and then where would they be? Francis was like a restless, difficult child if he had nothing to occupy him. This book meant that he spent long hours in his study, presumably working on it. It would not be at all convenient for Mrs Cleveland to have him hanging about the drawing-room, wanting to be amused. After nearly thirty years of married life she had come to take very much for granted the handsome, distinguished husband whom she had once loved so passionately. Indeed, she even thought poor Francis rather a bore sometimes. She was two years older than he was, a sensible, kindly woman, stout and grey-haired, with many interests in her life,

16

although vastly different ones from those of her youth. For now she never thought of seventeenth-century love lyrics but only of her house and daughter and the generations of undergraduates, who sometimes needed her help as a friend or even as a mother.

Miss Doggett sailed majestically into the shabby, comfortable drawing-room. That chintz has faded, she thought with satisfaction; I knew it would. But it's no use telling Margaret anything, she won't listen.

'Margaret,' she said, addressing Mrs Cleveland, 'who was that young man who went just now?'

'Oh, that was Simon Beddoes,' said Mrs Cleveland casually. 'His father used to be British Ambassador in Warsaw, or something like that.'

'Really?' Miss Doggett looked interested and thoughtful. She glanced at Anthea, who seemed a little confused when her father asked her what Simon had thought of the first editions. 'Then he must be the son of Sir Lyall Beddoes, who died a year or two ago,' said Miss Doggett. 'I believe he left a considerable fortune. He was a kinsman on his mother's side of Lord Timberscombe . . .' Miss Doggett wandered on happily. She had a good deal of information from *Debrett* and *Who's Who* tucked away in her head. 'I don't remember who Lady Beddoes was before her marriage. Nobody distinguished, I think. She lives in Chester Square.'

'Well, he seemed to be a very nice boy,' said Mrs Cleveland, as if this was hardly to be expected of young men whose mothers lived in Belgravia.

'He's third year, reading History,' said Anthea, feeling that something was expected of her.

'The vicar and Mrs Wardell,' announced Ellen,

opening the door. 'And Miss Morrow,' she added, as an afterthought.

The Reverend Benjamin Wardell, vicar of St Botolph's, came into the room, followed by his wife, Agnes. He was a short, jolly-looking man, while Mrs Wardell was tall and thin, with a vague expression, and clothes which were untidy through absent-mindedness, rather than from any other cause. She was wearing a smocklike garment of flowered shantung over a blue skirt. On her feet were heavy shoes, the heels caked with mud.

'Margaret, my dear,' she said, looking down at them. 'I've just realised that I've come in my gardening shoes.'

'Were you gardening on a Sunday?' asked Francis Cleveland, in tones of mock disapproval.

'On a Sunday?' repeated Miss Doggett, in a different tone.

'Yes. Do you think it wrong to garden on a Sunday?'

'Well, if your conscience allows you to,' said Miss Doggett gravely.

'My conscience?' Mrs Wardell laughed. 'My husband or his parishioners are far more likely to stop me than my conscience.'

'You are lucky, Mrs Wardell, in having a husband who is something more than just a husband,' said Francis Cleveland.

'I think it's really quite enough for a husband to be just that,' said Mrs Wardell. 'It's certainly a whole-time job, isn't it, Ben?'

'Supper's ready,' said Mrs Cleveland.

'I forgot to put out the beetroot,' said Anthea, hurrying from the room.

'And what would Sunday supper be without

18

beetroot?' said Miss Morrow brightly.

'Ah, Miss Morrow, I didn't notice you,' said Miss Doggett. 'I see that you are here.'

'She can hardly deny that,' said the vicar, chortling with laughter, as he always did at his own jokes.

'I might,' said Miss Morrow. 'A companion is looked upon as a piece of furniture. She is hardly a person at all.'

They went into the dining-room and sat down. Mrs Cleveland carved the cold beef at the sideboard. Mr Cleveland sat staring down at the tablecloth, while Anthea passed round beetroot and potatoes in their jackets.

'I've let Ellen go out,' said Mrs Cleveland apologetically. 'Another of her cousins has come down from Manchester. Why is it always Manchester, I wonder?'

But the others were talking about the new curate.

'His name's Stephen Latimer, and he's got red hair,' said Mrs Wardell. 'I think he's awfully good-looking, don't you, Ben?'

'I can't say that I really noticed,' said her husband. 'He seems an able young man. Quite cultured too, I should think.'

'Where's he going to live?' asked Anthea.

'Ah, that's the point. "Ay, there's the rub", I might say.' Mr Wardell's eyes brightened and he looked rather mysterious. 'He tells me that he doesn't want to be in lodgings but would prefer to live with a family in the parish.'

'I can understand that a cultured young man would wish to live with people of his own class,' said Miss Doggett.

'I don't know if we could have a curate here,' said Mr Cleveland doubtfully, as if it were some strange kind of animal.

'As a matter of fact I was thinking that perhaps, that is just *perhaps*, Miss Doggett might like to have him,' said the vicar, bringing out the words with a rush.

Everyone looked at Miss Doggett doubtfully, but to their surprise she seemed very much taken with the idea.

'Of course I don't pretend to be a young woman,' she declared in a measured tone. 'I don't think I could spend my time running up and down stairs with glasses of hot milk and poached eggs.'

'Oh, I would do that,' broke in Miss Morrow eagerly.

'Well, I hardly think it would be necessary,' said the vicar seriously.

'Oh, Ben, you know it wouldn't be *necessary*,' said his wife, 'but it always happens with curates. Don't you remember Willie Bell?' she added, referring to a former curate who had lodged with a widow and eventually married her.

The vicar looked rather embarrassed. 'I hardly think that this is the same sort of thing,' he said hastily.

'No, Mr Wardell, it is not. Mr Latimer would be quite safe in *my* house,' declared Miss Doggett.

'There are no widows in Leamington Lodge,' said the vicar, in a hearty tone.

'But there are two spinsters,' whispered Anthea to Miss Morrow. 'Surely that's just as dangerous?'

'Won't the poor young man be fussed over at all?' said Mrs Wardell regretfully.

'I can see to his material welfare,' said Miss

20

Doggett, 'and I believe he will find the atmosphere of my house an extremely cultured one.'

Miss Morrow thought of the dining-room on a wet Sunday afternoon, with the rain dripping off the dark branches of the monkey-puzzle, and the bright, jangling music from Luxembourg.

'And,' continued Miss Doggett, 'I shall be able to keep an eye on him—insofar as that is necessary in one of his profession.'

3

A SAFE PLACE FOR
A CLERGYMAN

The Reverend Stephen Latimer's first sight of Leamington Lodge was on an October evening. Preparations were already being made for the Fifth of November, and there was a smell of fireworks in the air. Ever afterwards this smell reminded him of his arrival in Oxford. The street lamps were already lit, and the Victorian-Gothic house looked mysterious and romantic in the misty half-light. Its ugliness was softened and the monkey-puzzle and the dingy laurels were blurred masses of darkness.

Miss Morrow heard the scrunch of feet on the red gravel but took no notice of it. Mr Latimer was not expected until seven. Miss Doggett, who had gone out to tea, was coming back at six. It was now only half past five.

Miss Morrow was in her bedroom putting rouge on her cheeks. She was experimenting. She had read that if you put the rouge far out on the cheek-bones, and smoothed it in carefully so that no hard line showed, it gave roundness to a thin face. A touch on the chin was another trick, but it didn't say what that gave. She had got as far as putting on some lipstick, and two large dabs of rouge on her cheeks and a smaller one on her chin, when Florence tapped at the door.

'Please, Miss Morrow, I'm sorry to disturb you,' she said, 'but Mr Latimer is here.'

'Mr Latimer here, *now*?' echoed Miss Morrow incredulously. She spoke with her back turned, so that Florence should not see her face. 'Well, tell him I'll be down in a minute. Miss Doggett wasn't expecting him till seven.'

'No, miss, but the sheets are on the bed,' said Florence virtuously. 'I'll tell him what you say.'

I don't suppose he'll want to go to bed at half past five, thought Miss Morrow, who was now in a flurry of agitation. There was no time to change her dress, but she washed her hands and sprinkled herself lavishly with Parma Violet, as if to make up for it. Then, with her handkerchief, she scrubbed at her lips and cheeks, but the cosmetics she had used were of an indelible brand, and while the scrubbing took some of it off, it by no means removed all of it. This was especially noticeable with the lips. Miss Morrow thought, with sudden shame but also with some amusement, of the advertisement on the little card to which the lipstick had been fixed. Something about your lips never having looked so tempting. How humiliating it was to be caught out in such folly! She assured herself that nothing had been further from her mind than the idea of tempting anyone. The very possibility of Jessie Morrow's tempting anyone was so ludicrous that it

22

made her feel like blushing.

At last, when she had ruined a white linen handkerchief and removed what seemed to her nearly all the unnatural colouring, she hurried downstairs. Whatever would Miss Doggett say, she wondered, when she discovered that Mr Latimer had arrived nearly two hours too early? Miss Morrow felt that in some inexplicable way she would be blamed for it, and so her greeting of Mr Latimer when she entered the drawing-room lacked warmth; indeed, it was hardly a greeting at all.

'I don't know what Miss Doggett will say,' she burst out in a breathless voice. 'She isn't here yet.'

Stephen Latimer, who had been prodding the little cactus with his finger, turned round, rather taken aback by this welcome. It was not at all what he was accustomed to. Women usually gushed with delight when they met him. He saw a thin, fair woman standing in the doorway, nervously clasping her hands. She had very bright eyes and such a high colour on her cheeks and lips that for a moment he wondered if it could be natural. But then he told himself that his suspicions were ridiculous. She didn't look at all the sort who would use make-up. By instinct and from experience he distrusted all women under the age of fifty and some over it, for he was an attractive man with a natural charm of manner and had been much run after. Once, indeed, he had even got himself caught in the tangles of an engagement, so that before he knew what he was doing he found himself strolling with a young woman before the windows of Waring and Gillow, looking at dining-room suites. But fortunately they had not got beyond looking, although there had been some unpleasantness and nearly a breach of promise case. He turned hastily from these uncomfortable recollections and was thankful that he had chosen to live with an old lady and her companion in North Oxford, where he hoped he would be safe from the advances of designing women. He did not imagine that many such would call at Leamington Lodge.

'I'm terribly sorry,' he said easily, 'but I found myself catching an earlier train, and I thought I could probably leave my luggage here, even if you weren't ready for me.'

'Oh, we are ready, really,' said Miss Morrow, remembering the sheets on the bed. 'But Miss Doggett isn't here,' she added hopelessly. She was quite taken aback at the sight of Mr Latimer. Mrs Wardell had told them about his red hair, but it was auburn, really, and so thick. He was tall, too, with broad shoulders, and yet he didn't look like the Rugger Blue type, who would preach about the Game of Life.

'Well, as you're here, I'd better show you your room,' she said doubtfully, still thinking of Miss Doggett.

'Thank you, that would be very kind.'

Miss Morrow led the way upstairs. She knew that she was doing a wicked thing, but she quieted her conscience by reminding herself that she could hardly be blamed for Mr Latimer's early arrival, and that she could hardly have refused to see him until Miss Doggett came back.

'Your room faces the garden,' she said, 'and you can look away into the distance. It gives one such a feeling of space. The rooms are very big,' she added hastily, 'but you know what I mean. It takes you out of yourself, beyond all this.' With a wave of her

24

hand she seemed to indicate the landing, with its dark turkey carpet and indefinite oil paintings.

'Yes, I suppose we do occasionally need taking out of ourselves,' said Mr Latimer thoughtfully, as if the idea had not occurred to him before.

'I think you will find it so when you have lived here a bit,' said Miss Morrow without elaboration.

Mr Latimer laughed. 'Oh, well, if I find I want it as much as all that I can always go somewhere else,' he said.

'Yes, of course,' said Miss Morrow in a disappointed tone. She felt as if she had offered him a precious possession and had it thrown back at her.

They were standing in the room now.

'This is the study and the bedroom leads out of it. I feel like a landlady doing all this,' said Miss Morrow, anxious to make bright, normal conversation.

'Well, it seems very comfortable,' said Mr Latimer, looking round at the reassuringly Victorian room with its good, solid furniture. He glanced approvingly at the hard, uninviting-looking sofa. Hardness and uninvitingness were, he felt, just those qualities which the sofa in the study of a bachelor clergyman should possess. No chance of amorous dalliance here. It was too narrow and slippery. He went over to the enormous roll-top desk. 'I can see myself writing sermons here,' he said. 'The dark green walls are so restful. The curtains too'—he touched their dull, stuffy folds—'so very soothing. What's the tree growing outside the window? A monkey-puzzle?'

'Yes,' said Miss Morrow. 'There's one on the front lawn too. It shuts out the sun,' she added in a faint voice. Surely it wasn't natural that a good-looking young man should *want* to shut himself up in a prison, even if he *was* a clergyman? 'The bedroom is through here,' she said, opening a door. 'I believe it has all the usual conveniences. Miss Doggett insisted that the largest washstand in the house should be put here. I don't know why.'

'There is supposed to be some connection between cleanliness and godliness,' said Mr Latimer, making a curately joke. 'It's certainly a magnificent piece of furniture. I think its presence is justified simply because of that.'

'Yes,' agreed Miss Morrow. '"A thing of beauty is a joy for ever". It reminds me of the altar of Randolph College chapel. So much marble and mahogany.'

'What's this engraving?' said Mr Latimer, going to the wall.

'Oh, that's one of the Bavarian lakes,' explained Miss Morrow. 'Miss Doggett has a whole set of them. This is the biggest.'

'What a very dry-looking lake it is,' said Mr Latimer thoughtfully. 'One can't imagine that the water could ever be wet.'

They both laughed. Mr Latimer sat down by Miss Morrow on the bed. They were still laughing when Miss Doggett came in. The sound of their laughter was the first thing that she heard before the shameful sight met her eyes: the sight of Miss Morrow—painted like a harlot—sitting laughing on the bed with a handsome clergyman whom she had just met for the first time, the new curate whose welcome Miss Doggett had planned so carefully. It was too bad. Miss Doggett cast about in her mind for words strong enough to describe Miss Morrow's

26

perfidy and deceit, but could find none.

It was certainly a bad beginning, and nobody was more conscious of this than Miss Morrow. But Mr Latimer leapt up entirely without embarrassment. His natural, easy manners made the washstand, its rose-garlanded china and the large double bed seem no more out of place than the ordinary furniture of a North Oxford drawing-room. Miss Doggett, who had so far said nothing but a rather cold 'Good evening', was completely pacified by his profuse apologies for having arrived earlier than was expected. He very tactfully made no reference to Miss Morrow, thus giving the impression that although he had indeed arrived, he had not yet been welcomed. And so Miss Doggett found herself with something definite to do and began showing him the rooms all over again.

Miss Morrow slipped away to her bedroom and began scrubbing at her cheeks and lips with the already ruined handkerchief. Completely indelible, it had said in the advertisement; won't come off when you're eating, smoking or being kissed. I suppose if I had suddenly kissed Mr Latimer, she thought detachedly, it would have left no mark. She went to the washstand. Surely soap and water would remove it? Ten minutes later she went downstairs, her face flushed and shining, but flushed only because she had had to rub so hard with her soapy face flannel. She hoped Miss Doggett hadn't noticed. But Miss Doggett was quite taken up with Mr Latimer and did not see her companion until she was sitting in a chair on the edge of the room.

'Ah, Miss Morrow, I was wondering where you were,' she said, turning her head. 'I wanted you to hold my wool.' She produced a rough navy skein, which was to be knitted up into a balaclava helmet for a seaman.

Fierce was the wild billow,
Dark was the night,

thought Miss Morrow, as she arranged the wool on her hands.

Wail of the hurricane
Be thou at rest.

Some versions had 'Wail of Euroclydon', which was much grander. Surely Mr Latimer ought to be holding the wool? Wasn't it one of the chief functions of curates, or had she been misinformed? It was just another of those small disillusionments which make up our everyday life on this earth, she decided.

'Do you like a hot water bottle at night, Mr Latimer?' asked Miss Doggett. 'And do you prefer China or Indian tea? A fire will be lit in your room every morning, of course.'

But it's only the twenty-eighth of October, thought Miss Morrow indignantly. So this is how it's going to be. She glanced at Mr Latimer, who sat like a handsome, complacent marmalade cat, telling Miss Doggett all his little fads. I'm certainly not going to fuss over him, thought Miss Morrow, jerking the wool vigorously round her thumbs; *I* won't wait on him.

While Miss Morrow was steeling herself to resist Mr Latimer's charms, Miss Doggett was telling him about the inhabitants of North Oxford and her own relations in particular. She became quite coy and

28

skittish about Anthea's romance.

'I happened to go into the drawing-room yesterday evening,' she said, 'and there were the young people sitting on the sofa, very far apart and *rather* pink in the face. Of course *I* knew what they'd been up to. We're only young once, aren't we?' She wagged her finger at Mr Latimer, who seemed to draw back a little.

Miss Morrow, too, was surprised. Miss Doggett usually disapproved of young people, especially of girls who 'made themselves cheap', as she called it. But of course, reflected Miss Morrow, it all depended on who was at the other end of the sofa, so to speak. If it was the only son of a sometime British Ambassador in Warsaw, whose mother lived in Belgravia, who took you to expensive restaurants and bought you orchids and whose college battels each term would have kept somebody like Miss Morrow clothed for many years, then Miss Doggett adopted a come-kiss-me-sweet-and-twenty attitude and observed that we are only young once. But supposing it had been a young man from one of the poorer colleges, who came from Huddersfield and had a state scholarship and wouldn't wear suède shoes even if he could afford them? Supposing they had been sitting together, holding hands by the light of a gas-fire in a dreary room in one of the more remote streets leading off the Cowley Road, talking seriously about their future? Miss Morrow could see the room, the gas-fire flickering and popping, the table with its red or green baize cloth piled high with mathematical textbooks or Latin authors, while in Simon's rooms in Randolph College, the table was strewn with bills, invitations to luncheons and sherry parties, and even love letters. Or so Miss

29

Morrow, who was highly imaginative, pictured it.

'. . . son of the late British Ambassador in Warsaw,' she heard Miss Doggett saying to Mr Latimer. 'A brilliant young man. I think dinner is ready now. I hope you can take veal?'

They walked into the dining-room, talking happily about dyspepsia. Miss Morrow followed, feeling rather young and sprightly.

After dinner there was more wool-winding and some general conversation about Italian churches, central heating, ravioli, the unemployed, winter underclothes, plainsong chants and various other subjects, which seemed to follow each other quite easily. At ten o'clock they retired to bed.

Good, thought Mr Latimer, as he climbed into the high, wide bed, laden with far too many bedclothes; there was a bedside lamp. He had so often in his life had to patter across cold linoleum in bare feet to turn off a light by the door. He believed that he was going to be very comfortable here. Of course Miss Doggett made a fuss of him, as all women did, but he rather liked this, as long as he wasn't expected to give anything in return except the politeness and charm which came to him without effort. And, after all, what else could he be expected to give to an old woman of seventy? He liked the companion too, an amusing, sensible little woman, who wasn't likely to throw her arms round his neck, for poor Mr Latimer had experienced even that. His last thought before he went to sleep was that he liked Leamington Lodge.

In the Clevelands' house nobody was asleep, although they were all in bed. Francis Cleveland was shouting through the communicating door to his wife's room that he had a new pupil called

30

Barbara Bird, who had written a remarkably fine essay on the love poems of John Donne.

Mrs Cleveland made some suitable remark and then went back to her calculations about eggs for pickling. They seemed to get through such a lot of everything with these young men always coming to the house. And even when they were in love with Anthea they seemed to have enormous appetites.

Anthea was lying in bed on her stomach, with her face buried in the pillow. She was, as usual, thinking about Simon, with whom she had been out that evening. She was wide awake and it was no use trying to go to sleep, because even in the dark she saw his bright eyes looking at her. She tossed and turned and then lay on her back, regretting that these romantic evenings with much wine always made one so frightfully thirsty afterwards. She gulped down two glasses of water, then went to the window and leaned out. 'Is he thinking about me?' she whispered to the night, solemnly blowing kisses in what she imagined was the direction of Randolph College, but which was actually, and most unsuitably, the nearest way to a seminary for Roman Catholic priests.

Simon was not thinking about her. He was lying happily awake in his college bedroom, going over a speech he hoped to make at the Union debate on Thursday. Of course he adored Anthea, but 'Man's love is of man's life a thing apart', especially when he is only twenty and has the ambition to become Prime Minister.

4

MISS BIRD

'Now, Miss Morrow, you ought to be in your place at the stall,' said Miss Doggett sharply, moving about the room giving orders. Every year she made herself the chief figure at the winter Sale of Work, although she did little to help in the preparations beyond knitting a few garments out of inferior wool or sending a quantity of junk out of her house.

This afternoon she was a regal figure in maroon with a skunk cape, quite alarming in her magnificence, although every woman had smartened herself up a little for the occasion. Even Miss Nollard and Miss Foxe, two dim North Oxford spinsters, were wearing new hats, and Miss Nollard's hair looked suspiciously as if it had been waved. Only Mrs Wardell remained reassuringly the same. Everyone knew that the curiously out-of-season straw hat she wore was only her old garden hat trimmed with a bunch of cherries from Woolworth's, and some with sharper eyes were able to notice that the cherries had been sewn on with greenish darning wool, probably left in the needle after she had finished darning the vicar's socks.

This year Mr Latimer was the chief attraction at the sale, and his presence helped them to forget that they had not been able to get anybody distinguished to open it and so had been obliged to fall back on Mrs Cleveland, who was always very ready to do anything she could, and whose husband *looked* very distinguished, even though he was only a Fellow of Randolph College.

She performed the opening ceremony swiftly and competently. As she had forgotten to ask what the sale was in aid of and there seemed to be no clues anywhere, she was not able to give any really convincing reasons why people should spend their money on the not very attractive things displayed on the stalls. But she was a conscientious woman and did her best, and when she had made her speech she walked round in her best lizard-skin shoes, which hurt her corn, and bought a great deal of jam and cake—always useful for the Sunday tea parties—and as many other things as she thought could possibly be used in any way. But no crowd of obsequious church workers followed her, as is usual on such occasions. All the women who were not serving at the stalls were occupied elsewhere. They were clustering round Mr Latimer.

Miss Morrow, who was somewhere at the outer edge of the throng surrounding him, watched him with dispassionate interest. His smooth remarks came as easily as if he had put on a gramophone record, she thought. He praised everything on every stall, tasted every different variety of home-made cakes, sweets and even jam, and had a compliment ready for every lady who asked him, as many did, how he liked her dress.

Miss Morrow would never have dreamed of asking a man such a question, she had for so long now worn the sort of clothes about which nobody could possibly say anything complimentary without telling lies. Her clothes were no more than drab coverings for her body. How do you like this grey jumper suit, Mr Latimer, with its sagging cardigan and dowdy-length skirt? How do you like this felt hat of the sort of grey-beige which goes with everything and nothing? How do you like this blouse which I bought in Elliston's Sale two years ago because it was, and still is, that shade of green which even the prettiest girl can't get away with?

But Mr Latimer was glad when, by some movement of the crowd, he found himself next to Miss Morrow. If he had analysed his feelings he would have realised that he turned to her with relief, as one does to a person with whom one need not make conversation. But there was no personal quality in his feeling for her. He regarded her simply as a man might regard a comfortable chair by the fire, where he can sit with his slippers on and a pipe in his mouth.

Miss Morrow felt this, but it did not worry her. Inanimate objects were often so much nicer than people, she thought. What person, for example, could possibly be so comforting as one's bed? And although she hardly dared to imagine that he thought as highly of her as of his bed, she was nevertheless conscious of a certain easy relationship between them which pleased her. She knew that they both had the same opinion of Miss Doggett, although they never actually spoke of her. Mr Latimer's coming to Leamington Lodge had certainly brought pleasure into their lives, and Miss Doggett had less time to nag at her companion now that she had a curate to dote upon.

'How much longer will it last?' he asked in a low voice. 'It's five o'clock now.'

'It will last as long as *you* stay here,' said Miss Morrow. 'Surely you can see that?'

Mr Latimer heaved a scarcely perceptible sigh. 'Do you think that if a thunderbolt suddenly fell out

34

of the sky onto this hideous embroidered tea cosy it would end then?' he asked.

'The tea cosy would be spoilt and nobody would be able to buy it, but why should the Sale of Work end?' said Miss Morrow.

'Are there no sick people I ought to visit?' asked Mr Latimer hopefully.

'There are no sick people in North Oxford. They are either dead or alive. It's sometimes difficult to tell the difference, that's all,' explained Miss Morrow.

'Oh, Mr Latimer,' said an eager don's wife, 'you must have a pair of these bed-socks. They'll save your life if you ever sleep in a cold, damp bed.'

'Or in a cold, open field with the raggle-taggle gipsies O?' laughed Mr Latimer, putting on his gramophone record. 'They are beautifully knitted.'

'Are you interested in Morris dancing?' asked somebody else.

'Have you tried my chocolate cake?'

'You *must* come to supper on Sunday night!'

And so it went on. Mrs Cleveland decided to go home. She would be conferring no honours on the eager church workers by making conversation or taking tea with them, and nobody minded or even noticed when she hurried away to change her uncomfortable shoes and have tea in her own drawing-room.

As she went in through her gate she saw a young woman, wearing a scholar's gown over a wine-red tweed suit, propping up her bicycle against the laurel bushes. That must be Miss Bird going for a tutorial with Francis, she thought intelligently. What a pretty girl she is.

'Do come into the drawing-room and get warm,'

said Mrs Cleveland pleasantly, as they went into the house together. 'It isn't quite half past five yet.'

Barbara Bird followed her. As always before her tutorial she had that half-terrifying, half-thrilling shakiness at the knees and a sinking feeling inside. Her hands, clutching her essay on 'What seem to you to be the main features of the Metaphysical style in poetry?', were damp with sweat. But as she entered the drawing-room she seemed outwardly composed, a tall, dark girl with beautiful eyes who looked somehow older than her twenty years.

'Do sit down,' said Mrs Cleveland, moving a bundle of Anthea's dressmaking off the sofa. 'I'm sorry this room's so untidy, but somehow it always is, especially when anyone calls. You know how it is,' she laughed.

Barbara laughed too. If only Mrs Cleveland weren't quite so nice, she thought. And yet she obviously wasn't the right wife for Francis. She was older than he was and didn't seem to be any sort of an intellectual companion to him. One couldn't imagine them reading poetry together, she thought, this being her main idea of a happy marriage.

'Have you time for a cigarette?' asked Mrs Cleveland, offering a packet of Gold Flake.

'Thank you, I have a few minutes,' said Barbara, thinking that a cigarette might be a good thing to steady her nerves. 'I believe Mr Cleveland has somebody else before me this evening.'

'Yes, it's Michael or Gabriel. I never can remember which is which, except that one is dark and the other fair. They always say exactly the same sort of things.'

Barbara sat on the edge of the sofa and smoked nervously. At last there was a knock at the door and

Michael bounded into the room. 'Oh, Birdikin,' he said, addressing Barbara, 'do go quickly and soothe poor Mr Cleveland. I hadn't done my essay and he was *heartbroken*. He needs womanly comfort.'

If only he really did need me, thought Barbara, who had indulged in all the usual dramatic dreams about saving his life or ministering to him when he was romantically ill. She collected her things and started on the familiar walk to his study. Past the oak chest with the flowers in a pewter jug—bronze chrysanthemums today—and the willow-pattern plates on the wall behind it, round the little bend, then up the stairs with the worn beige carpet, whose tread had to be altered every spring because it was wearing so thin. Along the little passage where Mrs Cleveland had hung all the pictures they didn't like but couldn't give away for fear of offending the donors, and then there was the study door, and behind it Mr Cleveland—Francis—was waiting to stand up and say 'Good evening, Miss Bird, and what have you got for me today?'

Barbara reminded him of the subject of her essay and sat down.

'Oh, yes. Well, let's hear what you've made of it.'

He always said this and then waited for her to read. Sometimes he sat in a chair smoking a cigarette, or paced about the room, or stood and looked out of the window. Today he stood with his back to her, looking out of the uncurtained window at the Banbury Road, with its ceaseless stream of dark, shining cars.

Barbara began to read in a clear, colourless voice. Not even when she read the lines of Donne that always made her think of her tutorials –

For love all love of other sights controls,
And makes one little room an everywhere

– did she show any feeling.

She finished reading and there was a pause. 'That's all,' she said, her voice trembling a little. This was the worst moment of the whole evening, when the essay was finished and she was waiting for his verdict. Her mouth was dry inside and she could feel her heart beating. Her eyes strayed nervously round the room, noticing little things which had suddenly become important. An invitation card on the mantelpiece, a volume of Saintsbury's *Caroline Poets* upside down in a bookcase, some cake crumbs on the desk, a cobweb in one corner of the ceiling. She looked up at Francis in desperation.

He was completely taken aback. At one moment she had been no more than one of the better-looking young women, who had just read him an extremely good essay, and then suddenly he found her beautiful dark eyes looking at him in such a way that he was startled into asking himself how long it was since any woman had looked at him like that. He thought of his colleagues in the Senior Common Room at Randolph: old Dr Fremantle, Lancelot Doge, Arthur Fenning, Arnold Penge . . . One couldn't imagine a woman gazing at any of *them* in such a way.

Francis felt rather pleased with himself and leaned forward a little, as if to make some attempt at returning the passionate glance. But, as so often happens, the moment had passed. He was too late. Barbara was looking down at her hands now, examining her nail polish with a critical frown.

'Well, Miss Bird,' he said, feeling rather flat, 'that

38

was a slippery subject, wasn't it, but you grasped it pretty well. Yes, pretty well,' he repeated, trying to remember what the essay had been about.

'I'm glad it was all right,' said Barbara, her voice faint with relief now that the tension was broken.

'There are one or two points that we might discuss,' he went on, as the subject of the essay came back to him. 'But have a cigarette.' He pushed the box towards her. 'The yellow ones are Russian; people seem to like them.'

Barbara took just any cigarette and lit it, her hands still trembling a little. She always enjoyed the discussion which followed her essay. It was the one time when she and Francis seemed to have so much in common, she thought simply.

That look, he thought, making mechanical jokes about Wordsworth's colloquialisms; had he imagined it? If he had, he must be getting peculiar in some way. Elderly or middle-aged dons were known to be peculiar. But she was a very beautiful girl. Why had he never noticed that before? It had somehow never occurred to him that there *were* beautiful female undergraduates. Well, now you know, said a chirpy voice inside him. What are you going to do about it?

5

THE VICAR OF
CRAMPTON HODNET

It was the last Sunday of Michaelmas term. Mr
Cherry was sitting happily in the Clevelands'
drawing-room, telling a sympathetic audience about
his political views. How different coming to tea
here was from going to Miss Doggett's! he thought.
People were listening to him as if even a Socialist
had a right to his own opinion, and one young man
in corduroy trousers was actually agreeing with him.
The only person who wasn't listening was Anthea,
and she kept fidgeting and looking at the clock until
at last, just before six, she got up and slipped quietly
from the room.

Going to see Simon, thought Mrs Cleveland. Of
course it would never do to say anything, mothers
nowadays knew nothing, absolutely *nothing*, but she
couldn't help thinking it rather a pity that Anthea
saw so much of Simon. Of course he was a *nice* boy,
she hadn't really anything against him, except the
vague fear that he might make Anthea unhappy.
It would be so much better if they could just be
friends, thought Mrs Cleveland, peering anxiously
into the teapot and hoping that nobody would ask
for more tea, though young women nowadays didn't
seem to be content with that. It was either being in
love or nothing. After all, Anthea was only nineteen
and there were in Oxford so many other more
suitable people. A vague company of dull but steady

men rose up before the anxious mother's eyes, young dons who wouldn't at all mind acquiring a wife so long as the courting and marrying of her didn't disturb their research in the Bodleian. It was an excellent thing for a husband to have something like research to occupy his time. After the first year or two of married life one no longer wanted to have him continually about the house. Mrs Cleveland hardly noticed now whether her husband was there or not, and she was too busy doing other things ever to stop and ask herself whether she was not perhaps missing something. The best she could say of Francis was that he gave her no trouble, and she thought that that was a great deal more than could be said of many husbands.

But Anthea, hurrying along St Giles', could hardly be expected to have arrived at this enviable state of 'calm of mind all passion spent'.

This evening, she thought solemnly, as she stepped into the lodge of Randolph College, we won't spend all our time lying on the sofa. I'll show Simon I'm *intelligent*. We'll really talk about something. She wasn't sure what—perhaps the Foreign Policy of His Majesty's Government, she thought, stepping into a puddle and splashing her stocking. That was the sort of thing they were always debating at the Union. She reached the bottom of the staircase where Simon's rooms were and started to climb the worn stone steps. She stood for a moment outside the doorway with his name painted over the top, knocked, went in, and the next thing she knew she was in his arms.

The room was dark except for the glow of the fire, for Simon understood the value of a romantic atmosphere. He was also a very tactful young man and had put away all his photographs except those of his mother, his aunt Constance and his friend Christopher. Outside in St Giles' it was raining, and the comforting sound of the Salvation Army band playing hymns made a dear and familiar Sunday evening background for lovers. At this hour time seemed to stand still. In the half-darkness Anthea could see the *Sunday Times* spread out on the floor. A flame leapt up in the fire and illuminated the headlines. Something about the Foreign Policy of His Majesty's Government.

The Salvation Army went on playing half-recognised hymns, the rain fell softly but steadily, and from different parts of Oxford came the sound of the various bells calling people to evensong. After a time the smell of cooking rose up in the quadrangle of Randolph College, rough young voices were heard down below and on the stairs, and a bell began to ring, a loud bell that disturbed the young men and the young women who had come to tea with them. Lights were turned on to reveal the happy lovers blinking like ruffled owls, the honey toast lying cold and greasy on a plate in the fireplace, the tomato sandwiches curled up at the edges, and the Fuller's walnut cake a crumbly mess because it had been roughly cut by inexperienced hands.

Anthea and Simon got up from the sofa and stood looking out of the window at the wet, shining quadrangle, crowded now with hurrying figures in gowns.

'Simon!' called a loud raucous voice from below. 'Are you coming into hall?'

'Oh, God, it's Christopher,' said Simon, looking down at a group of young men under his window.

He drew Anthea into a more prominent position and kissed her hand. He was the only one of his set who had a young woman in love with him.

The young men shuffled off, and Simon and Anthea went downstairs and out into the street. They walked along holding hands and looking into each other's eyes, completely unconscious that there were other people on the pavement.

Thank goodness for love, thought Miss Morrow, as she slipped past them, with a hand up to shield her face.

'That was Anthea Cleveland and her young man,' she explained to Mr Latimer, who was walking just behind her. 'I think we'd better slip along Parks Road. We're less likely to see anyone there.'

'All right, though Parks Road is usually so deserted that if we *do* meet anyone we know they're all the more likely to notice us,' said Mr Latimer.

'What a good thing the vicar was preaching tonight,' said Miss Morrow, hurrying along. 'Though of course he'll wonder what's happened to you.'

'I wonder what I ought to tell him,' said Mr Latimer thoughtfully.

'Why, the truth, of course,' said Miss Morrow, as if the possibility of a clergyman's doing anything else had not occurred to her.

'The truth?' said Mr Latimer doubtfully.

'Yes, I think he'd understand. Say that you took advantage of Miss Doggett's being away from home to go for a walk on Shotover. That you walked right over the other side and then discovered that you couldn't possibly get back by half past six, even if you got a bus straight away. And then no buses seemed to come and it started to rain and it was seven o'clock before you were back in Oxford,' Miss Morrow finished up triumphantly.

'But it sounds so silly. It makes me out to be such a feeble, inefficient sort of creature,' said Mr Latimer, protesting.

'Well, men *are* feeble, inefficient sorts of creatures,' said Miss Morrow calmly, 'but you can lay the blame on me if you like. Women are used to bearing burdens and taking blame. I have been blamed for everything for the last five years,' she continued, 'even for King Edward VIII's abdication.'

'Oh, I can't bring *you* into this,' said Mr Latimer, in a shocked tone of voice.

'Why ever not?' asked Miss Morrow, genuinely surprised.

'Well . . .' Mr Latimer hesitated. 'There might be a scandal. People might talk. You know what I mean,' he went on quickly, sensing a mocking quality in her silence. 'When people think of us walking about on Shotover Hill in the *dark* they might easily take it the wrong way.'

'But it wasn't dark then,' said Miss Morrow, aggravatingly literal. 'It didn't get dark till we were on the road trying to get a bus. You really have the most curious ideas. If you think anyone could make up a scandal about *me*, you flatter me.'

'No, I don't,' he said with sudden irritation. 'I'm only looking at the facts and imagining how other people might interpret them. You can't be so unworldly as to be ignorant of what I mean.'

'I still think you flatter me,' said Miss Morrow, striding along with her arms full of berries and branches. 'Companions to old ladies are supposed to be essentially unworldly. To imply the contrary

44

is surely a compliment. It conjures up pictures of silver fox furs, and perfumes to suit every occasion, and reading *Vogue* instead of the *Church Times*.'

Mr Latimer could hardly help smiling at this, but he was still annoyed with Miss Morrow for not seeing his point of view. An unmarried clergyman could never be too careful, and he had already had a good deal of experience of the consequences of the very slightest indiscretion. He had thought Miss Morrow so very safe and sensible, essentially the sort of person who could be relied upon to do the right thing. Was she going to turn out like all the others? Was she going to noise it about North Oxford that *she* had been the cause of the curate's non-appearance at evensong? For it *had* really been her fault, he told himself, working up his feelings against her. She had said that she knew the way back and how long it took, and where and when one could get a bus. Perhaps she had deliberately trapped him, he thought, getting more and more angry; perhaps she hoped that she was going to catch him. His mouth set in a firm line and he walked on without speaking.

'Do you honestly imagine,' said Miss Morrow, quickening her step to catch up with him, 'that Miss Doggett would have left us alone together in the house if she had thought that anyone could *possibly* think anything of it? She herself would be the first person to make a scandal; she always is. And yet she goes and leaves us together in the house. What do you think of that?'

'Well, she couldn't have taken me to Tunbridge Wells,' said Mr Latimer obstinately. 'I'm not a pet dog.'

Miss Morrow felt that she wanted to giggle. 'And

45

she never takes me because she moves in rather high society there, and she likes to leave somebody at home to see that the servants behave and don't poke among her things. So it was quite natural that she should leave us both. I really think you're making an unnecessary fuss.'

'Well, I didn't start it,' said Mr Latimer crossly.

'And I'm sure I didn't,' said Miss Morrow. 'Anyway, nobody will ever know about it unless *you* tell them. I only said you could blame me if you wanted to.'

'We're getting into the Banbury Road,' said Mr Latimer suddenly. 'It seems to be full of people. I suppose I ought to go into church. I shall only have missed about three quarters of an hour.'

'*Only* three quarters of an hour!' Miss Morrow said. 'You're so anxious to conceal your movements, and then you suggest going into church in the middle of the service! Why, it would cause a sensation. Every member of the congregation would wonder where you'd been, whereas if you don't go in, nobody but the vicar will know that you ought to have been there.'

'Yes, I suppose you're right,' said Mr Latimer. 'And in any case I'm rather wet. What are the servants going to think when we arrive like this?' he said suddenly. 'All wet and bedraggled, and you carrying all those trailing things?'

'I often go out for a walk and come back carrying trailing things,' said Miss Morrow calmly. 'In any case Florence will have gone out, and old Maggie never notices anything. Just be quite calm about it,' she added reassuringly. 'I don't suppose Maggie will see us anyway. We can slip upstairs.'

Mr Latimer rather disliked the idea of slipping

46

upstairs. It sounded almost as if there were something immoral about it. But he said nothing. Miss Morrow, thank goodness, seemed to be behaving sensibly after all. Perhaps she was not trying to catch him. He felt almost annoyed.

The front door of Leamington Lodge was of the old-fashioned kind, which can be opened from the outside without a latch key, and so Miss Morrow and Mr Latimer were able to do their slipping upstairs very successfully. Old Maggie, who was sitting in the kitchen, reading a story about a girl who was a Mother but not a Wife, did not even hear them come in.

'Well now, that's all right,' whispered Miss Morrow, when they were standing under the stained-glass window on the landing. 'You'd better go and have a bath, or you'll catch cold.'

Why, she's quite a nice-looking woman, thought Mr Latimer suddenly, and, indeed, Miss Morrow looked not unpleasing in the dim light. The rain and the exercise of walking had freshened her complexion and brightened her eyes, and such hair as showed under her unbecomingly sensible felt hat had curled itself into little tendrils. When her hair was tidy it was so tightly scraped back that one would never have suspected that it could curl. If she were decently dressed, thought Mr Latimer . . . but then pulled himself up. What on earth was he thinking about?

'Yes, I think I ought to have a bath and take some aspirins,' he said seriously. 'I don't want my rheumatism to come on.'

'And perhaps you ought to put some mustard in the bath and have a hot drink,' suggested Miss Morrow.

47

Could it be that she was making fun of him? he thought, glancing quickly at her. But her expression was perfectly serious, and she even told him that there was some mustard in the bathroom cupboard.

Miss Morrow went into her bedroom. She felt that she wanted to laugh, a good long laugh because life was so funny, so much funnier than any book. But as sane people don't laugh out loud when they are alone in their bedrooms, she had to content herself with going about smiling as she changed her clothes and tidied her hair. She went to the wardrobe to get out her brown marocain with the beige collar, but as she was looking among the drab folds of her dresses, her eye was caught by the rich gleam of her blue velvet. It had been bought to attend a wedding. Miss Doggett had thought it an extravagance. The brown marocain with a new collar would have done just as well. Nobody would expect Miss Morrow to be grandly dressed. It had been quite a success at the wedding, but Miss Morrow had never worn it since. She felt happier in the brown marocain, which Miss Doggett's eye would regard with approval, if it regarded it at all.

I'll wear the blue velvet tonight, thought Miss Morrow, it's silly to keep things. It would give her pleasure to wear it, and she wouldn't be embarrassed by any comment from Mr Latimer. Men never noticed things like that.

At twenty minutes to eight she was down in the drawing-room. With sudden recklessness she went to the fireplace and piled more coal on the fire. They would be coming out of church any time now. Supposing the vicar were to call to find out why Mr Latimer hadn't been at evensong? What should she say? She hoped he would soon come down, so that

48

he could deal with the situation in his own way.

She took her knitting out of its cretonne bag and examined it to see when she could start casting off for the armholes. She was in the middle of a row when the front door bell rang. Oh, dear, she thought, that must be the vicar. She flung her knitting onto the sofa and ran swiftly to the window to see if she could catch a glimpse of whoever it was, but all she could see was a dark shape that looked more like a woman than a man. Where was Maggie? Why wasn't she answering the door? At last, after what seemed a very long time, Miss Morrow heard her shambling old footsteps in the hall. Then the drawing-room door was opened.

'It's Mrs Wardell,' said Maggie.

'Oh, Mrs Wardell, good evening. How are you? Do sit down.' Miss Morrow began scurrying about the room, picking up her knitting and putting it down again, clearing imaginary objects off chairs and sofas.

'Well, well,' said Mr Latimer, coming into the room rubbing his hands and looking very pleased. 'I had a splendid bath.' When he saw Mrs Wardell he stopped in the middle of the room, his hands suspended in mid-air. 'Oh, good evening, Mrs Wardell, how nice to see you,' he said in a hurrying tone. Then, evidently feeling that some explanation was needed as to why he had been having a bath when he should have been assisting at evensong, he plunged into a long and complicated story about how he had suddenly received a message from a friend who was vicar of a distant parish in the Cotswolds, asking him to go over and take evensong. 'I went on my bicycle,' he said, 'and got rather wet coming back, so I thought it would be wise to have a hot bath.'

Miss Morrow listened to this story in amazement. She wondered if it showed in her face, for she had never before, as far as she could remember, heard a clergyman telling what she knew to be deliberate lies. And what a hopeless story! she thought pityingly. If Mr Latimer had thought it necessary to give some explanation of his splendid bath, surely he could have done so without involving himself in such an account, the falseness of which could easily be proved by judicious enquiries. Why couldn't he have said that he had a bad cold and leave it at that? Mrs Wardell might have accepted a cold, but, as it was, she would probably go asking awkward questions about this friend and his parish in the Cotswolds, which Mr Latimer might find difficult to answer. Nor was Miss Morrow mistaken; before she could think of anything to say, Mrs Wardell was asking in an interested tone the name of the place where he had been.

'Crampton Hodnet,' said Mr Latimer glibly.

Was there such a place? Miss Morrow wondered. She was sure that there was not. She waited nervously for Mrs Wardell to make some comment and sat rapidly knitting purl instead of plain, not daring to look at anybody.

'What a nice name,' said Mrs Wardell. 'I don't think I've been there. Ben wondered what had happened to you, if you were ill or something, so I thought I'd better just slip in and see.'

'I think I've managed to stave off a cold,' said Mr Latimer, in a high, rather sickly voice. He clutched at his collar and gave a determined cough.

'It's a pity you weren't in church, Miss Morrow,' went on Mrs Wardell pleasantly. 'Old Lady Halkin

50

had one of her *turns* and had to be taken out. It was really quite exciting.'

'Miss Morrow has a cold,' said Mr Latimer quickly.

Mrs Wardell suddenly burst out laughing. 'You *poor* things,' she said, 'I think I'd better say that you *both* had colds. Ben's very understanding, and I haven't forgotten what it's like to be young myself.'

'But I'm not young,' protested Miss Morrow in agitation.

Mrs Wardell wagged her finger and stood up to go. 'But you're looking very nice in your blue velvet,' she said. 'I must rush off now. Old Dr Fremantle and his wife are coming to supper. So depressing.' She sighed. 'Reminiscences of Oxford in the eighties, with a few daring little academic jokes. And poor Olive's so dreary.'

They went out into the hall together.

'What pretty berries,' said Mrs Wardell, examining the ones Miss Morrow had picked in the afternoon, and which lay on a chair in the hall, waiting to be put in water.

'Yes, aren't they?' agreed Miss Morrow. 'I got them on Shotover this afternoon.'

'Oh, did you go there this afternoon?' said Mr Latimer, in a ridiculously casual voice. 'I've heard it's a very nice walk.'

'Particularly when it's raining and you ought to be assisting at evensong,' said Miss Morrow, when they had got Mrs Wardell safely out of the door.

'Oh, *what* an experience!' said Mr Latimer, flopping down on the sofa.

'Well, I really think you made it worse,' said Miss Morrow. 'Your story was ridiculous. Heaven knows what Mrs Wardell thinks we've been doing. She spoke almost as if . . . well, you know what I mean.' Miss Morrow, although unworldly, had a natural delicacy which would not allow her to speak plainer than that. But Mr Latimer understood and felt that it was an uncomfortable situation.

'I really feel quite exhausted,' he said, slipping out of it easily. 'Is there by any chance any sherry in the house?'

'I don't keep a secret bottle in my bedroom,' said Miss Morrow, 'but there is some in the sideboard. Miss Doggett only brings it out when we have company or when she feels she needs reviving.'

'Well, we have just had company, and we certainly need reviving,' said Mr Latimer.

'All right, I'll get some. I too have undergone a shattering experience,' said Miss Morrow, thinking that the first time one heard a clergyman telling deliberate lies could surely be called that. 'Luckily the glasses are in the sideboard, but I shall have to hide them and wash them myself, otherwise Maggie and Florence might think things. Florence is such an intelligent girl,' she added.

Miss Morrow came back with the sherry.

'You must let me propose a toast,' she said. 'I think we should drink the health of your friend, the vicar of Crampton Hodnet.'

Mr Latimer looked at her uneasily. He was beginning to realise that he had put himself completely in her power. Could he trust her? He disliked the idea of depending on her for his good reputation—or his bad one, for that matter. He felt he ought to say something but he hardly knew what, and, as the sherry brought warmth and contentment to his body, his mind grew lazy, so that he said something which, although it was the first thing that came into his head, was not perhaps a very wise choice. 'What a pretty dress you're wearing,' he said. 'Blue is my favourite colour.'

6

AN AFTERNOON IN THE BODLEIAN

'Well, this is a cosy sight,' said Francis Cleveland, coming into the drawing-room on a cold December afternoon. 'What are you doing?'

'Well, Anthea's reading and I'm mending your socks,' said Mrs Cleveland patiently. 'What have *you* been doing all the afternoon?' she asked.

Mr Cleveland came and stood in front of the fire, thus shielding it from everyone else. 'Oh, I've been doing some work,' he said vaguely. 'I don't know how you can sit about all afternoon doing nothing.'

'Well, dear, you can come and mend your own socks, as you seem to think it less arduous than what you've been doing,' said Mrs Cleveland placidly. 'What are you going to do now?' she asked. Francis seemed to be in what she called one of his 'loose-endish' moods this afternoon.

'Why do you always ask that whenever I come into the drawing-room?' he said rather irritably. 'Can't I stand in my own drawing-room and talk to my family? Isn't that doing something?'

Anthea looked up from the romantic novel, which she was finding more sympathetic reading than the dull book on economics she had hoped to get through. 'I know what you're doing,' she said.

53

'You're keeping all the fire off me.'

'Oh, then I suppose I'd better go and sit down somewhere,' said Mr Cleveland in an offended tone. He went to the farthest edge of the room and sat down on a hard chair in a direct draught.

'Oh, Father, come and sit on the sofa,' said Anthea impatiently, moving her knitting. 'There's plenty of room.'

'It's only three o'clock,' said Mrs Cleveland. 'Why don't you go along to the Bodleian until teatime? You might see Arnold Penge or Edward Killigrew or somebody. That would be nice.'

'Very nice, to listen to Arnold Penge droning on about Virgil, or to Edward Killigrew saying that Mother doesn't like him to be late for tea,' said Mr Cleveland coldly.

'Well, you could be alone and work,' persisted his wife. 'Or perhaps you'll find a nice young woman working there and take her out to tea,' she added brightly.

'You certainly seem to want to get rid of me,' said Mr Cleveland, 'so perhaps I *will* go to the Bodleian. It's a comfort to know that there is at least one place left in Oxford where scholars and elderly people can spend a peaceful afternoon.'

'Take your overcoat, dear,' Mrs Cleveland called after him. 'Remember how cold it is there.'

Francis is so much better when he has something definite to do, she thought contentedly. If he walked it would take him twenty minutes to reach the library. He might spend twenty minutes talking to somebody or looking up books in the catalogue and then, by the time he had walked home again, it would be teatime and his afternoon would have been nicely filled in. Only of course if he took a bus

54

he would get home sooner.

Francis Cleveland, hunched in his grey overcoat, walked gloomily into the Bodleian quadrangle and up the stairs into Duke Humfrey's library. There was something he had meant to look up, but he had forgotten now what it was. TALK LITTLE AND TREAD LIGHTLY said the notice. Mr Cleveland trod as heavily as he could and would certainly have talked much, had he seen anyone to talk to. When he looked in at his usual seat by the hot water pipes, he found it occupied by a young clergyman, who gave him a startled glance but who stood his ground and offered no apology. Mr Cleveland sat down in the empty and more draughty seat beside him and with unnecessary fuss began to move his books from the young clergyman's desk onto the new one. When he had got them all together he decided that he did not want to read any of them, so he got up and began walking about until he came across Edward Killigrew, a senior assistant in the library, who was always ready for a good gossip.

Edward Killigrew sat at his desk, wearing a leather golf jacket and grey hand-knitted mittens. He was a tall, vague man of uncertain age, with a fussy, petulant voice. He lived with his old mother in the Woodstock Road. He was reading a catalogue of second-hand books and marking certain items, but he did not in the least mind being interrupted in his work. He kept Mr Cleveland entertained with spiteful bits of gossip about various members of the University and the library staff until nearly four o'clock. Then he stood up and said, 'Well, I must go now. Mother will be annoyed if I'm late for tea. She always likes it punctually at half past four.'

55

Left to himself once more, Mr Cleveland wandered through the Upper Reading Room, brushed aside the dark, mysterious curtain leading to the Tower Room, and hovered indecisively by the bookcase where the dictionaries and encyclopaedias were kept.

Oh, supposing he comes in here, thought Barbara Bird in a panic. So great was her agitation that she hardly knew whether she wanted him to come or not. She crouched in her seat by the radiator, with her fur coat around her shoulders, trying desperately hard to concentrate on her work.

Mr Cleveland went on hovering in the entrance to the Reading Room, peering inquisitively among the desks. He was bored, and it was always rather a comfort to watch other people working. And then he saw Barbara and realised that she was just what he needed. He wanted to be with somebody who appreciated him. He went up to her desk with an ingratiating smile on his face.

'Do come out and have some tea with me,' he said. 'I'm sure you've been working quite long enough this afternoon.'

He could see her hands trembling slightly as she looked up from her book. They were pretty hands with long, rose-coloured nails. Unacademic-looking hands, he thought.

'I'd love to,' she said, looking up at him with eyes which Mr Cleveland might have described even more warmly.

She stood up and arranged her books neatly on the desk, looked at her face in a small mirror and put on her gloves. She was purposely taking her time so that she could compose herself and think of what she should say to him when the time came for

56

intelligent conversation.

They walked out of the Reading Room and down the stairs.

'Don't you get depressed working in that place after the end of term?' said Mr Cleveland. 'I should have thought you'd rather go home.'

Go home with the chance of seeing you in Oxford? thought Barbara. Why, if I'd gone home this wouldn't be happening to me. 'It's impossible to work at home,' she said. 'One simply can't get any peace.'

'Where do you live?'

'In North Wales, by the sea.'

'Oh, do you? We often go to Llanfaddyn in the summer. We sometimes take reading parties there,' said Mr Cleveland. 'I dare say you may have seen us.'

'Yes, I have, but that was before I knew you properly, and before you knew me at all,' said Barbara, remembering one day when she had gone into the village shop to buy something and had found him standing there, wrestling with a long list of groceries. 'It was such a surprise to see you.' She laughed. 'I'd always thought of you as you were lecturing at the Schools, and then I saw you in shorts, buying tins of baked beans and spaghetti. It made you so much more human.'

'Well, I am human, quite human,' said Mr Cleveland, rather pleased at the idea of himself being anything else. 'And now we seem to be at the door of Fuller's. Shall we go in here?'

'Yes, I think it's a very suitable place,' said Barbara. 'Quite the right sort of place for a tutor to take his pupil.'

'His *favourite* pupil,' said Mr Cleveland, with

rather stiff gallantry. 'I shall expect you to eat a lot of cakes.'

They went upstairs and looked around for a table. 'Do you like the new part down the steps?' asked Mr Cleveland. They stood at the top of them, looking down at the groups of North Oxford spinsters, dons' wives and families, who were taking some refreshment after their Christmas shopping.

'I think the other part is nicer,' said Barbara.

'Yes,' agreed Mr Cleveland. 'Less full of chattering women.'

'Let's sit by the window,' said Barbara.

When the tea came she found that he liked his with milk and two lumps of sugar, just like so many other people: Peter, her brother, or that dull young man from St Wilfrid's Hall, who was always asking her to go out with him. It was a wonderful thing for Barbara to have found out how Francis Cleveland liked his tea. She began to pour hot water into the teapot, trying at the same time to appear intelligently interested in what she was saying. But really she was taking in her surroundings, so that she could have many details stored away in her memory, each of which might have the power to bring this afternoon back to her. She noticed the big pink chrysanthemums with heads like mops, the cakes in their cellophane coverings, even the people sitting at the tables near them. There was a tall, handsome woman, perhaps the wife of a don, with her three little boys, chattering about Christmas presents and fingering the cakes. One day those little boys would grow up, and although they would never know it, they would somehow all be linked together by this experience. Barbara suddenly felt a warm, all-embracing love for everybody in Fuller's

58

that afternoon, even for the chattering dons' wives and North Oxford spinsters, who were sitting in the other part of the café, anxiously wondering whether they had bought the right things or whether that cushion cover that Ella had given them last year could possibly be used as a present for anybody else without fear of discovery.

But if most of them were thinking more prosaic thoughts than Barbara, two at least were in some way sharing in her experience.

'Of course,' said Miss Morrow rather timidly, 'Mr Cleveland *is* her tutor. It seems to me that it's quite an ordinary thing for a tutor to take his pupil out to tea.'

'I am not denying that,' said Miss Doggett, 'but the circumstances here seem to me to be *quite* different. It would be a perfectly natural thing for a tutor to ask a pupil to tea at his house, where his wife or housekeeper or some elderly person could act as hostess. But to sneak off to a café in the town, and then to rush off so unceremoniously when he sees somebody he knows . . . well, Miss Morrow, you can hardly say that that is quite an ordinary thing.'

Miss Morrow was silent for a moment, silent in admiration at Miss Doggett's capacity for twisting the facts of a situation so that it appeared to be something completely different. 'But, Miss Doggett,' she persisted, 'I don't think they *did* see us. I don't think either of them did. They came here to look and found that it was crowded, so they went into the other part of the café. It seems to me perfectly simple.'

'Miss Morrow,' said Miss Doggett in a warning tone, 'you are not a woman of the world. You cannot possibly know what goes on outside Leamington Lodge.'

Miss Morrow went rather red, not so much from mortification as from a desire to giggle. She was thinking that if she did not know what went on *outside* Leamington Lodge, Miss Doggett was just as ignorant of what went on *inside* it. For she obviously had no idea of the conspiracy between her and Mr Latimer, the secret of the walk on Shotover, the vicar of Crampton Hodnet, the splendid bath and the sherry. Thinking of these things, Miss Morrow bent her head and said nothing. The last thing she would ever claim to be was a woman of the world.

Encouraged by Miss Morrow's silence and bent head, Miss Doggett went on to speak of what she thought they ought to do. 'I believe it may be my duty to speak to Margaret about it,' she said thoughtfully. 'Don't think for a moment that I'm suggesting that there could possibly be anything in it,' she said, turning to the unworldly Miss Morrow, 'but you know what I mean. There are some things that one cannot let pass without comment. It is a duty one has to other people, not always a pleasant or an easy duty, but one which must be performed. Will you have another cake, Miss Morrow?' she asked, putting on her skunk cape, fastening the buttons on her gloves, and obviously preparing to get up from the table.

'No, thank you, Miss Doggett,' said Miss Morrow virtuously.

'Well, then, we may as well go home,' said Miss Doggett, standing up. 'I don't like leaving Mr Latimer alone; I feel he needs company.' She turned suddenly to Miss Morrow. 'When we pass

60

Francis and that young woman,' she said, 'I shall merely nod, and you must do the same. Just an acknowledgement, simply that. We don't want to be either cold or effusive.'

They walked up the steps into the other part of the café. Miss Doggett took out her lorgnette and looked round. Then, fixing it on Barbara and Francis Cleveland, she gave a curt nod and passed on.

Miss Morrow, struggling with gloves, handbag, umbrella and a great many parcels, made an odd sort of dipping movement with her whole body, as if she were genuflecting before an imaginary altar. She hoped that this expressed neither coldness nor effusiveness, but she suspected that it merely looked ridiculous and expressed absolutely nothing. And in any case Mr Cleveland and the young woman were so deep in conversation that they hadn't even noticed that they were being acknowledged.

'Do let me walk back to your college with you,' said Francis, as he and Barbara were preparing to go their different ways.

'Well . . .' Barbara hesitated. 'I had been going to do some work, but it hardly seems worth it now before dinner. But I've left all my books in the Bodleian.'

'We can go round that way. I'll wait while you get them.'

Barbara ran up the wooden stairs, leaving Mr Cleveland to wait for her at the bottom. He sat down on one of the broad window-sills and absent-mindedly took out his cigarette case.

'Now, now, no smoking here, Cleveland,' said the playful, slightly petulant voice of Edward

61

Killigrew, who was just coming down the stairs at that moment. 'What are you doing here lurking in the shadows?' he asked.

'I'm waiting for somebody,' said Mr Cleveland shortly.

'Oh, *ho*,' said Mr Killigrew with ridiculous coyness.

'Here I am.' Barbara came running down with her books.

'Well, I must be off,' said Mr Killigrew, raising his eyebrows.

When he had gone out of earshot, Barbara began to laugh. 'I'm sorry,' she said, 'but I always think he's such a funny young man.'

Young man, thought Mr Cleveland, remembering that he himself wasn't much older than Edward Killigrew. He began to feel quite sprightly. 'Let me carry those books for you,' he said.

'Well, it isn't part of a tutor's duty to be so polite to his pupils,' said Barbara.

'Yes, but I'm not your tutor now.'

There was a pause, as if both were considering their new relationship, whatever it might be. They walked on in silence over Magdalen Bridge. Barbara tried hard to think of some intelligent remark to make. He'll think I'm so stupid if I don't say *anything*, she thought desperately, and I may not get another opportunity to be with him like this again.

How sympathetic she is, thought Francis. She doesn't spoil the magic of a beautiful evening— it happened to be a particularly raw December evening—by making conversation. One could enjoy it in peace. She seemed to know one's feelings. If he went for such a walk with Margaret she would

62

be chattering all the time about unimportant things, something they ought to get done in the house or some trivial bit of North Oxford gossip. One somehow couldn't imagine Barbara talking about things like that. He began to see himself as a sensitive, misunderstood person, who had at last found a soul-mate.

'Well, here we are,' he said with real regret in his tone, as they came to the gates of her college.

'I must go,' she said, lingering by the gate and not going.

Francis put out his hand and daringly touched her dark, furry sleeve. It was really just the right moment for a kiss, he thought, and he was sure that she felt it too.

Oh, *why* can't I think of anything intelligent to say. So anxiously had Barbara been racking her brains for the sort of remark an intelligent woman well read in English Literature would make that she had not even noticed his tentative advance, the touch on her sleeve.

At that moment a dark shape could be seen hurrying down the drive. It was Miss Rideout, the Principal, a good-natured woman who had unwittingly cut short many a good-night kiss.

'Good night,' said Francis quickly.

'Good night and thank you,' said Barbara in a small voice, disappointed with herself. She hurried upstairs and into her room, still going over all the things she might have said.

It was really a good thing, she thought, looking around her, that men weren't allowed in the women's rooms. The majority of them were so sordid and unromantic. Even Barbara's, which was sometimes quite nice, was not looking at its best

63

this evening. The folding washstand was open, there were stockings drying over the back of a chair, the chrysanthemums were dying and the desk was littered with her attempts at a Middle English paper. It was not the kind of room she would have liked to entertain Francis in, although it was better when it was tidy. Barbara thought of it as quite a good setting for herself, with its books and flowers and the large reproduction of a Cézanne landscape over the mantelpiece. But there was nowhere really comfortable to sit except the bed, and it didn't seem quite right to think of Francis sitting there, among the cheap, gaudy cushions.

There was a knock at the door, and her friend Sarah Penrose came in. She was a heavily built, fair girl, always overburdened with work.

'Oh, *Birdy*,' she wailed, 'I wonder if you could help me with *Sir Gawaine*. I simply *can't* translate it. I've been at it *all* afternoon, from two o'clock until now. I thought perhaps we might go through it together.' She flopped down on the bed, exhausted.

'Have a cigarette,' said Barbara, 'and wait while I tidy things up. I've been out to tea.'

'Out to tea?'

Yes, out to tea, thought Barbara. My heart is like a singing bird, just because I've been out to tea . . .

'I've had tea,' said Mr Cleveland, as he stood in the drawing-room doorway.

'I should hope you have,' said his wife, laughing. 'It's after six, and you certainly won't get any here. Did you have it in the town?'

'Yes, I did,' said Francis shortly.

Francis sounds rather huffy, thought Mrs Cleveland. Perhaps he's annoyed about what I said. 'You can have more tea if you *like*, dear,' she said,

64

not very encouragingly.

'But I've *had* tea. Why should I want any more?' he said impatiently.

'I don't know. I just thought you might. You do sometimes want odd things, you know,' she said. 'Who did you have tea with?'

Really, Margaret was exasperating sometimes, he thought, sitting down by the fire. 'I had tea with Killigrew,' he said defiantly. It was the first time, as far as he could remember, that he had ever told his wife a deliberate lie. It made him feel fine and important, a swelling, ranting Don Juan with a dark double life, instead of a middle-aged Fellow of Randolph, ignored or treated with contempt by his wife and daughter.

'Oh?' said Mrs Cleveland. 'How is old Mrs Killigrew?'

'I don't know, just the same as usual, I imagine. We went to Fuller's. We talked about Milton,' he said, enlarging on the fiction. 'Killigrew was quoting *Paradise Lost*. The beauty of the work is certainly lost through a mouthful of walnut cake. He looked ridiculous.'

Dear Francis, thought his wife affectionately. Was it possible to recite Milton over the tea table and not look ridiculous? 'Won't you recite some now?' she asked solemnly.

'Whatever for?'

'Don't you remember . . . ?' she began, but she stopped, because she was herself being ridiculous now. For there was surely something essentially ridiculous in remembering how Francis had once recited the whole of Marvell's 'To His Coy Mistress' to her over tea in Boffin's.

'Did you see Aunt Maude and Miss Morrow in

65

Fuller's?' she asked. 'They may have been there when you were. I know they were going shopping, and they usually have tea there if they stay in town.'

'Oh, no,' said Francis confidently, 'I didn't see them.' But the news that they might have been there made him a little uneasy. He couldn't really remember noticing anyone, except Mrs Furse and her three little boys, and the café had been very full. Supposing they had been there and had seen him with Barbara? One must consider that possibility. If they had seen him, Aunt Maude would be sure to tell Margaret. She would consider it her duty. And yet there was nothing *wrong* in taking Barbara Bird out to tea. Margaret had herself suggested that he should do something of the kind. It was only that he had told her that he was with Killigrew, and she would probably wonder why he had told a lie about it. He didn't really know why he had. The whole thing was Margaret's fault, he thought unreasonably. She oughtn't to have turned him out and sent him to the Bodleian on a cold afternoon. And she ought to have told him as soon as he came in about Aunt Maude's probably having been in Fuller's. Then he would have been warned.

'Did you see anyone else that we know?' persisted Mrs Cleveland.

There she was, going on about it again, he thought, exasperated. 'The whole of North Oxford was there, I should think,' he said in an even tone. 'It usually is in the vacation. So you can gather that I probably saw almost *everyone* we know.'

7

MR LATIMER GETS AN IDEA

'If I were you, Miss Morrow,' said Miss Doggett to her companion, 'I shouldn't say anything to Mrs Cleveland about what we saw in Fuller's last week. You are inclined to be impulsive, you know, and well-meaning busybodies often do more harm than good in matters like this.'

'Oh, no, I never thought of mentioning it,' said Miss Morrow meekly, without attempting to protest against the injustice of Miss Doggett's implications. 'I shall *certainly* not say anything.'

'I do not think it is really our business,' said Miss Doggett. 'We will let the matter drop,' she added, having no intention of doing anything of the kind. It was quite possible that there would be further incidents in the story. It would be much more interesting to wait. It was really not her duty to tell Margaret about last week, but it might very well be to confront her with a complete and convincing story of her husband's unfaithfulness.

'Is it this evening that the vicar and his wife are coming to dinner?' asked Mr Latimer, coming into the room.

'Yes,' said Miss Doggett with a sigh. 'He is such a boring little man, but we must do our duty.'

How smooth he is, thought Miss Morrow, as she listened to Mr Latimer criticising, quite respectfully, of course, the vicar's sermons. Every remark that he made was taken up eagerly by Miss Doggett and, as it were, magnified.

'In the old days,' declared Mr Latimer, 'nobody would have tolerated a sermon lasting only ten minutes or a quarter of an hour. Mr Wardell thinks he is still in those old days. He has material for a ten-minute sermon, but he tries to spin it out for half an hour. The result is—well'—he turned to Miss Doggett with his charming smile—'you have seen that for yourself. Ideas have changed now.'

Certainly they have, thought Miss Morrow with amusement. Clergymen nowadays apparently think nothing of telling deliberate lies. She wondered whether Mr Latimer would claim that the change was for the better.

'Of course Mr Wardell has none of that dignity one associates with the clergy,' said Miss Doggett. 'He looks more like a grocer. When I see him in church, I imagine he ought to be slicing bacon.'

So these were the thoughts that were in Miss Doggett's mind during Divine Service, reflected Miss Morrow, with interest. Sometimes one could tell, or at least imagine, what people were thinking, but that Miss Doggett should imagine the vicar slicing bacon was something entirely unexpected. By her grave and reverent demeanour, one would have thought that her mind was fixed on God, a large, solemn, bearded God, who might, if He were on earth, very well live in a house like Leamington Lodge, with its massive furniture and general air of gloomy dignity.

'I think he's quite a good sort of man in his way,' said Mr Latimer condescendingly.

'Oh, yes, one never hears anything definite said against him,' agreed Miss Doggett reluctantly, 'but I never feel he is quite at his ease among people like us.'

'Well, we must do our best to make him feel at ease tonight,' said Miss Morrow seriously. 'He must be in a permanent state of uneasiness, considering how often he comes here.'

'The vicar and Mrs Wardell,' said Florence, opening the door.

Mrs Wardell strode into the room, her husband scuttling behind her like a crab. Miss Morrow had a brief vision of him in a white coat and apron, slicing bacon.

'How nice Miss Morrow is looking,' said Mrs Wardell. 'I *do* like that blue velvet.'

Miss Morrow smiled rather stickily. She did not want anyone to notice or make any comment on her dress. She had already been made to feel that she had done the wrong thing in putting it on, first by Miss Doggett's raised eyebrows and then by the startled, appealing look Mr Latimer had given her when he saw it. It was as if he were afraid that the very wearing of it would make her betray his secret.

'Have they been knitting for you already?' said Mrs Wardell, plucking at the grey pullover which Mr Latimer wore. 'I see nothing but lovesick young women hanging round the church these days. You mark my words,' she said to Miss Doggett, 'we shall be losing Mr Latimer soon.'

Mr Latimer gave her a wan smile. One never knew what Mrs Wardell was going to say. He certainly did not want any reference to be made to that fatal Sunday evening, although she and Miss Morrow were the only ones who had heard his foolish story. He had made the excuse of ill-health to the vicar, and it had been accepted without question, and with a bottle of Dr Armstrong's Influenza Mixture thrown in. Mr Wardell was a very easy-going little man and had not seemed in the least curious. He was smiling now as he thought about what his wife had said about Mr Latimer and Miss Morrow. She had some wonderful story about them, almost as if there were something between them. Just like dear Agnes, thought the vicar affectionately. There was nothing she enjoyed more than a nice romance. Even now she was chattering away to Miss Doggett about a new one she had discovered.

'Really?' said Miss Doggett indulgently. 'Don't tell me it's Mr Killigrew and Miss Morrow.' She tittered. 'They'd be a nice pair.'

'No, it's even nearer to you than that,' said Mrs Wardell triumphantly. 'But I'll leave you to guess.'

Mr Latimer could feel his face getting hotter and redder every moment. Whatever would she be saying next? he wondered angrily. He dared not look at Miss Morrow.

'Well,' laughed Miss Doggett, in high good humour, 'I can only think you mean Mr Latimer and *me*.'

'I'm afraid Miss Doggett would hardly stoop to notice a humble curate,' said Mr Latimer, recovering his gallantry. But he wished, all the same, that they could change the subject. It was amazing how, even with the restraining presence of Miss Doggett, they always seemed to be talking about *love*, or what passed for love in a circle consisting of clergymen and spinsters.

Thinking things over in bed that night, Mr Latimer came to the conclusion that he might have to take some action in the matter himself, if only for his own safety and peace of mind. After all, he was thirty-five years old, old enough to know his own mind and yet not so old that he would behave as those elderly clergymen one read about in the cheaper daily papers, who married a servant or a chorus girl of eighteen. He was a man of private means, good-looking and charming. It was obvious that he could never expect to have much peace until he was safely married. Besides, there was something comforting about the idea of having a wife, a helpmeet, somebody who would keep the others off and minister to his needs without being as fussy as Miss Doggett was. Some nice, sensible woman, not too young.

And at this point, in the high, wide bed, heaped with too many bedclothes, he fell asleep. And he soon began to dream violently. Somehow, he didn't know why, he had asked Miss Doggett to marry him, and the ceremony was to take place on Shotover Hill. They stood on the hill, the vicar and his wife, the Clevelands, Miss Morrow, and a strange clergyman, perhaps the vicar of Crampton Hodnet, who was to perform the ceremony. And then suddenly Mr Latimer was struggling to get back to Oxford, running along a wide, deserted road, looking for a bus which never came. And he remembered that he had all his packing to do, and how could he possibly manage it when he was on this road so far away from Oxford? He would never get there in time . . .

He woke up in a sweat and flung off the heavy crimson eiderdown. He knew now that it had been a dream, because he could see the dark masses of the trees against the window and hear the sound of the steadily falling rain. He switched on the light, deciding to read. There was only a Bible on his bedside table, so he opened it at the Acts of the

Apostles and started to read from the beginning. But somehow the narrative did not grip him, for he found his thoughts wandering again to the question of marriage.

And it was then that it occurred to him that he might do worse than marry Miss Morrow. The idea framed itself in precisely those words—that he might do *worse* than marry Miss Morrow. Besides, he thought, warming up a little, he liked her, and as she too was a person of discreet years, he felt that she would understand the way in which this plan had come to him: not as a wild, romantic love; he had known that as a young man of nineteen, and although it had been an experience which had enriched his life, he had now reached an age when he preferred something less disturbing. Love was all very well for *young* people; he was sure Miss Morrow would understand that.

This time he fell into a dreamless sleep, which lasted till morning.

8

SPRING,
THE SWEET SPRING

Spring came early that year, and the sun was so bright that it made all the North Oxford residents feel as shabby as the still leafless trees, so that they hurried to Elliston's, Webber's and Badcock's, intending to buy jumper suits and spring tweeds in bright, flowerlike colours to match the sudden impulse which had sent them there. But when they found themselves in the familiar atmosphere of the shop, they forgot the sun shining outside and the thrilling little breezes that made everyone want to be in love, and the young lady assistant forgot them too, because, although she may have felt them walking down the Botley Road with her young man on a Sunday afternoon, they were not the kinds of things one thought about in business hours. And so, after a quick, practised glance at the customer, out would come the old fawn, mud, navy, dark brown, slate and clerical greys, all the colours they always had before and without which they would hardly have felt like themselves. It would probably be raining tomorrow, and grey, fawn or bottle green was suitable for all weathers, whereas daffodil yellow, leaf green, hyacinth blue or coral pink would look unsuitable and show the dirt.

But one afternoon Miss Morrow went impulsively to Elliston's and bought herself a dress of tender leaf green and hid it in her wardrobe among her old, drab things, where it might have to wait many weeks before she had the courage to wear it. Only young people, like Anthea, could suddenly put on a new and pretty dress without fear of damping remarks and disapproving raised eyebrows.

Barbara Bird, also, was able to say to herself when she woke up on a bright March morning, 'I'll wear my new green suit today and my yellow jumper.' While she lay in bed thinking about shoes and other details, she realised that the sun was shining, and that must be because it was today that she and Francis had arranged to meet in the Botanical Gardens at half past two.

The chapel bell started to ring and Barbara

leapt eagerly out of bed. But as she poured the enamel can of hot water into her basin, she began to wonder how she was going to get through the six long hours before it would be half past two. It was a wonder that she managed to do any work at all these days, for even writing essays for Francis had lost some of its attraction. He didn't seem to listen very attentively now and even stopped her sometimes, before she had finished reading, and began talking about things that had really nothing to do with tutorials. Barbara believed that Francis liked talking to her, and that she was able to bring into his life something which had been lacking in it before—sympathy, understanding, perhaps even love. But of course Francis wasn't like the men in jokes who told young women that their wives didn't understand them. He never spoke of his wife and daughter, except casually, and as they appeared to take so little interest in him, she supposed that there was nothing wrong in her meeting Francis occasionally and going for a walk or having tea with him. She had no intention of stealing him from his wife, and it never occurred to her that he might begin to return her love, and that it might be a different kind of love from her rather schoolgirlish passion, which could live happily on a smile or a kind word and asked nothing more than long walks and talks about life and poetry and themselves. Barbara was an intelligent girl, but she had never been in love with anyone of her own age and had cherished many impossible, romantic passions for people she scarcely knew, or had perhaps seen only once. She was not interested in undergraduates; they were so unintelligent and lumpish, and the few that weren't were so conceited and effeminate that one couldn't possibly take them seriously.

She dressed quickly, not bothering to put on any make-up. Very few people in college did for breakfast, except that minority who were always elegant, or whose pride would not permit them to show their faces in their natural state. She hurried into the dining hall and, after collecting tea, cornflakes and fish, sat down in her usual place by her friends. They were already talking, mostly about work. Snatches of their conversation floated over her head.

'I said *"Bloody* old Beowulf", and she must have heard, because she turned round and gave me such a *look* . . .'

'I shall cut Boggart-Smith's lecture today. He hasn't said anything so far that's not in the *Cambridge History* . . .'

'Sir Stafford Cripps is speaking at the Labour Club tonight, you ought to come . . .'

'I'm going to spend the *whole morning* at the Bodleian.' This in a full, resolute tone, which promised four hours of concentrated work.

'Why, Birdy's got a new suit!' exclaimed somebody, suddenly noticing her. 'Isn't it a pretty green? Oh, Birdy, wasn't the Modern English paper *bloody*?'

And so the morning went on and on, and after a very long time it was twenty-five past two, and Barbara was hurrying over Magdalen Bridge. She stopped on the bridge and looked down anxiously into the Botanical Gardens and saw him, standing outside one of the hothouses and peering in. She could go straight there now. There would be no need to loiter in Rose Lane or Christchurch Meadows, in case she should be too early.

'Hullo, I hope I'm not late,' she said, coming up behind him. 'What were you looking at?'

'A curious orchid. They're rather beautiful, aren't they?'

'Yes,' she said happily. 'I told you there were lots of lovely things here. This is one of my favourite haunts. I had to show it to you.'

'I should feel ashamed of myself for not knowing it better,' said Francis, 'but I have the excuse of being an Oxford resident, who has never seen anything in Oxford, though of course I *have* been here, you know. But never with you,' he added in a different tone.

'Shall we look at the rock plants and bulbs and then go into the hothouses?' said Barbara.

'I'm entirely in your hands. You shall be my guide.'

'Do you like flowers?' she asked. 'I mean, *really* like them?'

Francis thought for a moment. He always made himself out to be a keen gardener, although he never did anything but snip off an occasional dead flower. 'Yes, I like them,' he said, feeling somehow that he had to be more honest with her, 'but perhaps I don't feel that every flower enjoys the air it breathes.'

'I really think I do,' said Barbara. 'When I was a little girl I could never bear to see flowers thrown away before they were dead. I used to imagine they suffered. I believe I'm still a bit like that.' She laughed, as if ashamed of herself.

They walked in silence into one of the hothouses. In the middle of the floor was a raised square pool, full of water plants and goldfish.

'Oh, this is nice,' said Francis, wanting to say

76

something to show that he was enjoying himself, although he really preferred to listen to Barbara talking.

'I know these fishes quite well,' she said. 'I believe some of them must be quite old, and perhaps when we're dead there'll be some who will remember that we came here. If fishes *have* memories, that is,' she added, 'I don't know if they have. Did you ever see those wonderful old horny fishes at the Petit Trianon?' she went on. 'They crowd under the bridge to be fed, masses of them. They must have seen Marie Antoinette, because some of them are supposed to be two hundred years old. I couldn't stop thinking about it when I was there, it seemed so marvellous.'

'You think of things that wouldn't occur to other people,' said Francis solemnly. He couldn't imagine Margaret thinking that about the fishes. If they ever went sightseeing she was always preoccupied with uncomfortable shoes or whether they would be able to get tea somewhere. 'It must be wonderful to go on a holiday with you, Barbara,' he said rather wistfully. 'You make me see things that I could never see by myself.'

Barbara looked up at him, but just at that moment two old ladies came in and started poking at the fishes with the tip of an umbrella.

Barbara and Francis moved off into another hothouse.

'What a pity I can't pick you some of those red lilies,' he said.

'Oh, you couldn't do that. It's not allowed. Besides, they look so nice growing there,' said Barbara.

If I were thirty years younger, thought Francis

77

regretfully, I'd have no hesitation in breaking them off and giving them to her. But only young men like Simon Beddoes did things like that. Not middle-aged dons with grown-up families. They didn't even *buy* lilies for anyone, not even for their wives, and certainly not for pretty female undergraduates.

'It's awfully hot and steamy in here,' said Barbara. 'I'm sure we ought to be outside in the sunshine.'

'Let's walk round here,' said Francis, indicating a secluded path. He felt suddenly excited at the prospect of being alone with her. It was spring. Spring, the sweet spring. There was nothing at all unusual in feeling that one needed a little excitement. Everyone felt it. Arnold Penge had been seen in the High wearing knickerbockers and a green Tyrolean hat, and that morning Bodley's Librarian had come into the Upper Reading Room humming a little tune. Even Edward Killigrew had now discarded his leather jacket and mittens. Undoubtedly there was something about the spring that made people behave differently, thought Francis hopefully.

He flung his arm round Barbara's shoulders, but the position was an awkward one, and they walked along stumbling in their efforts to keep in step with each other.

They had been wandering like this for some time, when the silence was suddenly broken by the sound of familiar voices somewhere near.

'Michael and Gabriel,' said Barbara quickly. 'We don't want them to see us.'

'Let's hide in these bushes,' said Francis impulsively.

78

The footsteps came nearer and the voices grew louder.

'. . . the décor was *tolerable*, but the choreography was simply *frightful*. Talk about Diaghileff turning in his grave!'

'I always imagined it something like *this*,' said Gabriel, leaping up into the air.

'Yes, *exactly*,' agreed Michael.

They began to dance very prettily in the path.

'They haven't seen us,' whispered Francis, crouching uncomfortably.

But as they moved off, Michael said in a whisper, 'My dear, did you *see*?'

'They've gone now,' said Barbara. 'We can get out of here.'

'Oh, must we? I think it's rather nice,' said Francis, uncomfortable and ridiculous though he felt. 'Don't you think so?'

'Oh, yes,' said Barbara doubtfully.

'It could be even nicer,' said Francis boldly. He put his arm round her and gave her a tentative peck on the cheek. Not very successful, he felt. It was so difficult not to overbalance.

'I think we'd better be platonic,' said Barbara nervously. 'It makes things so difficult if we aren't.'

'Yes, of course, I suppose it does,' said Francis regretfully. It's too dangerous, he thought. We can't trust ourselves. Those dark, passionate eyes. All or nothing.

Barbara rose eagerly and brushed the dust off her skirt. She hoped he wasn't going to be like *that*. So many beautiful friendships had been spoilt because of *that*.

'How are you getting on with your book?' she asked quickly. 'You promised to tell me about it.'

'Did I?' he said vaguely. It was so long since he had spoken to anyone about his book, so long, indeed, since anyone had taken it seriously, that he found himself at a loss to know what to say about it. He could talk about his book any time, with Doge or Fenning or Edward Killigrew. It was a waste of a spring afternoon to talk about it with a beautiful girl whom he wanted to kiss.

'Love that's in contemplation placed is Venus drawn but to the waist,' he thought, remembering one of his ancestor's neat couplets. How odd that his book should suddenly have come alive. But it wasn't at all the sort of thing he could quote to Barbara. He began to feel rather ashamed of himself for having thought of it when Magdalen clock struck the half hour, and Barbara leapt to her feet.

'I simply must go,' she said. 'I've got to be at Headington by four, and I must go back to college first.'

'Oh, I hoped you'd have tea with me.' Francis looked and felt disappointed, even jealous. A tea party with some young men, he supposed, or perhaps one special one, for such an attractive girl must surely have many admirers.

'I'm awfully sorry,' said Barbara. 'I should have liked that very much, but I'm afraid it can't be helped. And I've got to write an essay for you, you know,' she added.

Damn the essay, thought Francis. 'Your company does me much more good than an essay,' he said gallantly.

'Well, I don't do them for *your* good,' Barbara replied, and then she was gone, leaving him standing forlornly under a tree.

He watched her hurrying over Magdalen Bridge and hoped that she might look down into the garden. But she kept her eyes straight in front of her. He stood looking after her for a moment and then decided that there was nothing to do but go back home to tea.

The thought of tea and his family made him feel slightly guilty about the way in which he had spent the afternoon, and as he walked along the High and turned into Catte Street, he busied himself finding reasons to justify his behaviour. A few harmless walks and talks were really nothing, he decided. Margaret would be the last person to mind anything like that. She never minded anything. Not that there had ever been anything for her to mind, for that matter. Of course he didn't intend to tell her, because, although he knew she wouldn't mind, she would be sure to want some sort of explanation, and explanations invariably got one into difficulties. Francis Cleveland had kept away from difficulties for as long as he could remember, and he had no intention of going to meet them now.

But suddenly, as he walked along Broad Street, he came upon a little flower shop, and in the window was a jar of red lilies, exactly like the ones he and Barbara had seen in the hothouse. Without waiting to consider whether it was wise, he went in and bought them and asked that they should be sent to Miss Bird at her college. He wrote a message on a card and slipped it into an envelope. It was all done in five minutes.

He walked out of the shop and nearly collided with Edward Killigrew, who was going home for his tea.

'Well, Cleveland, buying flowers?' he said.

81

'Ordering a wreath for a deceased relative from the look of you,' he added. 'Not lost but gone before.'

Francis smiled. Yes, that was what everyone would think. Flowers for a funeral or a sickbed, or a dutiful husbandly offering, not red lilies for a beautiful girl, he thought, feeling very pleased with himself. He was willing to bet that Killigrew had never done such a thing in his life.

'How is Mrs Killigrew?' he asked politely.

'Oh, Mother is very well, thank you,' said Edward. 'Full of beans as usual,' he added, his tone losing a little of its joviality. He knew that it was wicked and unfilial of him, but he sometimes wished that Mother was not quite so full of beans.

They went on talking about various academic matters on the bus, and then Mr Killigrew got off and walked through Canterbury Road to his house. He hurried, because Mother didn't like him to be late for tea.

Francis Cleveland did not bother to hurry. Nobody minded whether he was late for tea or not. He found his wife with Anthea and Simon Beddoes in the drawing-room. Nobody asked him where he had been. Mrs Cleveland was reading, while Anthea was measuring a pullover against Simon, who was refusing to keep still. The tea, with no cosy on it, was stewing in the pot, and there appeared to be nothing left to eat except a dry-looking piece of fruit-cake and a leathery crumpet in a dish in the fireplace.

'Oh, Simon, why can't you keep *still*?' said Anthea plaintively. 'It'll be too short if you don't let me measure, and then you won't wear it.'

'Darling, I'll wear it whatever it's like,' said Simon soothingly. 'I'm sure it's going to be wonderful, anyway. Oh, hullo, sir,' he said, springing up when he saw Mr Cleveland. 'Do come and sit here. I seem to be taking up all the room.'

'Will this tea do for you?' said Mrs Cleveland, peering doubtfully into the pot.

'Oh, yes, we haven't had it long,' said Anthea casually. 'You don't mind, do you, Father?'

'Miss Beaton rang up. She wanted to know whether you could take any more of her young women,' said Mrs Cleveland cryptically.

'Well, what did you say?'

'I told her I didn't know, of course, dear. I said you'd ring up yourself.'

Francis groaned. 'Never be an English don,' he said to Simon. 'It's a dog's life.'

Simon, who was convinced that he would certainly be Prime Minister or the leader of some new and powerful political party long before he was Mr Cleveland's age, smiled and said that he was sure he would never rise as high as that.

Francis looked pleased. He began to think that he rather liked Simon. Margaret had thought he was too conceited and full of himself, but she wasn't *always* right. By no means, he thought, getting his teeth into the leathery crumpet and devouring it with every appearance of enjoyment.

Francis looks different, thought his wife. Almost sprightly, which is an odd thing for a middle-aged don to be, even in spring. Still, there was something very disturbing about the spring in Oxford. Even she had felt it this year, walking up the Banbury Road on a fine morning to do her shopping. It was the sort of feeling one had had thirty years ago, going to meet one's love—Francis, she thought, almost with surprise—or thinking that one might see him by accident in the town. It was not the sort of feeling a busy don's wife had time for, so she had put it from her and gone into Elliston's to see about the new curtains for the bathroom, but even when she got absorbed in check gingham and flowered oilskin she knew that the feeling was still there. Perhaps Francis felt it too, but somehow one didn't talk about things like that now.

But Francis was wondering if Barbara had got the lilies yet.

As he was thinking of her, she had just come back from her tea party and undone the paper. She took out the card, imagining that the flowers were from a persistent young man who had admired her at a lecture. She read what was written on it—*You shall have your lilies, even if I can't pick them for you*—and then of course she knew who had sent them. She touched them with her fingers and stood staring down at them, not quite knowing what to think. At the back of her mind she was conscious of a slight feeling of disappointment. She wished he had put a quotation from some seventeenth-century poet on the little card. It would have been so suitable somehow, so romantic. But perhaps he had been in a hurry. It was often difficult to think of an apt quotation when one was in a hurry.

84

9

BALLET IN THE PARKS

'I do not think Mr Latimer is very well,' said Miss
Doggett. 'He looks pale and seems rather nervous,
but the Sanatogen ought to pull him round, and
he's been taking a glass of milk every night, too. Of
course sensitive and intelligent people *are* nervous,
there's no denying that.'

'I think Mr Latimer is highly strung,' ventured
Miss Morrow.

'Yes, he is like a finely tuned instrument,' agreed
Miss Doggett.

Like an Aeolian harp, thought Miss Morrow,
pleased with the idea. But really a frightened rabbit
was nearer the mark. Mr Latimer had been quite
ridiculously furtive with her lately; indeed, ever
since the night of the walk on Shotover, now that
she came to think of it, and that was months ago.
Sometimes she had found it hard not to laugh out
loud at him and explain the whole thing to Miss
Doggett. It was a wonder she hadn't guessed that
there was some secret between them, for nowadays
Mr Latimer never addressed a remark to her
directly and always followed Miss Doggett out of
the room if there was any chance that he would
be left alone with Miss Morrow. But of course it
would never have occurred to Miss Doggett to
suspect anything. He was a clergyman, a finely
tuned instrument, whereas Miss Morrow, if she
was anything, was a harp with broken strings, an
old twanging thing that somebody might play in

the street. What could Mr Latimer have to say to a person like Miss Morrow? She turned her head away, smiling at her thoughts.

It was pleasant sitting in the Parks in the sunshine, which was as warm as June, although it was only the beginning of March. But Miss Doggett had not yet been tempted to put on what she called 'flimsy clothes' and still wore her skunk cape, gaiters and fur-lined gloves.

'I thought Mr Latimer's sermon last week was very fine,' she said, still on the same subject. 'He is a really gifted preacher, such a command of language. And those quotations were really quite obscure. Anyone can see that he is a very well-read man.'

No doubt he would appear so to one who read nothing but Tennyson, thought Miss Morrow, but it was not really so difficult to find quotations unknown to the average elderly female churchgoer to adorn a sermon. There were many excellent anthologies. Mr Latimer had several on his shelves, and Miss Morrow had seen him skimming through a Wordsworth one evening, where, as most people surely knew, one could prick an appropriate line about Man or Nature or both with a pin.

'It was clever to suit it to the time of year,' went on Miss Doggett. '"Behold, I make all things new", and how we see that borne out in Nature and in the new ideas which we often get at this time of year.'

'Yes, of course,' said Miss Morrow, thinking of Miss Doggett's new idea, which had been to move the silver-table in the drawing-room to the other side of the room.

'But I was glad to see that he remembered the need for moderation,' said Miss Doggett. 'New ideas are not necessarily better than old ones.' She paused, as if thinking of the silver-table, for the moving of it had cost her much anxious thought. 'It is unusual to find a young man who realises this. Mr Latimer knows as well as anybody that we can sometimes be too rash, and that we should ask for God's guidance at such times.'

'One always thinks of clergymen as realising things like that more strongly than other people,' said Miss Morrow. 'I suppose we are apt to attribute to them all the virtues they preach.'

'Yes, clergymen are better than other men,' said Miss Doggett, agreeing with her companion for once. 'They are chosen, you see, set apart. That is why there are not very many of them.'

'Oh.' This seemed rather a curious idea to Miss Morrow. She imagined God selecting half a dozen and saying, 'Well, that's enough for North Oxford. We don't need any more.'

Miss Doggett had now gone on to speak of secular things, although this particular topic of conversation was no less holy to her than sacred things themselves. Anthea and Simon had been up to London together last week, and she was saying how splendid it was that Anthea should have made such a good impression on Lady Beddoes.

'I believe she is very easy to get on with,' said Miss Morrow.

'Well, she has that graciousness of manner that one would expect,' said Miss Doggett, who did not somehow like the idea of her companion's finding somebody of Lady Beddoes's position 'very easy to get on with'. 'You see, Anthea is really nobody on her mother's side,' she went on, 'and even the Clevelands can hardly compare with the

Beddoeses.'

'But Anthea is such a sweet girl,' protested Miss Morrow. 'Anyone would like her. And Lady Beddoes's father was only an English professor teaching in Warsaw. She told Anthea.'

'Miss Morrow, I don't think you understand these things,' said Miss Doggett.

'No, I don't think I do,' said Miss Morrow humbly.

'It will be a splendid thing for Anthea, really *splendid*,' purred Miss Doggett. 'I wouldn't have thought she had so much sense.'

But sense is just what a girl in love doesn't have, thought Miss Morrow, who didn't understand these things.

'I feel the sun is doing us so much good,' she ventured.

'Yes, it is very beneficial if taken in small doses,' agreed Miss Doggett, 'but we mustn't sit still too long, or we shall catch cold.'

They moved slowly away, Miss Morrow adjusting her usually brisk step to suit Miss Doggett's more majestic one. They walked in silence, enjoying the sunshine and their surroundings.

Miss Morrow loved the Parks, especially in fine weather when they were full of people. In the spring there was a faintly ridiculous air about them, like Mendelssohn's *Spring Song*, but, as in the song, there was also a prim and proper Victorian element which chastened the fantasy and made it into something quaint and formal, like a ballet. Dons striding along with walking sticks, wives in Fair Isle jumpers coming low over their hips, nurses with prams, and governesses with intelligent children asking ceaseless questions in their clear, fluty voices. And then there were the clergymen, solitary bearded ones reading books, young earnest ones, like chickens just out of the egg, discussing problems which had nothing to do with the sunshine or the yellow-green leaves uncurling on the trees. There were undergraduates too, and young women with Sweet's *Anglo-Saxon Reader* or lecture notebooks under their arms, and lovers, clasping each other's fingers and trying to find secluded paths where they might kiss. But for Miss Morrow the lovers were only a minor element; the North Oxford and clerical elements were stronger and gave more character to the ballet. She felt that even she and Miss Doggett could be principals in it, together with all the other old ladies who were being walked or wheeled about by their companions to get the fresh air. As they passed such couples, they could hear snatches of their conversation.

'Do you know Archdeacon Liversidge?'

'What?' This in a querulous tone.

'I said, do you know Archdeacon LIVERSIDGE?' Very loudly and clearly.

And then they would pass out of hearing, and Archdeacon Liversidge would remain forever an unknown quantity.

Miss Morrow listened with delight to all she could hear and was glad that Miss Doggett did not want to start a conversation of their own. They had been walking in silence for about ten minutes, when two young men ran up to them.

'Oh, Miss Doggett, what a *delight*!'

'It only needed a meeting with our dear Miss Doggett to make the day *quite* perfect.'

'Why, Michael and Gabriel,' she said, 'what are you doing here? You quite startled me, leaping about like that.'

'We feel we must express ourselves in movement,' said one of them. 'We've been playing Stravinsky's *Sacre du Printemps* all day, and we're simply shattered by it.'

'Michael wants to leap into that pool with one glorious leap,' said Gabriel.

'Wouldn't you frighten the ducks?' said Miss Morrow prosaically.

'Oh, no, we are quite at one with all the wild creatures today,' said Michael. 'I really think it's *wicked* that one should have to work. I've got a tutorial with Mr Cleveland after tea.'

'That *reminds* me,' said Gabriel suddenly, in a mysterious voice. 'Do you think we ought to tell Miss Doggett?'

'Tell her what?'

'What we saw in the Physick Garden?'

'He means the Botanical Gardens,' explained Michael. 'Of course it *was* the Physick Garden in the seventeenth century, wasn't it? We always like to use the old names.'

'What are you talking about?' asked Miss Doggett indulgently.

'Well, it's *rather* naughty.' Michael giggled.

'But it may be our duty to tell,' said Gabriel piously. 'Think how frightful it would be if we failed in our duty.'

'Yes, we always like to have a clear conscience,' said Michael.

'Well, it's about Birdikin and Mr Cleveland,' said Gabriel importantly.

Miss Doggett at once looked interested. One could almost say that her face lighted up, thought Miss Morrow, as she watched her.

'We were walking along a secluded path,' said Michael, 'and we saw them *crouching* in the bushes.'

'Perhaps they were playing Red Indians,' suggested Miss Morrow.

'Miss Morrow, this is no time for joking,' said Miss Doggett sternly. 'You must tell me all you can,' she said to Michael and Gabriel. 'It may be a very serious matter.'

'Oh, a scandal! How *thrilling*!' they cried.

'Oh, no, nothing like that,' said Miss Doggett hastily. 'My nephew suffers from rheumatism, and he ought not to be crouching in bushes,' she said, offering a somewhat unconvincing explanation for her interest. 'Did you notice anything else?'

'Well, of course, we're such innocent *lambs*,' Michael said, 'but we did think it rather *odd*.'

'It looked almost as if they were *hiding* from us,' said Gabriel. 'As if they didn't want to be seen.'

Miss Doggett smiled indulgently but absently. 'I think we must be going home to tea now,' she said, with the air of dismissing the young men. 'You must come and see me soon,' she added graciously.

'Oh, Miss Doggett, we'd *adore* to,' they said, melting gracefully away.

Miss Doggett and Miss Morrow walked on without speaking. Hiding in the bushes, thought Miss Doggett grimly. Obviously Francis had something to hide, something he was ashamed of. Well, she had no intention of interfering, not directly, that was. It was a thankless job talking to Margaret. Having no sense of duty herself, she did not seem to realise that other people had and that it might compel them to do things they would otherwise not have chosen to do. But when you compared Margaret with Miss Bird, you could hardly wonder at Francis's behaviour.

I've never liked Margaret, thought Miss Doggett, suddenly and surprisingly. There she was, quite happy and contented, making no effort to keep her husband interested in her. Wearing the same old jumper suit and comfortable shoes, the same musquash coat with its old-fashioned roll collar, bicycling into town to do the shopping, sitting by the fire smoking cigarettes, taking no interest at all in her house and family. Look at those faded loose-covers, thought Miss Doggett unreasonably, and the way Anthea has been allowed to go about with young men ever since she was fifteen or sixteen. Yes, Margaret was a bad wife and mother. It was no wonder that Francis was looking elsewhere. And yet Miss Doggett would have been the first to condemn Mrs Cleveland if she had suddenly started wearing smart clothes or spending money on beauty treatments, or if she had forbidden Anthea to go out with the eligible Simon Beddoes.

'Murder will out,' she said, with such suddenness that Miss Morrow was quite startled. 'These old writers are very wise,' she went on. 'Things happened in their day just as they do now.'

Miss Morrow could not but agree. 'Of course human nature doesn't really change much,' she ventured tentatively.

'Nor can the leopard change his spots,' said Miss Doggett gravely.

And so, with further exchanges of platitudes, the conversation was carried on until they reached the gate of Leamington Lodge.

10

RESPECT AND ESTEEM

'Hullo, Mr Latimer, going to take evensong?'

The bright, almost chirpy tones startled him, and Mr Latimer turned round to see Mrs Wardell standing by the vicarage gate, with a trowel in one hand and a young plant in the other.

'Yes, I am,' he said shortly. It was surely obvious that he was going to take evensong. Where else could he be going, with a cassock slung over his arm and a face as long as a fiddle?

'It seems a shame on such a lovely evening,' said Mrs Wardell chattily. 'You know, I think there's almost too much church in some ways. It would do you all more good to be digging in the garden. I'm going to have a *gorgeous* show of sweet williams here,' she went on, waving her earthy trowel in the air and depositing some of it on Mr Latimer's cassock.

'Well, I suppose I must be getting along,' he said, brushing off the earth rather ostentatiously. 'I mustn't keep my flock waiting.'

'Your *flock*! Really, you say the funniest things,' she called after him. 'As if they were a lot of sheep.'

'It's quite a usual expression,' said Mr Latimer rather coldly.

When he got to the church he found the usual weekday congregation there. Miss Doggett and Miss Morrow, old Lady Halkin, the Misses Grote, Mrs Allonby, Miss Nollard and Miss Foxe, Mrs Jason-Lomax and Jim Storry, a feeble-minded youth who did odd jobs in the church such as fetching vases and putting up wire frames for the ladies when they did the flowers.

Yes, this was the Church of England, his flock, thought Mr Latimer, a collection of old women, widows and spinsters, and one young man not quite right in the head. These were the people among whom he was destined to spend his life. He hunched his shoulders in his surplice and shivered. The church, with its dampness and sickly smell of lilies, felt cold and tomblike. He had the feeling, as he mumbled through the service, that he and his congregation were already dead. Even Miss Morrow, usually so bright and amusing, looked grey and corpselike in her dowdy hat—the one that went with everything and nothing—and her greenish tweed coat. Looking at her, Mr Latimer wondered whether he could possibly do worse than marry Miss Morrow.

After the service he lingered in the vestry, feeling disinclined to make conversation, but when he got outside he saw that he had not escaped. Miss Doggett and Miss Morrow were waiting in the porch. He felt like some pet animal being led home. As he walked by Miss Doggett's side, a sudden feeling of despair came over him, wrapping him round like the heavy crimson eiderdown which he so often tossed onto the floor when he woke in the night.

When they got to Leamington Lodge he sat in the drawing-room, waiting for dinner, while Miss Doggett knitted. At her request he read some extracts from *In Memoriam*. He chose them at random, but, as so often happens, the lines seemed to be appropriate.

Thou wilt not leave us in the dust,
Thou madest man, he knows not why,
He thinks he was not made to die—
And Thou hast made him—Thou art just.

Perhaps there was a message of hope here. It referred to a life after this. But he didn't want to think about that. What he was concerned with was how to escape from the life he was living now; he didn't care what happened afterwards. Oh, this place! These heavy velvet curtains, green-papered walls, high-collared clergymen of the eighties and nineties, Swiss water-colours and Bavarian engravings . . . His voice droned on through *In Memoriam*. Miss Doggett's needles clicked. The marble clock on the mantelpiece chimed to remind him that the days of man are three score years and ten and that he was sitting in a North Oxford drawing-room, reading Tennyson to an old woman. He felt he wanted to make some loud noise, to roar, bellow or scream at the top of his voice, as if by so doing he might have the same effect on the walls of Leamington Lodge as the trumpet on the walls of Jericho.

He put down the book and stopped reading. But all the noise that came out of him was a weak, faltering, bleating sound, something between a yawn and an 'oh'.

'Poor Mr Latimer, I'm afraid I've made you read too much,' said Miss Doggett. 'You must be tired after taking evensong. You shall have some Ovaltine before you go to bed.'

Mr Latimer slumped down in his chair. He was a creature without bones, a poor worm of a man. He laughed as he remembered his idea of marrying Miss Morrow. A creature without bones, a worm, marry? How was it possible? He was fated to live and die in a gloomy house in North Oxford, where the sun was not allowed to shine through the windows in case it might fade the carpets and covers.

'Mr Latimer, you look quite pale,' said Miss Doggett in a solicitous tone. 'I don't know if it is against your principles, but perhaps you would like a glass of sherry?'

I have no principles. I am a worm, thought Mr Latimer, gladly accepting her offer. 'You must have some too,' he said, with something of his usual gallantry. 'I can't drink alone.'

'Well . . .' Miss Doggett hesitated. 'Perhaps I could do with something. Elderly people need stimulants sometimes, you know.'

Mr Latimer emptied his glass in one gulp and then suddenly and without warning burst out,

'O for a beaker full of the warm South,
Full of the true, the blushful Hippocrene,
With beaded bubbles winking at the brim . . .'

Miss Doggett looked at him with some anxiety, but before anything could be said, the door opened and Miss Morrow came into the room, wearing her new dress of leaf green. She had meant to slip in quietly, but now her entrance only added to the dramatic quality of the scene. The appearance of Miss Morrow in this most unsuitable dress combined with the sight of Mr Latimer standing on the hearthrug waving his empty glass and reciting Keats was too much for Miss Doggett.

96

'Really, Miss Morrow,' she began, '*really* . . .' and then muttered a word that sounded like 'popinjay'.

'Doesn't she look splendid?' said Mr Latimer. 'Every woman should have a new dress in the spring.'

Miss Doggett said nothing. Perhaps in her opinion Miss Morrow hardly counted as a woman, certainly not the kind to be associated with spring and new dresses.

'I think dinner is just going in,' said Miss Morrow in a hurrying tone, to hide her embarrassment.

'Allow me to escort you, Miss Morrow,' said Mr Latimer, offering his arm.

'Mr Latimer isn't feeling very well tonight,' said Miss Doggett, as if explaining away his courtly gesture. 'I persuaded him to take a glass of sherry.'

I don't imagine he needed much persuading, thought Miss Morrow sardonically.

'I took a glass myself,' went on Miss Doggett deliberately. 'It has considerable medicinal value.'

'And Miss Morrow is the only person who hasn't had any,' said Mr Latimer eagerly. 'She must have some.'

'I don't want any, thank you,' said Miss Morrow. 'I am feeling perfectly well.'

Dinner was a strained meal and nobody said very much. Miss Doggett darted occasional glances of disapproval at her companion, who seemed unconscious of having done anything wrong. Miss Morrow knew that she was looking nice this evening, or as nice as it was possible for her to look, and she was feeling happy and excited, as one does on an unexpected sunny morning in winter. She realised as she sat eating her boiled mutton and caper sauce—the kind of food calculated to bring anyone down to earth again—that this was a most unsuitable state of mind for the companion of an elderly lady. It was the feeling that had made her plunge boldly among the drab dresses in her wardrobe and take out the new green one, which she knew she ought to be keeping for some special occasion that would never happen.

'Do have some cheese, Mr Latimer,' said Miss Doggett. 'You are eating hardly anything.'

Mr Latimer took some without seeming to know what he was doing. The moment he had seen Miss Morrow in her green dress it had all come back to him—the realisation that he might do worse than marry her. Of course that was what he should do. He would ask her tonight, before anything could change his mind. How pleased she would be! They really ought to be quite happy together: that was perhaps the most one could expect of any marriage and more than many people got. He could hardly wait for dinner to be over and for Miss Doggett to have gone to bed, which she usually did between half past nine and ten.

But tonight it seemed as if things were being specially arranged to suit him, for before dinner was over Florence came in to say that old Lady Halkin's companion had telephoned to ask whether Miss Doggett would go and play bezique with her ladyship. Miss Doggett, who had never been known to refuse an invitation from a titled person, sent Miss Morrow running upstairs for her hat and skunk cape and did not even wait to have her coffee.

'Well, well,' said Mr Latimer. 'We shall have an evening to ourselves.'

'Yes,' said Miss Morrow. 'I wonder if there's

anything good on the wireless.'

'Oh, don't let's have the wireless,' said Mr Latimer quickly. 'We so seldom have a chance to be by ourselves. Let's make the most of it.'

Miss Morrow sat down and assumed an attitude of patient expectation, as if ready to receive suggestions as to how this might be done.

'I think we always get on very well together,' began Mr Latimer.

Miss Morrow laughed. 'A curate and an old lady's companion?' she said. 'But what else would you expect?'

Mr Latimer wished she hadn't put it like that, making them sound slightly ridiculous. It was a bad beginning, he felt. But he was not yet discouraged. 'I meant that in some ways we seem to be very close to each other, very near,' he went on.

Miss Morrow took her knitting out of its bag and began to count stitches.

Mr Latimer looked round the room, as if expecting to receive inspiration from the objects in it. Oh, Canon Tottle, he thought, gazing at a faded sepia photograph, how would you do what I have to do this evening? How would you lead up to it? What words would you use? Looking at the heavy, serious face with its determined expression, Mr Latimer decided that with Canon Tottle there would be no leading up to it. He would plunge straight in and say what he had to say quickly and definitely. That was obviously the right thing to do if one had the courage. He looked round the room again. The sherry and glasses were still on one of the little tables.

'There's no need to look so furtive,' said Miss Morrow, following his glance. 'It's quite natural to want cheering up occasionally. I'm not sure that sherry *after* a meal is the correct thing, though. Shouldn't it be port?'

'Oh, I suppose so,' said Mr Latimer, impatient at the turn the conversation was taking.

'Still, if you're considering only its medicinal value I shouldn't think it matters when you drink it. I should have some now if you feel like it,' said Miss Morrow.

A glass of sherry would not do much for him, but Mr Latimer felt encouraged. 'How well you understand me,' he said. 'You must feel it too, the gloom here, the sense of being imprisoned . . .' He fluttered his hands in hopeless, birdlike gestures.

'Of course I have,' said Miss Morrow briskly. 'I warned you about it when you came. It's different for me, I'm a paid companion and as such I expect gloom; it's my portion. But on the whole I'm lucky and I really enjoy life.'

'You enjoy life?' asked Mr Latimer, as if this were something new to him.

'Yes, of course I do. And you ought to even more because you're young.'

'But I'm not,' said Mr Latimer. 'We're neither of us young, if it comes to that. But we aren't old yet.' His voice took on a more hopeful note. 'Oh, Miss Morrow—Janie,' he burst out suddenly.

'My name isn't Janie.'

'Well, it's something beginning with J,' he said impatiently. It was annoying to be held up by such a triviality. What did it matter what her name was at this moment?

'It's Jessie, if you want to know, or Jessica, really,' she said, without looking up from her knitting.

100

'Oh, Jessica,' continued Mr Latimer, feeling a little flat by now, 'couldn't we escape out of all this together?'

Miss Morrow began to laugh. 'Oh, dear,' she said, 'you must excuse me, but it's so odd to be called Jessica. I think I rather like it; it gives me dignity.'

'Well?' said Mr Latimer, feeling now as completely flat as any man might who has just proposed marriage and been completely ignored.

'Well what?' echoed Miss Morrow.

'I said, couldn't we escape out of all this *together*?'

'Do you mean go out this evening?' she said, with a casual glance at the marble clock on the mantelpiece. 'To the pictures or something?'

Mr Latimer was now so exasperated that he was determined to make her understand. Surely her stupidity must be intentional? She was trying to irritate him. 'I am asking you to marry me, to be my wife,' he said in a deliberate tone.

'Oh, I see,' said Miss Morrow. 'I thought you meant just to go out for this evening.'

Oh, I see. Had anyone proposing marriage ever before been so answered? 'You might at least give me an answer,' he said coldly.

'But are you really serious?' asked Miss Morrow. 'You don't sound as if you were, but I suppose you must be. A man would hardly propose to me as a joke, in case I might accept him.'

'You're a very charming woman,' said Mr Latimer sulkily and without any enthusiasm whatever.

'Well, I am certainly flattered that you should have wanted—or thought you wanted—to marry me,' said Miss Morrow calmly, 'but I'm afraid my answer must be no.' She paused and went on in a solicitous tone, 'I don't think you're quite yourself this evening. Perhaps you're overtired. I'll ask Florence to make you some Ovaltine, shall I?'

'You might at least give me the credit of knowing my own mind!' said Mr Latimer angrily. 'I respect and esteem you very much,' he went on in the same angry tone. 'I think we might be very happy together.'

'But do you *love* me?' asked Miss Morrow quietly.

'Love you?' he said indignantly. 'But of course I do. Haven't I just told you so?'

'You have said that you respect and esteem me very much,' said Miss Morrow without elaboration. 'But you said something about escaping together? Hasn't it occurred to you that if we did, you would soon find yourself wanting to escape from a marriage with a woman you didn't love? And how much more difficult that would be than just finding new lodgings!'

'I don't believe in divorce,' said Mr Latimer stiffly. 'And anyway, I shouldn't want to escape.'

'Oh, no.' Miss Morrow smiled. 'Clergymen aren't the escaping sort, but you'd feel you wanted to and that would be just as bad.'

'You don't seem to realise that one can learn to care,' said Mr Latimer pompously.

'No, I don't,' said Miss Morrow firmly. 'Learning to care always seems to me to be one of the most difficult lessons that can be imagined. How does one set about it? Perhaps we might do it together, like Russian, in the long winter evenings?'

'Now, Jessica, you're just being frivolous. I have

102

asked you to marry me and you have refused. Is that it?'

'Yes,' said Miss Morrow in a low voice. 'We don't love each other, and I'm sure you could do better. There will be something else for you, I know there will.'

'And what about you?'

'Me? Well, my life will go on just the same as usual,' said Miss Morrow, giving point to her words by picking up her knitting again. 'But I shall always be flattered to remember your proposal,' she added more graciously.

'Jessica . . .' began Mr Latimer.

'I think it had better be Miss Morrow and Mr Latimer,' she said gently. 'We don't want Miss Doggett to notice anything, do we?'

Mr Latimer made no reply but a groaning sound. 'I think I shall go for a walk,' he said.

'Yes, do,' said Miss Morrow soothingly. 'It's quite a nice evening.'

But Mr Latimer was already in the hall putting on his Burberry.

Well, thought Miss Morrow, looking down at her new green dress, so it had been an occasion after all. A man had asked her to marry him and she had refused. But did a trapped curate count as a man? It had been such a very half-hearted proposal . . . poor Mr Latimer! She smiled as she remembered it. 'I respect and esteem you very much . . . I think we might be very happy together . . .' *Might*. Oh, no, it wouldn't do at all! Even Miss Morrow's standards were higher than that, so high, indeed, that she feared she would never marry now. For she wanted love, or whatever it was that made Simon and Anthea walk along the street not noticing other people simply because they had each other's eyes to look into. And of course she knew perfectly well that she would never get anything like that. It was only sometimes, when a spring day came in the middle of winter, that one had a sudden feeling that nothing was really impossible. And then, how much more sensible it was to satisfy one's springlike impulses by buying a new dress in an unaccustomed and thoroughly unsuitable colour than by embarking on a marriage without love. For, after all, respect and esteem were cold, lifeless things—dry bones picked clean of flesh. There was nothing springlike about dry bones, nothing warm and romantic about respect and esteem.

Miss Morrow got up to look at the *Radio Times*. In spite of her commonsense reasoning, she could not help feeling a little sad. She liked Mr Latimer; they had little jokes together, and that was surely something.

A concert of contemporary music, variety from Newcastle, a verse drama about some character in classical mythology she had never heard of— somehow she did not feel that any of these would fit her mood. Perhaps a continental station would have something better. She turned the knobs until music of a Viennese nature filled the air—all the romance of Vienna in the days of the Emperor Franz Josef was suddenly brought into a North Oxford drawing-room. Miss Morrow went on with her knitting and thought about the film *Mayerling*, which she had seen with Miss Doggett, who approved of anything historical and connected with royalty, however immoral the tone of it might be. But people said it hadn't happened like that at all, really . . .

'I met Mr Latimer out walking,' said Miss Doggett, when she came in, 'but he didn't see me. He was striding along without a hat. I hope he won't catch cold.'

'He said he wanted exercise,' lied Miss Morrow.

'Well, of course, there isn't much for him to do when I'm not here. I expect he was bored.'

'Yes, I expect he was,' said Miss Morrow, without raising her eyes from her knitting.

'A young man needs stimulating and intelligent company,' went on Miss Doggett. 'Mr Latimer is really very cultured.'

'Yes,' said Miss Morrow.

'Why, Florence hasn't taken away the sherry glasses,' said Miss Doggett, seeing them still on the table. 'You mustn't let her get careless, Miss Morrow. It seems that I can't be out of the house for an hour without something going wrong.'

Miss Morrow said nothing.

It had started to rain outside. Mr Latimer strode along without knowing or caring where he was going. He was thinking of nothing, certainly not of the woman who had just rejected him. The feeling that had possessed him earlier in the evening was something fierce and elemental. It could not live in the drawing-room at Leamington Lodge.

On he went, taking no notice of anybody, until he bumped into a group of young men who were coming away from a political meeting. One of them was Simon Beddoes. He was feeling very pleased with himself, because he had asked a clever question that the speaker hadn't been able to answer at all satisfactorily. He said 'Good evening' to Mr Latimer, whom he had met once before, hoping that he would stop, so that they could lead the conversation round to it.

But Mr Latimer looked straight through him and walked down in the direction of the river.

And then suddenly he felt tired and rather silly. He no longer wanted to do wild things. He crossed the road and got on the first bus that came. And so there he was, he who had strode out into the night with the idea of escaping from it all, taking a twopenny bus ride home, letting himself in through the stained-glass front door, and creeping quietly up the ecclesiastical pitch-pine staircase so as not to wake anybody.

This is the way the world ends,
Not with a bang but a whimper.

The walls had closed round him again. There was no escape.

11

LOVE IN THE BRITISH MUSEUM

Nobody was surprised on a sunny May morning when Francis Cleveland announced at breakfast that he was going up to the British Museum that day to do some work on his book. It was not in the least unusual for him to go up to the British Museum. He did not think it necessary to add that he was taking Barbara Bird with him. Nobody would be surprised at that either. She was an intelligent girl and would be able to help him with various references that needed to be verified. His pupils had been helping him with his book for the past twenty years; it was really quite a wonder that it had not been finished before now.

'For goodness' sake give yourself a good lunch and tea, dear,' Margaret Cleveland had said. 'I don't know if they still have that depressing tea-room, but don't go there. I believe there are some quite good little restaurants in Bloomsbury.'

Francis had said rather shortly that he had no intention of going to the British Museum tea-room. He wished Margaret wouldn't fuss him so. The fact that she meant it kindly made him feel a little guilty, as if he were deceiving her about something, when really he was doing nothing of the kind. He was simply not mentioning Barbara, that was all. As nobody would think anything of it there was no need to mention it, he told himself rather defiantly.

He and Barbara had caught an early train from Oxford to Paddington, but as it was such a lovely morning they had first of all gone into Hyde Park and sat there for some time. This was very disappointing for Edward Killigrew, who also happened to be going up to the British Museum that day. He had seen them get into the train at Oxford, but at Paddington he had lost sight of them, and when he got to the Museum there was no sign of them in the Reading Room. He had quite assumed that this was where they would be going and had been unable to concentrate on his work all morning for wondering where they could be. Towards lunchtime all sorts of wild ideas came into his head and he was really a little disappointed to see them come into the Reading Room shortly before two o'clock. They sat down and appeared to be working quite hard, and at four they got up and went out. Edward Killigrew followed them. He was curious to see where they were going to have tea. Perhaps he might get near them and hear what they talked about.

But instead of going out of the Museum they turned to look at the autographs and manuscripts. Edward padded along behind them until he managed to get quite close. He was glad that he was wearing his shoes with crêpe rubber soles. He had found them very useful in the Bodleian and had been able to approach people and hear many interesting conversations without being seen or heard himself. He was afraid that he had missed something here, as he had been rather a long way behind them, but when he got nearer he heard that she was only talking about the book they were looking at.

'Milton's commonplace book,' she said in a rapt tone. 'Just to think of Milton *himself* writing in it! This must be *his* handwriting.' She bent lower over the glass case and peered down into it.

Edward Killigrew drew the curtain aside from an adjoining case and stood gazing at a letter from Lord Byron to his solicitor. This was dull, he thought, definitely dull. Mother had thought there might be something between these two. He had certainly expected something more interesting than a young woman going into raptures over Milton's commonplace book.

'I think it's so wonderful to see things like this,' she said. 'It gives me an indescribable feeling, so that I can hardly keep from crying. I know it's very silly, really.'

Edward Killigrew agreed that it was certainly

108

very silly, but Francis Cleveland seemed to think otherwise.

'No,' he said, 'it's not silly at all. It's just how you would feel. Oh, Barbara, I love you,' he said suddenly. 'I love you!'

There was a rapt silence. Edward Killigrew held himself very still, hardly daring to breathe. If they turned round now they would see him. But even so he had heard; those words could not be unsaid, that was the main point. He waited eagerly for her reply but the girl's voice was very low and the noise of somebody passing made it impossible to hear what she said. But luck was still with him, for after a moment or two Francis Cleveland said quite distinctly, 'And you love me too, don't you?' and Barbara's voice was not too low for Edward Killigrew to catch her 'Yes'.

Trembling with excitement, he padded swiftly away and out to get some tea. He found himself walking rapidly along without knowing where he was going. He stopped to think for a moment and then decided that he would give himself a treat and go to the big Lyons' Corner House. Mother always liked going there. He would have some splendid news for her when he got home tonight. Things in the library had been very dull lately, even the little feuds among staff and readers seemed to have died down. Fine weather was better for romances than for quarrels.

Edward ordered a pot of tea, a plate of cakes and something called a 'Beano', which he decided would fit the occasion very well. The orchestra began to play a rumba. He felt happier than he had felt for a long time. There had been nothing like this since that disgraceful affair of old Mr Pringle and the underground bookstore.

Barbara and Francis remained as if rooted to the spot, still staring at Milton's commonplace book. For a time they were silent, and then Barbara said uncertainly, 'I think I should like some tea.' When they were sitting down drinking tea, everything would be all right. They would become real people, themselves, again. Everything seemed unreal in this great building. Milton couldn't *really* have written in the book they had been looking at, just as Francis couldn't really have said those words and she have agreed with them. She felt rather funny, almost as if she were going to faint.

'Let's go out,' she said, drawing the curtain neatly across the glass case.

'Yes, we must talk,' he said. 'Where can we talk?'

'Here's a café,' said Barbara.

They looked into it. There was one other couple sitting in a corner, while two waitresses leaned against a counter spread with home-made cakes and jams.

'It's too quiet here,' said Francis abruptly, taking her arm and leading her out again. 'We must find somewhere else, some large place where people won't hear every word we're saying.'

'There's Lyons',' suggested Barbara doubtfully.

'Oh, yes, that will do.'

It would have been even more interesting for Edward Killigrew if he could have continued to hear their conversation, but as it was he considered himself to be most fortunate to have noticed them coming in and sitting at a table in the opposite corner of the great room. This would be something else to tell Mother. He went on happily eating his 'Beano', which turned out to be a poached egg on

110

baked beans, unaware that at that precise moment Francis Cleveland was asking Barbara Bird what they were going to do about it.

'What *can* we do?' she said, dealing rather inefficiently with the tea. 'There isn't anything we can do.' She was feeling more normal now, although still a little dazed, as if she had just woken out of a dream.

'But . . .' Francis went on stirring his tea, into which he had forgotten to put sugar. 'We love each other. I love you and you love me too, don't you?'

'Yes,' said Barbara doubtfully, 'I do, only . . .' How could she explain to him what her love was like? That although it was a love stronger than death, it wasn't the kind of love one *did* anything about? On the contrary, doing nothing about it was one of its chief characteristics, because if one did anything it would be different—it might even disappear altogether.

'Aren't you sure then?' he asked.

'Oh, yes . . .' she said uncertainly. She dug her fork into a cake and it broke into little pieces. She chased the hard bits unhappily round her plate.

'Poor little Barbara,' he said, 'don't look so unhappy. We'll find a way,' he said confidently, he who had never in his life found any way of doing anything except postponing evil days and unpleasant duties. If there was any way-finding to be done, it was always Margaret who did it. It would perhaps be asking too much even of her to find a way out of this.

'We seem to have got a carriage to ourselves,' he said hopefully, as they got into the train at Paddington.

But he had spoken too soon, for at the last

111

moment an old, birdlike man hurried in and sat nodding in a corner over his evening paper. Every now and then he darted an enquiring glance at Francis and Barbara, huddled miserably in the opposite corner, as if he were waiting for some sort of entertainment to begin. But they must have been a great disappointment to him, for they sat in silence, occupied with their thoughts.

What was to be done? Francis wondered. Obviously something would have to be done now that they had declared their love for each other. Barbara would expect something more than a declaration and would hardly be content to go on as before. He found himself getting quite agitated and thinking of wild, improbable things like divorce and remarriage. Perhaps a little house in one of the remoter Oxford suburbs . . . They wouldn't have much money, but Barbara was probably a domesticated girl and in any case it was natural for women to do housework. And yet, what a depressing prospect it was for a man getting on in years who was used to having every comfort! He didn't think he wanted anything like *that*; he was really so comfortable as he was. He looked at Barbara. She was supposedly reading, but it was many minutes since her hand had turned a page. Perhaps *she* would be able to find a way out, he thought hopefully. Women were better than men at things like that.

How awful, thought Barbara, that it should come to this! Was it *her* fault? Had she been wrong to see him so often? She looked back over their past association and decided that she had perhaps been at fault. That evening last term when he had sent the flowers—she ought to have been warned by that; she ought to have seen what was coming. Oh, why had she said that she loved him? She had been so surprised by his declaration that the truth had come out before she had had time to think what was the wisest thing to do. And now everything had gone wrong. Her beautiful love which had given her so much happiness would be turned into a sordid intrigue. Unless they could somehow forget about this afternoon, she thought hopefully, and go on as they had been before in those happy days which now seemed so far away.

Suddenly the old man leaned forward and said confidentially, 'I think I will go and wash my hands,' and with that he got up and left Francis and Barbara gaping after him, still trying to think of a suitable reply.

As soon as the old man had made up his mind as to the probable direction of the lavatory and finished hovering in the corridor, Francis turned to Barbara and said, rather dramatically, 'Thank God we're alone at last!'

'Yes, but only for a little while,' she said, with an anxious glance towards the door.

'Barbara, darling,' he said, edging nearer to her and putting his arms around her.

'Don't, he'll be coming back,' she said, carefully straightening her hat, which he had knocked crooked. She hated to be untidied in any way.

'Oh, what does *that* matter! I want to kiss you,' he said, feeling rather pleased with himself.

Barbara turned away. She found herself staring at the upholstery and wondering why it was so bright and glaring, not a warm, dull red as it usually was, but an ugly fawn with great sinister, sprawling flowers.

She knew exactly how she ought to feel, for she was well read in our greater and lesser English poets, but the unfortunate fact was that she did not really like being kissed at all. There had been one young man in her first term, and they had got on so well together, until, one Sunday evening when they had been walking by the river, he had suddenly seized her in his arms. She had been terribly distressed, and they had walked all the way back arguing miserably about intelligent platonic friendships. 'Man and woman created He them, Barbara,' the young man had said pompously, but all she could say was 'Yes, John, I know. But I only want to be *friends* . . .' after which she had run weeping into her college and a beautiful friendship between two intelligent people had been broken up. Since then there had been one or two casual kisses, which Barbara had endured simply because she felt that it was the only way of showing one's gratitude for a good dinner or a pleasant evening at the theatre.

But this was different, or it ought to be different. She and Francis really loved each other—they had said so in the British Museum. Naturally she must want him to kiss her. Of course he was her tutor; that may have had something to do with it. It seemed odd to be kissing one's tutor, whether one was in love with him or not. And the setting was not very romantic—that might be why she had these curious doubts. A hurried kiss, snatched in a railway carriage . . . there was something essentially sordid about railway carriages: one imagined the kinds of things one read about in the papers; to be kissed in a railway carriage was really quite the reverse of romantic. It hardly occurred to her that

114

another reason why the whole thing seemed odd and somehow wrong might be because Francis was a married man. Barbara had unconventional ideas about morality and had often discussed such matters with her friends over coffee and Ovaltine far into the night and early morning.

'Well, well . . .' Francis released her and wondered what he should say now. It was so long since anything like this had happened to him. But, fortunately perhaps, the old man chose this moment to come back and there followed one of those unreal conversations, this one being about the washing arrangements in English trains, the small, hard, non-lathering pieces of soap, the shortage of towels, the water that gushed forth in a boiling or icy stream or refused to gush at all, the smuts in the basin.

Barbara's thoughts went round in miserable circles, until she almost began to wish that she had never seen Francis Cleveland but had gone to old Miss Gantillon in her house in Norham Road and had calm, boring tutorials with no emotional complications.

'Is this Oxford?' asked the old man as the train slowed down.

'Oh, yes, this is Oxford,' said Barbara, forcing a smile. 'We're very punctual.'

'The Home of Lost Causes, that's what they call it, I believe,' he said conversationally.

'Yes, they do,' said Barbara politely.

'When I was a child Matthew Arnold came to our house to tea,' said the old man. 'An Inspector of Schools!' He shook his head and went shuffling out into the corridor, still muttering.

'May I see you back to your college?' said

115

Francis.

'Yes, if you like,' said Barbara. After all, it could hardly make any difference now.

They sat rather apart in the taxi and did not speak for a long time. As they approached Barbara's college, Francis said, 'Don't worry, everything will be all right.'

Barbara turned to him but found that she couldn't say anything. She felt a sudden impulse to cry on his shoulder, but that wouldn't do at all; nor was it what she really wanted. She felt that she must get to the seclusion of her room, where she could think things out in a familiar cloistered atmosphere that was nothing like a railway carriage or the British Museum.

'Good-bye,' she said, getting out of the taxi quickly. 'Thank you for a nice day.'

The tears were already starting into her eyes as she ran up the drive, and before she had reached her room she was openly crying. Miss Kingley, the Classics tutor, commented drily on the fact to Miss Borage, the Bursar. It was so unlike Miss Bird.

Francis Cleveland spent the evening in his own drawing-room and somehow it had never seemed so comfortable as it did now, when he supposed he ought really to be thinking of that little love-nest in one of the remoter Oxford suburbs, with Barbara doing all the housework. They wouldn't have such large rooms or such comfortable chairs as these, he thought, and where was he going to keep all his books?

'Francis, you're looking so odd,' said Margaret, glancing up from her novel. 'Have you got indigestion?'

'I don't think so,' he answered shortly.

116

'Then it must be the effect of the British Museum,' she said.

That was exactly it, thought Francis, suddenly blaming it all on the British Museum. Everyone knew that libraries had an unnatural atmosphere which made people behave oddly. He felt that he had somehow made a mess of things this afternoon. But of course he was not used to dealing with situations like this; he had had no practice. He had wasted his time sitting in libraries, doing research about things that were no good to anybody. He thought of his companions in the Bodleian: Arnold Penge, Edward Killigrew, Professor Lopping . . . They wouldn't have done any better either. Probably not as well. This reflection was some consolation to him, and he began to feel quite pleased with himself.

There was no need to *do* anything about it, he decided. They could just go on as they were. He was sure that it was not at all unusual for tutors and their pupils to declare their love for each other. He began to rack his brains for instances, but although he could not think of any at that moment, he was not discouraged. There was no harm in going on with Barbara just as before; that would be very nice. And, after all, it wasn't as if anybody else knew about what had happened this afternoon. They had managed to keep it all so very secret.

12

CONVERSATION
IN A TOOL SHED

'I hope my mother will know the right sort of thing to say,' said Simon uneasily. 'She isn't really used to opening church garden parties.'

'We are very fortunate in having persuaded your mother to come,' said Miss Doggett rather stiffly. It seemed unnecessary to add that Lady Beddoes would of course know the right sort of thing to say. Ambassadors' widows who lived in Belgravia were surely equal to any occasion; a church garden party was something they would take very easily in their stride. She was surprised that Simon should seem doubtful.

They were in the Clevelands' drawing-room, waiting for Lady Beddoes to arrive. It was a fine afternoon, but although the sun was shining there was a feeling of thunder in the air. Miss Morrow was carrying Miss Doggett's mackintosh cape and umbrella, and Mrs Cleveland had decided that she need not wear the large-brimmed hat which she disliked but which was supposed to be correct for such occasions. She would look much more sensible in her comfortable blue felt if it came on to rain. Anthea was looking charming in flowered chiffon and a hat trimmed with roses, but it was different for the young. They didn't mind and even enjoyed uncomfortable elegance.

'What is it in aid of?' asked Simon. 'I dare say I could help her with her speech, though'—he glanced at his watch—'there won't be much time if it's supposed to begin at three. My mother's hopeless about time. She may even mistake the day,' he added alarmingly.

'Oh, I hope not; I mean, surely she wouldn't?' said Mrs Cleveland in an agitated voice. 'Of course Dr and Mrs Fremantle promised to come,' she said, as if trying to find a possible substitute for Lady Beddoes should it be necessary. But one could hardly ask Olive Fremantle at the last minute. It would probably have to be herself in her old felt hat. She believed she was the only person who could safely be asked to do anything at the last minute without taking offence.

'Here's a car,' said Anthea, who had been stationed by the window. 'Come on, Simon, let's go out and meet her.'

Everyone felt relieved when Lady Beddoes came into the room. They had hardly known what to expect from the hints Simon had given them, but when they saw her they were reassured. She was tall and thin, and although there was a certain vagueness in her manner, she was undeniably elegant. She was really much smarter than anybody they had ever had to open the garden parties, except perhaps old Lady Halkin in the days before she began to have her 'turns'.

Lady Beddoes was talking so volubly to Anthea that it was some time before she noticed the other women in the room. Anthea had to interrupt her gently so that they could be introduced. She shook hands with them all and said what a good thing it was that it was fine and how glad she was to be coming to open the garden party. She loved doing things like opening garden parties, but now that poor Lyall was dead nobody asked her, because she wasn't important enough by herself. She then turned to Mrs Cleveland and said what lovely lupins she had in her front garden and how she wished she had a garden in Chester Square.

Miss Doggett, who had imagined herself having the monopoly of Lady Beddoes, decided that it was time to make a move. 'I think we should be going across to the vicarage,' she said. 'Time is getting on.'

'Yes, isn't it,' sighed Lady Beddoes, who seemed to have heard only Miss Doggett's last remark and was evidently taking it in a rather different way from that which had been intended. 'It seems only the other day since Simon was a little boy going to Eton for the first time, and look at him now, he's taller than I am.'

Simon began talking rapidly about something else. If they weren't careful, Mama would really get going and begin to tell them about that time in Warsaw when Marshal Pilsudski had taken him on his knee and asked him what he wanted to be when he grew up, and how Simon had said 'Prime Minister of England' and everyone had thought it so wonderful that a child should know what a Prime Minister was, at an age when most boys thought only of being engine drivers. She never told this story quite correctly, Simon felt, and although he liked nothing better than to be the centre of interest, he realised that as people were waiting for her to open the garden party, they would hardly be able to give the story the attention it deserved. He would save it for another time when they had nothing else on their minds.

The Wardells and Mr Latimer were waiting at

the vicarage.

'Oh, Lady Beddoes, how *good* of you to come!' exclaimed Mrs Wardell, rushing forward to greet her. 'Ben, isn't it good of her?'

'Yes, indeed it is,' said the vicar, although he was thinking that, as she had been invited and had promised that she would, it was hardly so *good* of her to have come. As always on these occasions he was fussing about, watch in hand, thinking of the last-minute things that ought to be done.

'Those chairs, Agnes, for the tea garden,' he called out in an agitated voice. 'Did you send Lily upstairs to bring some down from the bedrooms? I don't think there are going to be enough.'

'Oh, I expect everything will be all right,' said his wife vaguely. 'Why, Miss Morrow's wearing a new dress!' she exclaimed suddenly. 'What a pretty shade of green.'

'This is only the second time I've worn it,' said Miss Morrow, casting down her eyes demurely.

'I think you will probably be too hot,' observed Miss Doggett. 'It is a woollen material, isn't it?'

'I'm sure it's going to rain,' said Mr Latimer gloomily.

'Oh, well, it will do the garden good,' said Mrs Wardell, 'and we've several pairs of galoshes here and an old mackintosh of Ben's that he uses for fishing. I shan't mind getting wet,' she said, indicating her costume of green shantung, which was too long in the skirt. 'I love the rain. I sometimes walk for miles in it.'

'Now, now, it's nearly time,' said the vicar. 'We shall go out onto the lawn through the french windows, Lady Beddoes. I shall open the proceedings with a prayer; it is customary, you

121

know,' he added, as if in apology. 'And then one of the church wardens will introduce you.'

'And then you'll make your speech, darling,' said Simon. 'And remember it mustn't be too long, because people can never hear things in gardens anyway.'

'Well, I'm sure nobody would ever want to hear anything I have to say, even if they *could* hear it,' said Lady Beddoes obscurely.

'Let us pray,' said the vicar in a voice that was intended to be sonorous but succeeded only in being harsh and startling. 'O Lord God Almighty, look down and bless our humble endeavours and the cause for which we are working. Grant that we may be successful in our enterprise and that we may have fine weather, so that we may enjoy the fruits of the earth, which Thou in Thy mercy hast vouchsafed to us. Amen.'

Much safer to have used one of the orthodox prayers for such occasions, thought Mr Latimer scornfully; the vicar's efforts at extemporising were rarely successful. What fruits of the earth were they hoping to enjoy this afternoon? Early potatoes? There was certainly nothing else in the garden yet. His mouth twitched at the corners and he bent his head in a lower and more devout attitude, fixing his eyes on the root of a plantain which had been turned brown by weed-killer.

'I do hope Mama remembers what it's in aid of,' whispered Simon, as his mother got up to make her speech. 'She's so hopelessly vague.'

But everyone agreed that it was a lovely speech. She looked so gracious, standing there in her pretty hyacinth-blue dress and her elegant hat, and her voice was so attractive, that people hardly noticed what she said. If they had not been so charmed by her manner and appearance, they might have realised that she had almost given the impression that the garden party was in aid of the poor in Poland, about whom she spoke with great feeling for nearly ten minutes. And then, perhaps realising that she had wandered from the point, for she had quite forgotten to refer to her written speech, she ended up by saying that there were really a lot of poor people everywhere who needed our help, especially in London—in the East End, she added, frowning a little, for London to her meant Belgravia and she had not really seen much sign of poverty there. We ought therefore to buy as many things as we could. She herself was certainly going to buy a *great* many things.

After the votes of thanks, Lady Beddoes was led round the various stalls by Miss Doggett, who seemed to have taken possession of her, so that the vicar was compelled to follow at a respectful distance with the crowd of less important people. He walked along with his head bent, his eyes on the little holes which Lady Beddoes's high heels were making in the lawn.

Lady Beddoes and Miss Doggett kept up a running flow of conversation during their walk round the stalls. Miss Doggett was gratified to find that Lady Beddoes spoke to her quite unreservedly about all kinds of things. Simon was always saying how unwise it was to let his mother travel anywhere alone because she always began telling her life story to the most impossible people, but Miss Doggett did not know this, and even if she had known it she would have assumed that it was a natural sympathy between two gentlewomen of Belgravia and North

Oxford which made their conversation flow so easily.

They even began talking about the late Sir Lyall Beddoes.

'My husband would have liked these,' said Lady Beddoes, fingering a pair of hand-knitted blue bed-socks. 'It was always so cold in Poland in the winter, and he didn't like a hot water bottle. Blue was his favourite colour.'

'How you must miss him,' said Miss Doggett in a mournful tone.

'Well, I do in a way,' said Lady Beddoes doubtfully. 'I mean, it seems *odd* without him, though I've got used to it now. When you've been married to somebody for nearly twenty years, you get so used to seeing them about the house. When they've gone it's as if you'd moved a piece of furniture and left only a blank wall to look at, if you see what I mean,' she added.

Of course Miss Doggett agreed that she did see, but she could not help being surprised that Lady Beddoes should compare the death of her husband to the removal of a piece of furniture. It was not, somehow, what one expected.

'Funnily enough,' Lady Beddoes went on, 'we had a large mahogany sideboard in Warsaw that Lyall was very fond of, but we didn't bring it to England with us, and Lyall only lived in Chester Square for eighteen months. Perhaps it was an omen, though Lyall wasn't a large man. He was quite small, not really as tall as I am in high heels.'

'I'm sure you were devoted to him,' said Miss Doggett, doing the best she could, for she hardly knew what to make of this talk about sideboards. It was not the usual way in which widows spoke of

124

their late husbands.

'Oh, yes, I grew to be very fond of him,' said Lady Beddoes casually, 'and I tried to be a good wife, though I'm afraid I didn't always succeed very well. But of course one only *really* loves once in one's life, I think,' she added with a sigh.

And then there they were at the cake stall, so that it was impossible to continue a conversation about so intimate a matter. While Lady Beddoes bought several cakes, ones which Simon would like because she was *sure* he didn't get enough to eat, Miss Doggett pondered over the conversation they had had.

Could it be that Lady Beddoes hadn't really cared very much for her husband? She had almost implied that there had been Someone Else. Miss Doggett pursed her lips and shook her head. She was remembering what Anthea had told her of Lady Beddoes's origins. She had been nothing at all, just the daughter of an English professor teaching in Warsaw, and she herself spoke Polish fluently. Perhaps in Warsaw, one never knew . . . Miss Doggett began to imagine all sorts of rather dreadful things, but then she suddenly remembered that, after all, Lady Beddoes lived in Chester Square, and she visualised the smooth, unbroken line of the houses, all joined together, so that their inhabitants must be like one huge family, united in respectability, morality and the perfection of the upper classes. This was England, Miss Doggett's England, and it would have been a great shock to her if she had detected any crack in its façade. For one terrible moment she had imagined that Lady Beddoes might be a crack, but when she looked at her, so calm and elegant, talking so charmingly to the stallholders, she was ashamed of her suspicions. No doubt she had had several proposals of marriage since her husband died but had never been able to care for anybody else. She must have meant that when she had said that one only really loves once in one's life.

'Anthea is a *sweet* girl, isn't she,' said Lady Beddoes to Miss Doggett. 'I always wish I could have had a daughter.'

Miss Doggett was just going to say that perhaps she soon would have when a heavy spot of rain fell on her nose. 'Come quickly, Lady Beddoes,' she said. 'It's going to rain. We must shelter.'

A crowd of people was soon hurrying into the vicarage, stalls were covered up and tea things hastily abandoned to the fury of the downpour.

'What a pity, what a pity,' said the vicar, flapping his hands in confusion. 'I'm so sorry,' he added, as if feeling that the inadequacy of his prayers was to blame for the break in the weather. 'We'd all better go into the house.'

But Miss Morrow, who had somehow got separated from Miss Doggett, made for a little tool shed, which offered a nearer shelter than the crowded vicarage dining-room and drawing-room.

'Oh, it's you,' said a voice from among the lawn-mowers and rakes and spades.

Miss Morrow peered into the gloom and made out the red hair and clerical collar of Mr Latimer. 'I didn't follow you,' she said ingenuously. 'It seemed the nearest place to shelter.'

'Quite,' said Mr Latimer.

'Conversation in a tool shed,' went on Miss Morrow, in a pleasant, babbling tone. 'That would be a nice title for a poem, wouldn't it? A modern

126

one, I think, something rather obscure. Mr Auden or Mr MacNeice might be equal to it.'

'You do talk a lot of nonsense,' said Mr Latimer quite kindly.

'Well, I thought nonsense was better than nothing. I feel there's something awkward about a silence in a tool shed, and I hate silences if they're awkward.'

'I've got something to tell you,' Mr Latimer said. 'I've bought a car.'

They looked at each other. It was as if he had announced his return to sanity after the madness of the proposal.

Now, thought Miss Morrow, we shall behave like normal beings again. He won't rush out of the room after Miss Doggett rather than be left alone with me. So ends a Great Love. In a tool shed. She found the idea rather pleasing and began to laugh.

'Why is it funny?' he asked.

'Oh, the car? I don't really know,' she said, 'but I was just hoping that it might be rather an old-fashioned car, a high two-seater Morris-Cowley, perhaps.'

'As a matter of fact it is something like that.'

'Open cars are very draughty,' said Miss Morrow gravely. 'You must be careful not to catch cold when you go out in it.'

'It will be convenient for visiting people,' said Mr Latimer.

'I expect you will often be popping over to see your friend the vicar of Crampton Hodnet,' said Miss Morrow.

'Look, it's stopped raining,' said Mr Latimer. 'I think we might venture.'

'Perhaps we had better not be seen emerging

together from the tool shed,' suggested Miss Morrow. 'I'm becoming quite a woman of the world, you see.'

She picked her way across the sodden lawn and slipped quietly into the drawing-room, where Lady Beddoes, Miss Doggett and all the more important people were having tea. The conversation was dominated by Simon, who was explaining in a loud, clear voice and simple, non-political language the points he proposed to make in his speech at the Union on Thursday.

What a dull young man, thought Miss Morrow, who had managed to find an empty chair near Miss Doggett. Imagine being married to somebody like that. But of course Simon would never marry Anthea, she realised, with a sudden flash of worldly insight. He wanted to do things that people would remember, great things, and making a woman happy could hardly be called that. It was something that any man might do, a dull don, a bank clerk, a seller of vacuum cleaners, a clergyman, an undergraduate who had never made a speech at the Union. And of course one would hardly expect a person like Simon to be content with that. He probably didn't want to get married at all. Why should he? Young men of twenty-one didn't usually think about being husbands. They wanted a fine, romantic love to fill in the time when they were not busy with more important things, like making speeches or writing clever political pamphlets. But women, poor things, wanted more than that.

At this point Miss Morrow found herself being addressed.

'Where were you, Miss Morrow?' said Miss Doggett sharply. 'I told you to keep near me with

128

my mackintosh cape in case it started to rain. I couldn't see you anywhere.'

'Oh, Miss Doggett, I do hope you didn't get wet,' said Miss Morrow anxiously.

Miss Doggett, who was perfectly dry, did not answer. Whether she had got wet or not was hardly the point. 'Where is Mr Latimer?' she asked, peering round the room. 'Where is he?'

Miss Morrow almost expected that she might be blamed for his absence and sent to look for him, as she was sent to look for Miss Doggett's knitting, spectacles or library book. 'Perhaps he has gone to evensong,' she said, but the suggestion was a helpful rather than an intelligent one.

'Evensong at four o'clock!' said Miss Doggett scornfully.

'Well, I expect he is quite safe somewhere,' said Mrs Cleveland comfortably. 'After all, he is old enough to take care of himself!' It was a mistake to be always bothering about people, she thought. Much better to leave them alone.

'The rain has stopped,' said the vicar, clapping his hands. 'On with the motley! Come along, everybody!'

'I must buy *something*,' said Mrs Cleveland rather desperately. 'I suppose it had better be jam and cake, they always *come in*, don't they . . . ?'

'Needle-case in the form of a harp,' said Miss Morrow unexpectedly. 'I always think that sounds so pretty.'

'I've got a *darling* little thing,' said Lady Beddoes enthusiastically. 'But now I'm afraid I really must go. I *have* enjoyed myself. You must all come and see me whenever you're in London.'

Miss Doggett thanked her on behalf of everyone.

'We should of course let you know if we were coming,' she added.

'Oh, you needn't do that,' Lady Beddoes assured her. 'I love surprises.' Her face lit up as if in anticipation of one day peeping through the net curtains and seeing the whole of North Oxford on her doorstep.

After the car had gone, Miss Doggett and Miss Morrow walked slowly home. The sun shone into the drawing-room, bright gleams of it twisting through the dark, spiky branches of the monkey-puzzle. But it was the gentle evening sun which would not fade the carpet, and so it was allowed to come in.

Miss Morrow always enjoyed these summer evenings. The effect of light and sunshine on the heavy furniture, the dark covers, the silver-table, the Bavarian engravings, even on the photograph of Canon Tottle, gave her the idea that there might be a life beyond this, where even the contents of Miss Doggett's drawing-room might be bathed in a heavenly radiance. It was a confused and certainly quite wrong idea but a pleasing and comforting one, to imagine the whole of North Oxford, its houses and inhabitants, lifted just as they were into heaven, where all the objects would be the same in themselves but invested with a different meaning from that which they had on earth. They would all be dear, treasured things because they would be part of the heavenly atmosphere. It was not difficult, Miss Morrow thought, to imagine that heaven might be something like North Oxford. Certainly if there were any buildings there the architecture might well be Gothic—and why not the Victorian Gothic of North Oxford rather than the thirteenth-century Gothic of a continental cathedral? For one would surely feel at home in heaven, and who could feel at home in a cathedral? And really North Oxford was not as ugly as people who had never studied it were apt to think. It had many beauties, some of them not hard to find. There was winter, a time of leafless trees and evergreens, a comfortable season of wool-winding and brisk walks in rather too many clothes; then spring, with the first almond blossom seen in the light of a street lamp, the forsythia and the prunus. And when summer came there was almost too much beauty—the laburnum, the red hawthorn, the lilac, the syringa, and always the monkey-puzzle, somehow omniscient because it was there all the year round, never changing. And the people . . . here Miss Morrow's idea grew even more confused, for she sometimes found it hard to imagine any heavenly version of Miss Doggett which would still be at all recognisable as the earthly one. And surely we should all know each other in that fuller life?

'Lady Beddoes is a charming woman,' said Miss Doggett. 'So very interesting to talk to. She has had so much in her life.'

'I don't think she looks very happy,' said Miss Morrow.

'Well, of course, it is only a few years since her husband was taken from her. One could hardly expect her to look happy.'

'No, I suppose not,' said Miss Morrow doubtfully. 'I thought there was something rather pathetic about her, if you know what I mean. Something *lost*, as if her life were without purpose.'

Miss Doggett repeated that of course she had only lately lost her husband.

'But I think she's always been like that,' persisted Miss Morrow. 'I got that impression, anyway.'

'Dinner is just going in,' said Miss Doggett, ignoring her companion's remarks. 'It is rather late. We mustn't have a heavy meal.'

It seemed as if she hadn't got all she had expected out of life, reflected Miss Morrow, still thinking of Lady Beddoes. Perhaps she had now given up hope of getting anything, if there *was* anything. But was there? And if there was anything, wasn't it often much less than people expected? Wasn't it moments, single hours and days, rather than months and years? With her mouth full of ham and beetroot and rather tough lettuce—Miss Doggett always took the tender leaves for herself—Miss Morrow pondered on these problems. But by the time the cornflour blancmange arrived she had found no satisfactory answer, and Miss Doggett had gone on to speak of other things.

'Miss Morrow,' she said, 'I hope you are not allowing yourself to get silly about Mr Latimer. Mrs Wardell thought she saw you sheltering together in the tool shed.'

Miss Morrow bent her head. There was really nothing she could say. She could hardly explain to Miss Doggett that what Mrs Wardell had seen had been the end of a Great Love and not the beginning.

'I think I have passed the age when I could get silly over a man,' she said demurely.

'That is just the trouble,' said Miss Doggett in a warning tone. 'A plain woman no longer young is often the most likely to lose her head.'

Miss Morrow put up a hand to hers as if to reassure herself that it was still there. A

132

plain-looking woman no longer young. It was almost comforting to be described so neatly and in so few words, she felt. It made it impossible to realise that such a woman had had the chance of becoming Mrs Stephen Latimer. It stopped one from getting ideas, and that was surely a good thing.

13

EDWARD AND MOTHER
GIVE A TEA PARTY

'Well, Mother, who do you think will be the first to arrive?' said Edward Killigrew, pacing eagerly about the drawing-room. 'I think it will be Miss Doggett.'

'Did you remember to bring the cakes from Boffin's, dear?' asked his mother.

'Oh, Mother, you know I did,' said Edward, a little impatiently. 'You can't ask people to tea and give them nothing to eat.'

'No,' said Mrs Killigrew sardonically, 'even one's friends expect more than that. But this afternoon we shall have interesting news for them as well as cakes. That is good.' She took a little mirror out of her reticule. She was a fine-looking old woman of nearly eighty, very proud of her thick white hair and still good complexion. She was reputed to be of German origin and a slightly guttural quality in her speech sometimes betrayed this, although nobody knew for certain where she had come from. She had somehow always been in Oxford, first as a domineering wife and mother and then as a mother only. She did not entertain very much now but occasionally gave a tea party to which she asked her old friends. 'I cannot be bothered with young people now,' she used to say. 'It gives me more pleasure to see how much older my contemporaries look than I do.'

'I thought Olive Fremantle was looking *very* doddery at the Randolph College garden party,' she said in a satisfied tone. 'She ought to have let Herbert receive the guests by himself. He is quite capable of it.'

'The Master of Randolph College and Mrs Fremantle,' announced Esther, the stiff, old-fashioned parlourmaid.

'Dear Charlotte,' said Olive Fremantle in a quavering voice, 'you look *splendid*. I've been quite poorly.' She was a small, insignificant woman, who had always been overshadowed by her husband.

'I am sorry to hear that,' said Edward, hovering round with chairs and cushions. 'It's not quite so hot today, I think. I always find the heat rather trying myself. Ah, here are Miss Doggett and Miss Morrow. Now we are all here.'

'Well, Charlotte, you look younger than any of us,' said Miss Doggett.

'I expect she'll see us all in our graves yet,' said her son jovially. But behind his joviality there lurked a fear that it might be true. Of course Mother was his whole life and he would be quite lost without her, but he occasionally wondered if it might not be rather pleasant to be quite lost.

'How are you, Miss Morrow?' asked Mrs Killigrew graciously. 'It is many weeks since I have seen you.'

'I am very well, thank you,' said Miss Morrow, feeling that she ought to curtsy and say 'ma'am'.

She had been acknowledged now and could sink back into her usual comfortable obscurity. She found a chair, not one into which she could exactly sink back, but a low, curved one covered in tapestry. There was a great deal of tapestry in the room altogether. It would seem that Mrs Killigrew had spent the greater part of her life in working chair-seats and fire-screens. There were also antimacassars and cushion covers in Berlin wool-work and little tables covered with dust-collecting souvenirs from foreign lands. The room was in many ways like Miss Doggett's drawing-room, except that it somehow lacked the Victorian dignity of Leamington Lodge. There was something almost continental about Mrs Killigrew's room, Miss Morrow always thought. Perhaps it was the large gilt-framed mirror over the mantelpiece that gave it this air. One imagined supper for two in a gold-and-red-plush apartment somewhere in Vienna or Berlin in the seventies or eighties. It might well be that Mrs Killigrew's German origin was responsible for this atmosphere. But whatever it was, it was a flavour of something long dead, which made it a good setting for this afternoon's tea party.

'Edward went up to the British Museum last week,' said Mrs Killigrew, in a clear voice as if she were giving out the text for a sermon.

'What are you working on now?' asked Dr Fremantle. He was a tall, stooping man with a grey, bushy beard.

'I had to look at Gerard Langbaine's supposed translation of *The Gallant Hermaphrodite*,' he said in a precise voice.

'Oh, how *very* interesting,' said Mrs Fremantle,

135

clasping her hands. She had made this remark on every possible occasion during forty years of married life among academic society and had gained the reputation of being a sympathetic and intelligent listener.

'Doesn't Francis Cleveland specialise in that period?' asked Mrs Killigrew with an air of innocence.

Miss Doggett looked grim. 'Yes,' she said, 'he does.' It was obvious that the Killigrews had a piece of news, she decided. The realisation made her feel frustrated and angry, for ever since she had seen her nephew having tea with Miss Bird in Fuller's before Christmas and had heard of Michael and Gabriel's encounter in the Botanical Gardens, she had been looking out for further developments. And now it seemed as if somebody else had forestalled her. It was really most annoying.

'Yes, Edward saw him there.' Mrs Killigrew paused impressively. 'I wonder if you would pass me a piece of sandwich cake, dear? I can't take anything very rich.'

'Very wise of you, Charlotte,' said Miss Doggett. 'If only everyone would follow your example,' she added, with a glance at Miss Morrow, who was struggling with a piece of sticky fruit-cake.

'Miss Morrow and I are digging our graves with our teeth,' said Edward, helping himself to a piece of the same cake.

Oh, dear, thought Olive Fremantle, I hope they're not going to forget all about Mr Cleveland. It had sounded as if they had something interesting to say about him. One could always be sure that whenever dear Charlotte gave a tea party it was because she had some special piece of news to impart to her guests.

But the Killigrews had not forgotten. They were keeping their guests in suspense a little longer, so that the titbit they had for them might be all the more appreciated when it came.

'Now, we are not gossips,' said Mrs Killigrew. 'We do not tell stories about people for our own amusement.'

There was an almost perceptible pricking up of ears and drawing forward of chairs.

'But there are some things which ought not to be kept secret,' she went on, 'and this afternoon we are going to tell you something which we think too important to be withheld.'

We, thought Edward rather bitterly. 'It's my story, Mother,' he said petulantly. 'I think you'd better let me tell it.'

'Very well, dear,' said his mother encouragingly. 'Tell them what you heard and saw.'

'Yes, tell us. It is your duty, and we have a right to know,' said Miss Doggett impatiently. 'I am Francis Cleveland's aunt,' she added, giving the words a rather fuller meaning than was usual.

Edward then went on to tell how he had happened to see Francis Cleveland and Barbara Bird together and had followed them to the manuscripts and overheard their conversation.

'"I love you, Barbara. I love you",' he repeated solemnly and with a rather ridiculous attempt at fervour.

'And what did she say?' asked Miss Doggett eagerly.

'He asked if she loved him and she said "yes" in a very low voice. And then *they went away together.*' He gave these last words an awful emphasis.

'Where did they go?' asked Mrs Fremantle. 'Were you able to see?'

'To Lyons' Corner House,' declared Edward solemnly, apparently unconscious of any incongruity or falling-off in the ending to his story.

Miss Morrow bent her head down to hide a smile. After the declaration, they went to Lyons' Corner House. No doubt they had felt the need of a place like that. The atmosphere of the British Museum was too rarefied; there was too much past history and too many fragments of ancient greatness. 'How small a part of time they share' . . . 'Youth's a stuff will not endure' . . . one didn't want to be reminded of that. One wanted rather the cosiness and liveliness of a crowd of people eating and drinking—the gleam of the Britannia-metal teapots and hot water jugs, the smell of hot buttered toast and cigarette smoke. And perhaps an orchestra, dressed in Hungarian gipsy costumes, with white satin blouses and broad coloured cummerbunds. Miss Morrow knew the Corner Houses and found herself wondering what the decoration of that particular room had been. She remembered one with high, noble walls and ceiling and vaguely baroque carvings, a general atmosphere of white and gold, almost more suitable for sacred love than profane, perhaps hardly more sympathetic than the British Museum itself.

The whole of Edward's story, even the last part, had been received with gasps of horror and astonishment.

'Lyons' Corner House!' whispered Mrs Fremantle in such tones of shocked amazement that Miss Morrow wondered if she really knew what that great institution was.

138

'Did you actually creep up behind them and listen to their conversation?' asked Miss Morrow, whose mind was still occupied with unsuitable thoughts. 'How did you manage it?'

'Miss Morrow, I think that is hardly the point,' said Miss Doggett sharply.

'I was wearing crêpe rubber soles,' said Edward proudly, glad that he was being given some credit for his part in the affair. 'Look.' He lifted up his foot to show the sole of his shoe.

'What a terrible thing,' murmured Miss Doggett. 'Terrible . . . I feel quite shaken.'

'Shall I get you some brandy?' said Edward, springing up.

'No, thank you. I don't need a stimulant, but I should like some more tea. Miss Morrow, pass my cup to Mrs Killigrew. I am an old woman and this dreadful news has been a great shock to me,' she explained.

'I am sure that it must have been,' said Mrs Killigrew in a satisfied tone. 'But you have not said anything, Dr Fremantle. What is your opinion?'

They all turned to look at him, standing by the window, his hand absently burrowing in his beard.

'Well, I think it is really nothing,' he said surprisingly, 'or, at least, nothing very much.'

'You mean that you think there is nothing in it?' asked Edward incredulously.

'I do not say that,' said Dr Fremantle. 'There may well be *something* in it, but I do not believe it is as much as you think. After all, Cleveland is a handsome man in the prime of life. What could be more natural than for him to have a little affair of the heart? Man is by nature polygamous,' he declared. 'We all know that.'

139

Olive Fremantle shot a timid glance at her husband. Herbert polygamous! All these years of marriage, more than forty years now. She remembered one spring in Florence and an American woman who had afterwards appeared in Oxford in the long vacation. It did not do to enquire too closely. If Herbert said that man is by nature polygamous—well, all one could do was to leave it at that and hope for the best. At least he was still her husband, which was something. He was an old man, too, over seventy now. Perhaps that was even more.

'But, Dr Fremantle, the *disgrace* of it, it can't possibly be hushed up now,' protested Miss Doggett.

He smiled, but nobody saw the smile under his bush of beard. 'There will be no disgrace,' he said calmly. 'Nothing *need* come of it,' he added, with a warning glance at his hearers, 'and I prophesy that nothing will. You mark my words. There was something of the kind in the eighties—old Dr Baldwin—but he was in Orders, which made it rather a scandalous affair. But, of course, we mustn't forget that a man's a man however he wears his collar, must we?'

Miss Doggett looked as if she were about to protest that the wearing of a collar back to front was not the only thing that distinguished a clergyman from a layman, but Dr Fremantle stopped her with a peremptory wave of the hand.

'We don't want to make more fuss about this than is necessary,' went on Dr Fremantle. 'As you said, Charlotte, we are not gossips. We do not talk about these things for our own amusement,' he added, with a touch of malice in his tone. 'I cannot see that we shall do any good by meddling with things which do not at present concern us. I am sure that we all wish to do good, don't we? There is not really much else we can do now, at our age.' He laughed a rumbling laugh into his beard.

'But surely, Dr Fremantle, it is your duty to speak to my nephew about it?' persisted Miss Doggett. 'Think of the honour of the college.' She made a vague, sweeping movement with her hand.

'If as time goes on it appears to be my duty to say something, you can be sure that I shall say it,' Dr Fremantle reassured her, 'but in the meantime I do not see how the honour of Randolph College is going to be seriously affected by a declaration of love made in the British Museum.'

It certainly sounded very ridiculous put like that, thought Miss Morrow, but then perhaps all love had something of the ridiculous about it, and the realisation did not necessarily mean that Mr Cleveland's affair was not to be taken seriously.

'You know it's been going on for some time,' said Edward Killigrew, who was afraid that after what Dr Fremantle had just said his news might appear less important than it had done at first. 'I found him waiting for her to come out of the library one evening as long ago as last Christmas.'

'And he had tea with her in Fuller's before Christmas,' put in Miss Doggett. 'Miss Morrow and I saw them with our own eyes.'

'And then there was another time, in March, I think, when we had that nice weather,' said Edward. 'I met him coming out of a flower shop. I didn't think anything of it at the time. But now . . .' He paused significantly.

'Perhaps he was sending flowers to an invalid or

ordering a wreath for a funeral,' suggested Miss Morrow timidly.

'That's what *I* thought at the time,' said Edward.

'Don't be ridiculous, Miss Morrow,' said Miss Doggett sharply. 'He has no invalids among his acquaintance, and if a relative had died I should certainly have been among the first to know.'

'Yes, I suppose so,' agreed Miss Morrow reluctantly, for Miss Doggett delighted in deaths and funerals.

'Well, we all come to it, you know,' said Dr Fremantle indulgently. '"They are not long, the weeping and the laughter",' he quoted from a favourite poet of his youth. 'Come, Olive,' he called in a commanding voice, 'it's time we went.'

'Yes, Charlotte, I'm afraid we must be going,' said Mrs Fremantle regretfully. 'We have to go out to dinner tonight. It has been so delightful seeing you. You are looking *splendid*,' she quavered, putting a thin, spidery hand into Mrs Killigrew's firm white one.

'Yes, we have heard an interesting piece of news,' said Dr Fremantle, as if acknowledging the main purpose of the tea party. 'Mind you, I don't think it is quite as important as you seem to imagine, but one never knows,' he added, throwing them a fragment of consolation. A few words of advice from a man of the world, that was what Cleveland needed. He ought to have been more discreet about this little affair. It was surprising that a good-looking man like that hadn't had more practice. But of course Cleveland was lazy; he might drift into something without realising the consequences. Dr Fremantle flattered himself that he had ordered his own life a little more skilfully.

142

'They are not long, the days of wine and roses . . .' but he had certainly enjoyed them where he could. He chuckled, remembering some past episode. 'You mark my words, it will all blow over,' was his parting shot.

'I wish we could all take such an optimistic view of the matter as Dr Fremantle appears to,' said Miss Doggett in a gloomy tone, which yet seemed to be deeply satisfied. 'I am afraid there is going to be a great deal more in this than he thinks.'

'Yes, we felt we could not keep such a piece of news to ourselves,' said Mrs Killigrew. 'It would have been wrong to conceal it.'

And selfish too, thought Miss Morrow, as she walked home with Miss Doggett, on whom the news appeared to have acted like a tonic. Her step was more sprightly than when they had started out, and her voice had a new, firm quality about it.

'I blame myself for this,' she said. 'I ought to have acted sooner. I only hope it may not be too late.'

'Too late?' said Miss Morrow. 'Oh, I don't see how it could be too late.'

'Miss Morrow, you know nothing about such matters,' said Miss Doggett sharply. 'It may very well be too late. I would go into the house and tackle him with it now,' she added, as they passed the Clevelands' gate, 'but I feel that I must have time to think it over. This matter requires very careful handling,' she added obscurely.

As they sat having their supper, Miss Morrow listened in silence to the fascinating story of intrigue which was being unfolded before her. It was as good as one of the sixpenny novels old Maggie read, she decided. The middle-aged, handsome don, tired of a wife who made no effort to keep his love; the clever, sympathetic young woman, who was at the same time pretty; the reading of sentimental poetry together—this appeared to be Miss Doggett's idea of a tutorial—chance meetings followed by planned assignations, the Dawn of Love, an elopement, a divorce . . . in short, the breaking up of Francis Cleveland's home and the ruination of his academic career.

'But there must be so many middle-aged men who sometimes feel bored with their wives,' protested Miss Morrow, 'and just as many of them must sometimes meet attractive young women without anything very dreadful happening.'

'Miss Morrow, you do not know the world as I do,' said Miss Doggett in a warning tone. 'You look around you here and see upright men keeping their marriage vows.'

Miss Morrow agreed, but a little doubtfully, for at the moment she found it difficult to think of any married couples except the vicar and his wife, and she did not feel that she could make an observation which might only be frivolous.

'But unfortunately Francis is not an upright man,' went on Miss Doggett. 'He is not a churchman and he spends all his time studying the literature of a period when morals were lax and society was decadent. As a young man he was not steady, and his father, who married my eldest sister, was an unfaithful husband. It is hardly to be wondered at that Francis is what he is. We know that he has been deceiving his wife. I only hope that he may not have been doing even *worse* than that.'

Miss Morrow, feeling herself to be very much the unmarried lady who knew nothing of life, was silent.

'I have hinted to Margaret that there is something between him and Miss Bird,' continued Miss Doggett, 'but she was quite rude about it and as good as told me to mind my own business. I think it is time somebody spoke to Francis himself. I had thought of asking the vicar to do it, but I think Mr Latimer would be better. He is more of a gentleman and has stricter principles. And of course he believes in the celibacy of the clergy,' she added with a note of warning in her tone.

Miss Morrow could not help letting out an exclamation of surprise. Perhaps this accounted for the lukewarmness of his proposal, she thought, though she really could not see that it had much to do with the matter in hand.

'Mr Latimer is a very high-principled young man,' said Miss Doggett impressively. 'He has a fine character.'

Miss Morrow said nothing. Somehow, she felt that she did not admire Mr Latimer quite as much as other people did. Perhaps it was because she knew him too well. After all, he had nearly been her husband, and that surely presumed a degree of acquaintance which did not allow of excessive and unquestioning admiration. For, although she was in many ways a romantic, Miss Morrow could not help thinking that one usually married people in spite of faults rather than because of virtues.

Poor Mrs Cleveland, she thought, pondering over what they had heard that afternoon, what will she think when she hears about it? Will she mind? Perhaps one's feelings were mercifully blunted after twenty years or so of marriage. Twenty years was such a long time, long enough for a husband to change into many different kinds of people. Here Miss Morrow began to get rather involved with husbands, vipers in bosoms and wolves in sheep's clothing. But Mr Cleveland was always so mild; it was impossible to imagine him as either a viper or a wolf. Edward Killigrew had probably made the whole thing up. It must be dull working in the library in this lovely weather, and Miss Morrow had often noticed that clever people were inclined to be fond of spiteful gossip and intrigue.

14

THOUGHTS AT A LECTURE

'It's Mr Cleveland's last lecture,' said Sarah Penrose at breakfast one morning. 'I think we shall have to go, don't you, Birdy?'

'I don't think I can spare the time,' said Barbara evasively. 'I ought to be getting on with my revision.'

'But it would do you good to have a little relaxation,' said Sarah in a motherly tone.

'It will give us back our youth,' sighed an intense, untidy-looking woman who answered to the name of Fraser. 'We shall remember the first time we went to one of his lectures and how wonderful we thought he was and how we took down every word he said. We didn't have much to worry us in those days, did we?'

'"Alas! regardless of their doom, the little victims play",' quoted Sarah heavily. 'You must come, Birdy. You can't go on doing revision all the time.'

Barbara had woken up the morning after the visit to the British Museum feeling that she had been making a great fuss about nothing. After all, it was not so very unusual for intelligent people to be in love with each other, even if one of them was married. History and Literature were full of examples; indeed, it seemed almost essential that in a Great Love one of the parties should be married. There was no need to be melodramatic and never see Francis any more. There was no need even for their beautiful friendship to be turned into a sordid intrigue, for Barbara's ideas of love were very noble, and she had had no experience of any but completely abstract passions. Her ideas of how she and Francis were going to go on, now that they were two intelligent people admittedly in love with each other, were conveniently vague. She only knew that she was ready for whatever might be in store for her, and that she would welcome what came as an enrichment to a life which had so far been lacking in those experiences without which, if one was to believe all that one heard and read, no life could be really complete.

She had gone about in this state of mind for several days, waiting for an opportunity to see Francis and tell him, only in less prosaic words, of course, that everything was going to be all right. But her first meeting with him was under such different circumstances from what she had planned that it did not at all come up to her expectations. To begin with, the place had been unsuitable. They had come across each other in the Bodleian. She had been standing at the top of a ladder, searching for a pamphlet, feeling tired and dishevelled after a morning's work, and with an uncomfortable

147

suspicion that her petticoat was showing, when he had come to the shelf below her to get a book.

'Come down,' he said. 'I want to talk to you.'

She climbed down and followed him into the Tower Room. They leaned on the bookcase, which contained dictionaries and encyclopaedias, and he took out a volume which they pretended to be studying. Opposite them sat a blind man and his companion, who was reading aloud extracts from the *Cambridge History of English Literature* in a flat, monotonous voice.

'Barbara,' said Francis, hesitating a little, 'I want to speak to you. I've been thinking things over and I don't see—'

Here he had stopped abruptly and Barbara had heard the sound of footsteps and the peevish voice of Mr Killigrew and the booming tones of Dr Adder, the Librarian, coming towards them from the Upper Reading Room.

'I can't stay now,' said Francis abruptly, and he hurried, almost ran, out of the library, leaving Barbara hunched over the encyclopaedia, wondering what he had been going to say. She looked down and saw that it was open at an article on Poland, a vast, desolate country, which had forests and peasants and Chopin and Paderewski. Sad nocturnes came into her head and her eyes filled with tears. She felt hopeless and frustrated and there was a sick feeling at the pit of her stomach, which she did not recognise as a craving for her lunch.

But when she got back to college and helped herself to a great fish with its tail in its mouth, she found that she could hardly eat any of it.

That had been yesterday. Now, sitting listening

148

to Francis talking about the political significance of Dryden's *Absalom and Achitophel*, she felt more hopeful and confident. Her dear Francis. He loved her and she loved him. She looked round at the lecture audience. Those who had stayed the course consisted mostly of women, with a sprinkling of Indians and one or two plain-looking men.

The desire to shout out her secret came over her. She looked up at the ceiling and gazed at the figures of animals and birds which decorated it. There were two peacocks with their necks entwined and Barbara concentrated on them until the end of the lecture, while all around her conscientious women and Indians tried to take down all that Mr Cleveland said, which was not always easy. He seemed to be hurrying today, not bothering to make any jokes, and sometimes even turning his back on his audience, so that it was almost impossible to hear what he said.

At ten minutes to one he stopped rather abruptly and came striding down the room to where Barbara and her friends were sitting in the back row.

'Oh, Miss Bird,' he said in his lecture voice, 'I just wanted to ask you about those *Mac Flecknoe* notes . . .'

'I felt I had to talk to you after leaving you so suddenly yesterday,' said Francis, as they left the lecture room. 'May I walk back with you?'

'Yes, do,' said Barbara doubtfully. 'But I don't very well see how we can talk here.'

'Oh, well, we needn't talk about anything special,' he said evasively. 'What does it matter what we talk about as long as we're together?' he added.

'Oh, Francis,' said Barbara fervently. 'I feel that

149

too. Nothing matters as long as we're together. Do you remember the first time we ever walked over Magdalen Bridge?' she asked, smiling at him.

They continued to enlarge on this theme. Francis Cleveland was considered by many to be quite an authority on the seventeenth century and Barbara Bird was the Senior Scholar of her year, yet there was nothing in their conversation which would have led one to suspect this. It was not even enriched with suitable quotations from the great treasury of seventeenth-century love lyrics. It was quite remarkable how like Simon and Anthea they sounded as they walked into the college garden, arranging to meet later in the afternoon on Shotover Hill.

'There's Mr Cleveland again,' said Miss Borage, the Bursar, looking out of the Senior Common Room window. 'Smiling fondly at Miss Bird.'

'Oh, that man!' complained Miss Gurney, the English tutor, a tall, gaunt woman with grey bobbed hair. She turned and faced Miss Borage and the other occupants of the room, Miss Rideout, the Principal, and Miss Kingley, the Classics tutor. 'Men are the ruination of women,' she declared. 'The only girl who seems likely to get a First, and now look what's happening.'

'I can't say that I see anything very much happening,' observed Miss Rideout in a dry, good-humoured tone. 'We allow men to walk in the garden.'

'I often used to walk in the garden with my tutor,' said Miss Kingley sadly. 'Arnold Penge, you know . . .'

'Oh, we've all heard about him,' said Miss Gurney roughly. 'Miss Kingley walked in the garden

150

with her tutor, but nothing came of it.'

'No, nothing came of it,' agreed Miss Kingley in a tone of melancholy resignation.

'I wonder if anything will come of this,' said Miss Borage, looking out at Francis and Barbara, who were still talking.

'Mr Cleveland is a married man,' said Miss Rideout, with an air of putting an end to the conversation.

'So was Arnold Penge.' Miss Gurney cackled. 'Where there's life there's hope, isn't that so, Miss Kingley?'

'Nothing came of it,' repeated Miss Kingley patiently.

'There's the bell for lunch,' said Miss Borage.

'Mr Cleveland will be late for lunch,' said Miss Gurney triumphantly. 'He'll have to make an excuse to his wife. I wonder if he will tell her the truth.'

But there was no need for Francis to say anything. When he got home he found Margaret already carving the cold lamb, and he took his place at the table almost unnoticed while she speculated as to whether it would last another day.

'I shall want the car after lunch,' he said, but nobody seemed to care whether he took it or not. As he drove to meet Barbara he felt somehow cheated. He had been full of defiance, ready to tell his family to go to the devil, and all they had spoken of was cold lamb. And so it was really a direct result of their indifference that, as soon as he and Barbara had stumbled over the rough grass on the hill and found a secluded spot under a tree, he should take her in his arms and kiss her.

'I've got Schools next week,' said Barbara. 'I

shan't be able to see you at all then.'

'No, I suppose you won't,' he said. 'But you must stay up for a bit after the end of term, and then we can be together all the time.'

'*All* the time?' said Barbara in a surprised voice.

'Well, quite a lot of the time,' said Francis rather lamely. 'Oh, Barbara, I love you so much,' he said with sudden fervour, as he thought of the indifference of his family. 'I'm going to kiss you again,' he said, 'and then a thousand times more to make up for all the time I've wasted.'

While Francis was making up for his wasted time, Mrs Cleveland and Anthea were dragging round the shops on a hot afternoon, trying to choose materials for summer dresses.

'The whole afternoon wasted,' said Anthea peevishly, 'and all because I forgot to bring a bit of the stuff with me. I can't buy the check unless I'm sure it's going to match my blue coat.'

'What blue coat, dear?' said her mother.

'Oh, you *know*,' said Anthea crossly.

'What's the matter with you this afternoon?' asked Mrs Cleveland wearily. 'You're so impatient with me all the time.'

'Oh, it's so hot, and we're tired,' said Anthea hastily. 'Let's go and have a cup of tea in Elliston's.'

They went up to the café and found it already quite full of dons' wives, North Oxford spinsters and clergymen, with a sprinkling of undergraduates. The atmosphere, which was thick with smoke in the mornings, was quite clear now, and the place had an air of provincial respectability.

Anthea sat and brooded, while her mother ordered the tea. She did not want her to guess the reason for her bad temper. It was so silly to think that she should be feeling like this just because Simon had asked a young woman from Somerville to lunch. It was unintelligent, so boring, to be jealous, even if one knew that the woman was attractive, red-haired and clever. Anthea craned her neck out of the café window, but although she could just see the front of Randolph, Simon's rooms were farther along, and she could only wonder if the lunch party had taken its usual course and ended up on the sofa among the coral-coloured cushions and, as likely as not, a few bits of one of the essays that Simon always seemed to be in the middle of writing. But it was a quarter past four now. Surely she wouldn't *still* be there?

'What are we going to have?' asked Mrs Cleveland, pushing her hat back to an almost rakish angle because the band was a little tight and her head was aching from an afternoon's unsuccessful shopping.

'Oh, just tea,' said Anthea wearily. Her thoughts went on following the same desolate course. Simon was the sort of person who was sweet to everyone. It came naturally to him. The compliments flowed so easily from his lips. He had a way of suddenly taking hold of your hand when you were eating, and kissing your fingers or saying something so sweet that you went on chasing the food aimlessly round your plate because you couldn't do anything or even think when his eyes were on you. Oh, the lovely food that had been wasted in Randolph when two people in love had lunch together! A detached onlooker would have seen the funny side of those intimate meals—the abandoned fish, with the spiky bones peeping forlornly through the uneaten flesh, the wings of chicken lying desolate and untouched

153

in their cold gravy, the chocolate mousse, the peaches, the expensive cigarettes thrown into the fire before they were half smoked.

'Good afternoon, Mrs Cleveland,' said Miss Gurney, who was passing their table.

'Oh, good afternoon, Miss Gurney.'

'Now you tell your husband to keep away from my Miss Bird,' said Miss Gurney in her harsh, penetrating voice. 'I can't have him gadding about with her now; he must wait until the end of term. Schools begin on Thursday, and if she doesn't get a First I shall go into a nunnery!'

Anthea smiled.

'Well, I shouldn't look any worse than Sister Angelina,' retorted Miss Gurney, referring to a very plain-looking nun who frequently attended her lectures. 'I believe I might even look a little better.'

'I'll tell Francis to leave her alone,' said Mrs Cleveland soothingly. 'He's always very conscientious about his pupils, and I know he's very anxious for Miss Bird to get a First.'

'Well, he mustn't go tiring her out walking on Shotover then,' said Miss Gurney, moving off. 'And there's poor Miss Kingley, looking like a lost soul in the cake department. I'm coming,' she shrieked, causing a few people to look up from their tea in surprise.

'She's very blunt, isn't she?' Anthea giggled. 'If one didn't know her, one might imagine that Father was having a romance with Barbara Bird.'

'Don't be ridiculous,' said Mrs Cleveland, speaking more sharply than she had meant to.

Anthea raised her eyebrows and seemed about to make a remark, but what she had been thinking was hardly the sort of thing one could say to one's

154

mother, and so she said nothing.

'Don't mention what Miss Gurney said to Aunt Maude,' said Mrs Cleveland casually. 'You know how she is.'

'Yes, she'd probably think the worst,' agreed Anthea lightly.

They got up and went out of the café. How nice it must be when one is safely married, thought Anthea. Nothing to worry about except the lunch and easy domestic problems which needn't matter at all unless one wanted them to. But would being married to Simon be like that? She had a sudden depressing vision of their married life together, he so young and gay and ambitious and she trying desperately to Keep His Love, as they said in magazines. She glanced hopefully up at his windows as they passed Randolph and wondered if the woman was still there.

It was rather odd of Francis to go out with Barbara without saying anything about it, thought Mrs Cleveland when they were on the bus. Although, as Anthea had said, Miss Gurney was very blunt, one didn't like to think that people might be talking about them. Things like this could be so misunderstood and twisted round that they might seem to be something quite different. She would ask him about it casually sometime. It was much better to have things out rather than to brood on them.

She found an opportunity after supper when she and Francis were by themselves in the drawing-room.

'Miss Gurney says you're to keep away from her star pupil and not tire her out walking on Shotover,' she said lightly.

Francis looked a little startled, she thought, as if he had been found out in something.

'Oh, yes, I took her up on Shotover this afternoon,' he said, seeing that he could not very well conceal it. 'She looked as if she needed fresh air,' he added naïvely.

'You like her very much, don't you?' said Margaret placidly.

'Of course I like her. She's a very nice girl, very intelligent,' he said impatiently. 'I can't think why everyone's making such a fuss.'

15

ADVICE FOR
MRS CLEVELAND

'Old Mrs Killigrew coming *here*?' Mrs Cleveland raised her head from her book in sudden agitation.

It was a wet afternoon in July, and she and Anthea were sitting by the fire in the drawing-room.

'Yes, old Mrs Killigrew,' Anthea, who was looking out of the window, repeated. 'By herself, too.'

'But she never goes out,' said Mrs Cleveland in bewilderment, 'and it's such a wet day. Is there any cake in the house?' she asked frantically. 'I suppose we shall have to offer her tea.'

'There may be something,' said Anthea. 'I'll go and warn Ellen.'

'Oh, dear, oh, *dear*, she's so difficult to talk to,' wailed Mrs Cleveland.

'Mrs Killigrew,' said Ellen, standing in the

doorway.

'How do you do?' said Mrs Cleveland, advancing towards her rather uncertainly.

'Thank you, I am quite well.' Mrs Killigrew remained standing in the middle of the room, her sharp eyes taking in the faded loose-covers, the flowers that ought to have been changed and the general untidiness, Mrs Cleveland felt.

'Do sit down,' she said. 'It's so nice of you to come.'

'I do not know if it is nice,' said Mrs Killigrew, with a sudden sardonic grin. 'That is a matter of opinion, perhaps.'

Mrs Cleveland felt snubbed. 'Isn't it cold?' she said brightly. 'We have had a fire today,' she added, feeling that she ought to give some explanation of the fact that the grate was not filled by a vase of leaves or an embroidered fire-screen.

'I never feel the cold,' said Mrs Killigrew uncompromisingly. 'I have never given in to self-indulgence; that is why I am so healthy. You would never think that I was older than Olive Fremantle, would you?'

'No, you certainly wouldn't,' said Mrs Cleveland. She felt that she ought to make some remark about Mrs Killigrew's being wonderful for her age, but as she could not think of any more tactful way of putting it, she said nothing. 'Tea will be coming in soon,' she went on quickly. 'I hope you will stay and have a cup?'

'Thank you, no,' said Mrs Killigrew. 'I came only for a certain purpose. I have something to tell you, and as it can be said quite quickly I had better get it over. Mrs Cleveland, I have come to warn you.' She paused impressively.

157

Mrs Cleveland stared at her. There was something sinister, even alarming, about the old woman, sitting so straight in her dark foreign-looking ulster and stiff straw hat, which had a whole stuffed bird perched on the front of it.

'To warn me?' she said, when she had recovered from the first shock of surprise. 'What about?'

'About your husband,' said Mrs Killigrew simply.

'I don't know what you mean,' said Mrs Cleveland, rather stiffly, for it had now occurred to her that Mrs Killigrew might have heard some of this ridiculous gossip about Francis and Barbara Bird.

'He is going about with a young woman,' said Mrs Killigrew baldly. 'That is what I mean.'

'But there's nothing—'

Mrs Killigrew held up a black-gloved hand. 'Yes, there is something between them,' she said. 'I am afraid you do not know everything.' And then, before Mrs Cleveland could protest, she began to tell the story of what her son had seen and heard in the British Museum.

There was silence when she had finished. Mrs Cleveland's first impulse was to laugh. The British Museum! How like an Oxford don to choose such an unsuitable place to declare his love! But then it suddenly occurred to her that she hadn't even known that Francis was taking Barbara Bird up to London that day. He hadn't mentioned it; indeed, he had rather implied that he was going alone.

'What does the poet Shakespeare say?' asked Mrs Killigrew, breaking the silence with this rather surprising remark.

'Shakespeare?' echoed Mrs Cleveland.

'Yes. The poet Shakespeare says that men were

158

deceivers ever,' said Mrs Killigrew. 'I can see that you have had cause to know the truth of that,' she said in a satisfied tone.

'What makes you think so?' said Mrs Cleveland, suddenly hot with anger. She was angry, not because Francis had deceived her, but because he had put her in such a humiliating and ridiculous position. She shot a glance at Mrs Killigrew, sitting there so smug and splendid for her age, and there came over her a desire to squash down her stiff straw hat, to tear the bird off it and fling it into the unseasonable fire.

'You knew about it?' said Mrs Killigrew indulgently. 'Well, well, that may be. If I have told you something you already knew, then I have been an interfering old woman.' Again a sudden sardonic grin came over her face. 'I do not flatter myself that everything I do is right,' she went on. 'I thought I was doing my duty in coming here this afternoon, but it may be that I was mistaken.'

'Won't you stay and have a cup of tea?' said Mrs Cleveland, who had now recovered from her jungle impulse and was a polite North Oxford hostess once more.

'No, I do not think I deserve your hospitality,' said Mrs Killigrew, getting up. 'I have not done good this afternoon. I believe I may even have done harm. I must face that. It will be a burden for me to bear, the knowledge that I may have done harm,' she added, in a surprisingly light tone.

Mrs Cleveland stared at her, not knowing how to respond to her curious conversation.

'Husbands need to be watched,' continued Mrs Killigrew. 'I am an old woman and I have had some experience of husbands. I have seen two of them go to their graves. I have attended both their funerals.'

Mrs Cleveland looked a little startled. She had not realised that Mrs Killigrew had been twice married.

'One must be watching them always when they are alive,' went on the old woman reminiscently. 'When I was first married I lived in Dresden. We were walking in the Grossergarten one afternoon, Leopold and I—it must be nearly fifty years ago since then—'

She broke off and looked out of the window.

'Here is Agnes Wardell; she is carrying a basket of greens.'

'A basket of greens?' said Mrs Cleveland absently. 'But we have plenty in the garden.' She felt an unreasonable desire to hear the rest of the story about Mrs Killigrew and Leopold walking in the Grossergarten fifty years ago. Now she would probably never know what had happened, or even whether anything had happened at all.

'Well, Margaret, I've brought you some plants,' said Mrs Wardell, appearing in the doorway unannounced.

'Oh, I see, *plants*,' said Mrs Cleveland, who had imagined cabbages and purple sprouting broccoli. 'How nice of you!'

'I am just going,' said Mrs Killigrew, 'but I have not done any good.' She walked away with a firm step. Evidently she did not find the burden of having done harm a very heavy one.

'What on earth was she talking about?' asked Mrs Wardell.

'I hardly know,' Mrs Cleveland said evasively. 'Some involved library scandal. You know what Edward is.'

'Yes I certainly do. It's really the fault of the Bodley's Librarian,' declared Mrs Wardell surprisingly. 'There he is in the library, with a lot of idle assistants who have nothing to do but gossip.' And then to Mrs Cleveland's relief, she went on to talk about the plants and when they should be put in.

She had evidently heard nothing. Well, that was something. Indeed, when one remembered how fond of gossip dear Agnes was, it was really a great deal.

'We're just going to have tea,' said Mrs Cleveland. 'Do stay and have some.'

'I'd love to,' said Mrs Wardell. 'I'll take off my hat if you don't mind. I expect my hair's like a bush.'

Mrs Cleveland stood in the middle of the drawing-room in a state of unhappy bewilderment and indecision while Mrs Wardell made some attempt to tidy herself. What was she going to do about it? she wondered. Hope for the best and let things slide? Tell Francis that she knew? But that she knew *what*? It wasn't, after all, very much that she knew, only one 'I love you' that Edward Killigrew might or might not have heard him say in the British Museum. Tax him with his deception? Tell him that people were starting to gossip? But she hated nagging and jealousy; she had never *been* like that.

'Is it safe to come in again?' said Anthea, butting her head round the door. 'Has Mrs Killigrew gone?'

'Yes, she couldn't stay to tea,' said Mrs Cleveland absently. Anthea mustn't hear anything of this gossip, she thought; it must be kept from her at all costs. It was quite a relief to be able to put her problem aside for the moment and make ordinary conversation with Anthea and Mrs Wardell while they had tea.

'Did you know that old Mrs Killigrew has had two husbands?' she said, making a rather unfortunate beginning.

'How do you know?' said Mrs Wardell.

'Oh, it just cropped up in the course of conversation.'

'You must have had a funny sort of conversation,' remarked Anthea. 'Why were you talking about husbands with her?'

'Oh, my dear child. They're the sort of things that *do* crop up in conversations between married women,' said Mrs Wardell cheerfully. 'We have so little else to talk about.'

Anthea laughed. 'Don't I know it!' she said. 'And not only between married women. Simon's mother and I had the most intriguing conversation about husbands. Do you *know*,' she said impressively, 'she told me that she was in love with someone else when she married Lyall Beddoes!'

'How awkward,' said Mrs Wardell. 'Though by what I've seen of her I shouldn't think she'd ever be certain about anybody.'

'Oh, but one's always certain about a thing like that,' said Anthea confidently.

'It must have been awkward for her poor husband,' said Mrs Cleveland rather feebly.

'Oh, he didn't know about it,' said Anthea. 'He seems to have been rather frightful, as far as I can gather. Much older than she was and caring far more about Anglo-Polish diplomatic intrigues than about her happiness.'

'Well, poor man, I don't see what you could have

expected him to have done,' said Mrs Wardell.

'He ought to have given her a divorce or something so that she could have married this other man,' said Anthea firmly. 'Only of course I probably shouldn't have met Simon then,' she added irrelevantly.

'But she was quite happy with her husband, wasn't she?' said Mrs Cleveland hopefully.

'Oh, *yes*,' said Anthea impatiently, 'she was *fond* of him, but she *loved* somebody else. That's the point. Just think how frightful one's married life must be if it's like that. I couldn't bear it.'

Of course people of Anthea's age couldn't be expected to know much about marriage, Mrs Cleveland thought. How could they when they had no experience? They talked so glibly about divorce and remarriage, as if it were nothing more complicated than mincing up the cold beef and making it into a shepherd's pie. But of course, she told herself stoutly, there was nothing really wrong between her and Francis, just some silly gossip. Still, she found herself thinking about it when he came in to supper. If he was in love with somebody else, she thought, as she watched him eating plum tart with great enjoyment, she would have to give him his freedom, according to Anthea's philosophy. That was what it amounted to. But the whole idea was so fantastic. Francis simply hadn't got it in him to fall in love with somebody else and break up a comfortable home. If people wanted to gossip they would just have to. She wasn't going to interfere. She had always been broad-minded and tolerant; she hated to think that she might make a perfectly harmless friendship seem something else by adopting the attitude of a jealous wife.

163

'You must bring Barbara Bird to supper sometime,' she said, trying to sound casual, 'if she's still in Oxford. It's quite a long time since we saw her.'

That would show people, she thought. She must try and let it be known that Barbara was coming to supper with them. She must make a point of bringing it into any conversation she had with anybody. 'Oh, by the way, Barbara Bird is coming to supper tonight.' Of course that was much too blunt. She tried another way. 'How empty Oxford seems in the vacation, doesn't it? There are a few undergraduates still here, though: one of my husband's pupils, Barbara Bird . . . .'

She walked up the Banbury Road next morning practising this conversation, so much so that her first instinct on going into Sainsbury's to order some bacon was to say, 'Oh, Barbara Bird is coming to supper tonight.' She was sure that the assistant would have been quite equal to the occasion. 'Oh, yes, madam?' he would say. 'Perhaps you would care for a chicken? We have some nice young ones for roasting. Or perhaps you would prefer a boiler . . .'

But Mrs Cleveland had nearly finished her shopping before she met anyone that she knew well enough to stop and speak to. She was just coming out of Elliston's when she saw a little, bent figure in a shantung costume hurrying towards her. It was Olive Fremantle. She was almost running in her eagerness to prevent Mrs Cleveland's getting away.

'Oh, you *must* come in and see my new colour scheme,' she said breathlessly. 'It won't take a minute.'

Mrs Cleveland was caught off her guard, and

as she walked across the road to the Master's Lodgings she began to realise how odd it was that she should be asked to see Mrs Fremantle's drawing-room in the middle of the morning, especially when, as she stood in it, she saw that it was really no different from what it had always been. It was still greenish, gloomily magnificent and dominated by the frowning portrait of Dr Fremantle, which hung by itself on one wall.

'The room is charming,' said Mrs Cleveland, doing her best.

Mrs Fremantle did not seem to have heard and went on fussing nervously round the room, with one eye always on her husband's portrait, obviously as frightened of it as of the reality. At last she stood still by a tall jar of dried bulrushes and fingered them absently, as if ready to use them as weapons if necessary.

'The room isn't really any different,' she blurted out at last. 'I wanted to say something to you privately. Herbert won't be in till lunchtime,' she added, glancing furtively towards the door. 'I don't suppose he would approve of me speaking to you like this.'

Like what? thought Mrs Cleveland, sitting on the sofa clutching her shopping basket and waiting patiently for Mrs Fremantle to throw some light on this curious situation.

'He thinks I don't know anything of what goes on in the world,' continued Mrs Fremantle in an aggrieved tone. 'I may be an old woman and not very clever, but I have some experience of life. I'm not blind. I knew all about that time in Florence. A woman always does know, doesn't she?'

It began to dawn on Mrs Cleveland that Mrs

165

Fremantle was leading up to something more definite than general reflections on what goes on in the world; she was going to talk about Francis and Barbara Bird. She felt helpless, trapped in the great, dark drawing-room, but she just sat there feeling rather sick and clutching her shopping basket a little tighter while Mrs Fremantle went on.

'I just wanted to warn you not to listen to what people say,' she said, laying a thin, spidery hand on her arm. 'If you find your husband out in some little indiscretion, you mustn't at once think of divorce. They all have little lapses, and it isn't worth breaking up one's home for the sake of a little lapse, is it? You must think of your child, you know. The only way is just to pretend not to notice,' she added rather hopelessly.

'But I wasn't contemplating divorce,' said Mrs Cleveland, feeling that her voice sounded a little surprised, as well it might.

'Oh, but you must have thought of it,' said Mrs Fremantle, sounding disappointed. 'When I found out about Herbert and that American woman, my first thought was divorce. I know it was a wicked thought, because of course I don't really believe in divorce, do you?'

'Now, who is talking about divorce on such a fine sunny morning?' said Dr Fremantle, coming into the room.

'Oh, Herbert, I didn't know you'd be back so soon,' fluttered his wife apologetically.

'Well, I suppose I may come into my own house without asking anybody's permission,' he said, pleasantly enough. '"I am the Master of this college, what I don't know isn't knowledge",' he declared, laughing his rumbling laugh.

166

'I think I must be getting back now,' said Mrs Cleveland, standing up. 'Thank you so much, Mrs Fremantle. It has been so nice,' she added diplomatically.

'What has been so nice?' asked Dr Fremantle bluntly. 'Sitting in a sunless drawing-room listening to Olive's idle gossip?' He glanced round the room. 'I cannot see any cups or glasses or any signs of food. Olive, did you not offer Mrs Cleveland anything?'

'Oh, I never take anything in the middle of the morning,' said Mrs Cleveland, moving towards the door. 'It spoils one's lunch.'

'It spoils one's lunch. Ha-ha!' Dr Fremantle stood rubbing his hands, laughing at some private joke. 'You must not take any notice of what Olive says,' he added. 'She always gets hold of the wrong end of the stick.'

Mrs Cleveland walked home thinking about what Olive Fremantle had said. If she knew about what Edward Killigrew had seen, then it was obvious that her husband must know too. And it was evident that he did not take the gossip very seriously. This knowledge somehow comforted Mrs Cleveland. She saw Dr Fremantle as a symbol of North Oxford respectability, although she was not sure why, especially when she came to remember the hints Mrs Fremantle had given of his 'lapses'. That showed that he was not above suspicion himself. But then who was? The idea of Dr Fremantle's essential respectability persisted. Perhaps it was his beard, she thought, smiling to herself. One didn't somehow imagine that an old man with a beard could be wicked. Anyway, Barbara was coming to supper sometime, and she had to be given something to eat, so Mrs Cleveland found her thoughts turning to suitable summer menus: salads, cold meats, strawberries . . . There would be time enough for more serious thoughts later on.

But after all this planning Barbara did not come. When Mrs Cleveland suggested it to her husband he asked her *why* she was so keen on having Barbara Bird to supper. They had never had her before. They didn't want to get into the habit of asking all his pupils to supper; it would become a nuisance, a tie. And Mrs Cleveland, determined to say nothing of the gossip, had agreed that perhaps after all it wasn't necessary.

'If you want to ask somebody to supper,' Francis suggested, 'why not ask somebody with whom we have something in common—Lancelot Doge and Arthur Fenning, for example?'

And so they had a dull, academic little party and a not particularly enthusiastic discussion about the merits of the new Bodleian. Mrs Cleveland felt as if she had been cheated. It was true that Lancelot Doge and Arthur Fenning would be able to tell people what a devoted family the Clevelands were, but having *Barbara* to supper would have shown them even more. It occurred to Mrs Cleveland that Francis had been rather evasive about the whole thing, but, as it was the strawberry season and there was a great deal of jam to be made, she was really too busy to give the matter much thought, although she sometimes found herself brooding over it before she went to sleep at night. But that, as everyone knew, was the very worst time to think about anything. It was much more sensible to push all worries out of one's mind and to play a nice little alphabet game until one went off to sleep.

16

MR LATIMER'S HOLIDAY

'Well, tonight I shall be in Paris,' declared Mr Latimer at breakfast on the day when he was to start his holiday. Something of the delight and anticipation he felt in thinking of this gay city must have shown itself on his face as he stirred his tea, for Miss Doggett looked rather grave and said, 'I hope you know where you are staying in Paris. Have you got the name of a good, respectable hotel from Cook's?'

'Well, we haven't really decided,' he said. 'We'll find somewhere when we get there.'

'You ought to be very careful,' said Miss Doggett. 'Miss Morrow's cousin had a very unpleasant experience.' She turned to Miss Morrow. 'It was in Paris that your cousin Bertha had that experience, wasn't it?'

'Yes, it was, but I don't think Mr Latimer need be afraid of anything like that happening,' said Miss Morrow, thinking that, after all, Bertha had been a young girl of nineteen and Mr Latimer was a clergyman of over thirty.

'Well, you never know,' said Miss Doggett in a warning tone. 'Everyone ought to be careful in a place like Paris. I wonder where it was that Miss Jeremy—my friend who lives at Tunbridge Wells—used to stay. I remember her telling me about a very good hotel there. All the staff spoke English, the cooking was entirely English, and the visitors too. They were mostly clergy. She told me that on one occasion when she stayed there she had two, or I think three, Archdeacons at her table for dinner. It would be just the place for you and your friend.'

'It sounds very nice,' said Mr Latimer dutifully, although he privately thought that one Archdeacon was quite enough for anyone.

'It is really a good thing you are going away,' said Miss Doggett, with more seriousness than the occasion seemed to demand. 'North Oxford is no place for a young clergyman these days.'

'Something is rotten in the state of Denmark,' murmured Miss Morrow, pouring milk on her cornflakes.

'Denmark?' Mr Latimer looked up with an expression of polite surprise on his face.

'I am glad that you do not seem to have heard any gossip,' said Miss Doggett. 'You will be able to hear the whole story from one who knows the facts.'

Mr Latimer flung a startled glance at Miss Morrow, as if he feared some mention of Crampton Hodnet or the conversation in the tool shed. But his fears were soon set at rest. It was nothing to do with him, only some absurd story about Mr Cleveland that Miss Doggett seemed to have got hold of.

When she had finished telling it she paused impressively, waiting for some comment or exclamation of shocked amazement.

But Mr Latimer went on eating his breakfast and when challenged was inclined to pooh-pooh it and say that he frankly did not believe it. 'Mr Killigrew must have heard wrongly,' he said. 'I'm sure Mr Cleveland isn't that kind of man at all.'

'Mr Latimer, you are a clergyman, and it is natural that you should wish to see the best side of everything,' continued Miss Doggett. 'But I know

170

you would be the last person to shirk your duty.'

'My duty?' said Mr Latimer, his voice taking on a high note of alarm.

'Yes. I think it is your duty as a clergyman and friend of the family to speak to Mr Cleveland about it. I have done my best. Nobody will listen to an old woman. A clergyman's words carry more weight than anyone else's.' Miss Doggett put a corner of toast into her mouth with an air of finality.

'But even if it were my duty, what could I say?' said Mr Latimer.

'I must leave that to you,' said Miss Doggett. 'You should of course point out to Mr Cleveland how wrongly he is behaving, what unhappiness he is bringing to his wife and family, and how it will be the ruin of him if he goes on like this. I have seen things like this happen before. He can't break away and start a new life, you know.'

'But even if it were true, which I can't somehow believe, who am *I* to speak to Mr Cleveland about it?' said poor Mr Latimer in bewilderment.

'You are a clergyman,' said Miss Doggett in an emphatic tone.

'I know, but I am only a *curate*,' said Mr Latimer rather ridiculously and with a vague clutching gesture at his clerical collar. 'I'm no better than any other man. I can't go telling Mr Cleveland how he ought to behave. I am not worthy.'

'I should not like to think that what you say is true,' said Miss Doggett. 'It would be a poor thing if our clergy were no better than other men. But in any case you have a special duty, you know.'

'I think Mr Wardell would do it better than I should,' suggested Mr Latimer hopefully. 'He is a married man.'

'Well, Mr Latimer, I am surprised to hear you imply that a married man should be more worthy than a single man,' said Miss Doggett in a pained voice. 'Especially when you believe so strongly in the celibacy of the clergy.'

'But I don't,' protested Mr Latimer.

'But you told me so distinctly,' said Miss Doggett in amazement.

'Oh, well, I may have done,' said Mr Latimer casually, almost jauntily. 'I dare say I did believe in it once, but I've changed my mind now. I believe that a clergyman cannot possibly do good and help others unless he has had the experiences which other men have. His life is empty and unreal if he hasn't a woman with him. She can help him so much with everything; she can help him to know himself . . .' Mr Latimer went on talking almost to himself, as if he were unconscious of the presence of anybody else in the room.

'Well, Mr Latimer,' said Miss Doggett at last in a cold voice, 'there may be something in what you say, but I am sure that your views cannot have changed so much that you would condone adultery.'

'No,' said Mr Latimer in a vague, inattentive voice, 'I don't think I would do that.'

'I am sorry to hear that you are not more certain about it,' said Miss Doggett. She paused as if an idea had suddenly occurred to her and then said in a solicitous tone, 'Perhaps you are not feeling well?'

'Thank you, I am perfectly well,' said Mr Latimer absently.

'You must go on with the Sanatogen,' said Miss Doggett, 'and you ought to have milk or Ovaltine at bedtime. I expect it will be possible for you to get it in Paris. You know, we use up more energy

172

in the summer,' she added, remembering an advertisement she had seen somewhere, 'and you had a tiring day yesterday.'

That was it. He had a tiring day yesterday, thought Miss Doggett, suddenly relieved. He would be himself again tomorrow, not this strange, inattentive man who seemed suddenly to have lost all his principles.

But Miss Morrow knew that it was the beginning of the end. Mr Latimer was starting to break away, if he had not already broken. It would not be long now before Miss Doggett would have to be finding herself another curate, preferably an old, disillusioned one with no spirit left in him, who had long ago given up the struggle. One who would be thankful just to have a bed and food and a corner in a dark Victorian-Gothic house in North Oxford where he might end his days in peace. It was no use trying to keep young, handsome curates like Mr Latimer on the leash, however emphatically they might declare their belief in the celibacy of the clergy. Before many months were over they would be looking round for a way of escape.

They got up from the breakfast table, and Mr Latimer was at once busy with a hundred and one odd jobs. It was quite obvious that he would have no time to speak to Mr Cleveland that day.

Miss Doggett said nothing more about it. She had evidently decided that all she wanted was to avoid doing anything that might frighten Mr Latimer away from Leamington Lodge. It hardly mattered that he condoned adultery as long as he returned to her after his holiday. That was the chief thing.

At the last minute she sent Miss Morrow running

173

out after him with a small package.

'Here, don't go,' she called, waving it in the air. 'Miss Doggett thinks you ought to have this.'

'What is it?' he asked.

'Mothersill,' said Miss Morrow, 'for sea-sickness.'

'But I told her I was a good sailor,' said Mr Latimer plaintively. 'Good-bye!'

'Remember my cousin Bertha and her experience,' said Miss Morrow, laughing.

'I certainly will,' he called out as he drove away.

Miss Morrow watched the high two-seater with its tottering pile of luggage until it was out of sight and then walked slowly back to Leamington Lodge.

There was something particularly final about this departure of Mr Latimer's, she felt. Nothing would ever be quite the same again. It was like the closing of a door, she thought dramatically, this rattling of the car away from Leamington Lodge, up the Banbury Road, into St Giles' and then on to the road to Dover.

It was a lovely morning, when even the monkey-puzzle was bathed in sunshine. She clasped a branch in her hand and stood feeling its prickliness and looking up into the dark tower of the branches. It was like being in church. And yet on a day like this, one realised that it was a living thing too and had beauty, as most living things have in some form or another. Dear monkey-puzzle, thought Miss Morrow, impulsively clasping her arms round the trunk.

'Now, Miss Morrow,' came Miss Doggett's voice, loud and firm, 'you must find some other time to indulge in your nature worship or whatever it is. You look quite ridiculous. I hope nobody saw you.'

'Only God can make a tree,' said Miss Morrow

174

unexpectedly.

Miss Doggett did not argue the point but remarked that the trunk was dirty and Miss Morrow had probably soiled her dress.

Miss Morrow glanced down at her bosom, so appropriately clothed in dust-coloured Macclesfield silk with a bluish-grey stripe.

'I don't think it shows,' she said complacently. That was the best of drab clothes. One could be a nature worshipper without fear of soiling one's dress.

'The sheets must be taken off Mr Latimer's bed,' said Miss Doggett. 'Perhaps you would go and help Florence. The curtains can come down too; it will be a good chance to get them cleaned.'

Miss Morrow went into the house thinking about the trivial round, the common task. A companion asked really nothing; indeed, she had no right to, and Miss Morrow considered herself lucky to be able to occupy herself with those things that would furnish her with all she needed to ask.

'Room to deny ourselves; a road to bring us, daily, nearer God,' she thought, as she tugged the sheets off the bed. She felt no sentimentality as she did it. That heap on the floor was to her nothing more than a pile of sheets to be sent to the laundry. She was really a very lucky woman. It might well have been otherwise.

Meanwhile Mr Latimer was bowling along in his high two-seater. Although he was going on holiday he did not feel entirely carefree. There was an uncomfortable feeling at the back of his mind. 'We have left undone those things which we ought to have done; and we have done those things which we ought not to have done,' he thought, the words

175

coming automatically to him. Every Sunday the congregation of St Botolph's bleated it like sheep and he, who should have been their shepherd, bleated with them. He had *meant* to thank Miss Nollard and Miss Foxe for those alms-bags. He had *meant* to do that balance-sheet for the Boys' Club. He ought *really* to have been less feeble about the Cleveland affair. If only he had somebody to help him, to make him do these things, perhaps even to do them for him.

As he got near the end of his journey he began to feel that he didn't at all want to go to France. His friend, the Reverend Theodore James, was rather too serious a companion for a holiday. He couldn't think now why he had suggested that he should join him. It wasn't as if they had ever liked each other. Still, it was too late to do anything about it now, and at least they would be able to have a good talk about old times, rejoicing over those of their contemporaries who had not fulfilled their early promise and belittling those who had.

17

A CONFRONTATION

Ought one to dress up as if for a ceremonial occasion? Miss Morrow wondered, as she got ready in her bedroom. Was her brown marocain good enough, or should she have bought a flowered chiffon from Webber's? They had been showing some nice ones in the window. She set her beige straw hat firmly on her head, took her gloves and a clean handkerchief out of a drawer, and hurried downstairs.

Miss Doggett was already waiting in the hall. She was dressed in black, and her sombre magnificence made Miss Morrow feel light and summery and somehow inadequate.

'Have you got my smelling salts?' Miss Doggett asked. 'Give them to me. I may need them.'

'Here you are,' said Miss Morrow. 'Would it perhaps be better if I didn't come?'

'Of course you must come,' said Miss Doggett sharply. 'Your being there will make no difference one way or the other.'

Miss Morrow walked meekly along by Miss Doggett's side, a comforting neutral thing, without form or sex. There was something so restful in being somebody whose presence made no difference one way or the other.

'There will be no need for you to say anything,' said Miss Doggett, with her hand on the Clevelands' gate. 'I shall confront Francis with the facts and then wait for him to defend himself. If he can,' she added grimly.

Miss Morrow made no comment. She moved as if in a dream. Somehow, in spite of everything, she couldn't believe that there was *really* anything in it. Things like that could happen and perhaps they even did, but not in North Oxford, to people one knew.

'Well, Margaret,' said Miss Doggett in a falsely cheerful tone, 'we thought we'd come in and see you.'

'How nice of you,' said Mrs Cleveland. 'I'm sorry the room's so untidy.'

'Good evening, Aunt Maude and Miss Morrow,'

said Mr Cleveland, who had come into the room carrying a large enamel bowl full of gooseberries. 'Have you come to help with these things?'

'I'm making Francis useful.' Mrs Cleveland laughed. 'He's going to top and tail gooseberries.'

'I'm sure you women would do it better than I could,' he said. 'Everyone knows what a failure the academic mind is at anything like this.'

'I think if you set all the Fellows of Randolph to do it they'd be quite as good as we are,' said Mrs Cleveland. 'The academic mind is too often an excuse to get out of doing boring little jobs.'

'I'll help,' said Miss Morrow.

'Let's put the gooseberries on this little table,' said Mrs Cleveland, 'and all the bits must go in this basin. We shall soon get them done if we all help.'

'Many hands make light work,' said Miss Morrow happily. It would surely not be possible to discuss Mr Cleveland's infidelities now, and how much nicer to spend the evening topping and tailing gooseberries and gossiping of other things.

This is most unsuitable, thought Miss Doggett angrily. She sat stiffly upright, refusing to take any part with the others. Topping and tailing gooseberries, and in the drawing-room too! How like Margaret it was to have no sense of the fitness of things. It was going to be difficult for Miss Doggett to do her duty in such an atmosphere, but she was not going to shirk it.

'I came here because there was something I wanted to speak to you about,' she said firmly.

'Oh, really, what?' asked Mrs Cleveland without looking up.

'It concerns Francis, but of course it concerns you too,' said Miss Doggett deliberately. 'It is about

178

Miss Bird.'

For a second Mrs Cleveland faltered in her mechanical snipping of the gooseberries. Then, without glancing at her husband, she said casually, 'Oh, you mean the declaration of love in the British Museum?'

Miss Morrow let out a nervous giggle. She knew it was a serious matter, but it sounded so funny put like that.

Miss Doggett seemed taken aback, disappointed almost. Margaret knew about it. So either Francis had told her or somebody else had. In any case it was most annoying. It meant that she had been forestalled. Her bombshell had not exploded. But Miss Doggett belonged to a generation which had been brought up to believe that everything happens for the best and that we in our turn should try to make the best of everything. And so she did not let herself be too easily put off by what might be only a temporary setback.

'Well, Francis,' she said, 'how do you explain this?'

'I don't know what you're talking about,' he said shortly.

'You see, Margaret, he is still trying to keep up this deception,' said Miss Doggett. 'He has been leading a double life since Christmas,' she added dramatically. 'Miss Morrow and I saw him having tea with Miss Bird in Fuller's, Michael and Gabriel saw them together in the Botanical Gardens, Edward Killigrew heard their conversation in the British Museum, Miss Gurney saw them on Shotover and we cannot know what may have happened on other occasions,' she added in a dark tone tinged with regret at her inability to produce a

179

witness who had seen them in bed together.

'I don't know why you're telling me all this,' said Mrs Cleveland with admirable calmness. 'I know all about Francis's friendship with Miss Bird.'

Miss Morrow could see that Miss Doggett was having a more difficult time than she had anticipated, and she could not but admire her persistence as she plodded on. Some of the undergraduate generation at Oxford might well take a lesson from her. Miss Morrow could not help feeling glad that both the Clevelands were behaving so calmly. She liked exciting scenes in films and novels but found them embarrassing and distressing in real life. She knew that, when all is said and done, fiction is really stranger than truth, and was glad that it should be so. Margaret looked perfectly composed, while Francis showed none of the agitation one might have expected, except that he occasionally put the tops and tails of the gooseberries into the wrong bowl, but then even Miss Morrow found herself doing this sometimes, so she did not think it could very well be taken as a sign of a guilty conscience. Everything is going to be all right, she thought happily, and waited for the conversation to go on as if she had been listening to a play.

'Well, if you know about it, I suppose it is all right,' said Miss Doggett in a resigned tone. 'I know that one should never interfere between husband and wife, but I thought you ought to know how people have been talking about this affair. Gossip is not always entirely unfounded,' she added hopefully.

'No, no, of course not,' said Mrs Cleveland soothingly. 'Francis has admitted that he likes her very much, haven't you, dear?' she added, as if speaking to a child.

'Of course I like her,' he said sulkily. 'I make no secret of it. Why is everyone making such a fuss?'

What exactly did they know? he wondered uneasily. Various people had seen them together. Well, there was nothing in that. And they evidently knew about what had happened in the British Museum. But the way Margaret had spoken about it showed that she did not think much of that. She probably thought it impossible that he should have a love-affair, he thought, feeling suddenly aggrieved.

'Well, you know how people are,' Margaret was saying. 'They gossip about everything. Even I have heard gossip from various sources,' she added, 'but I didn't say anything to you because I knew that the whole thing was so fantastic. Why, the idea of you having an affair with Barbara Bird is quite ridiculous! I couldn't believe it.'

So it was ridiculous, was it? he thought resentfully. That was their idea. It was fantastic to suppose that a young woman should find him attractive.

'Of course,' said Miss Doggett, 'I have always thought it a great mistake for women students to go to men tutors. It is asking for trouble. Everyone knows how an older man's head can be turned by a little admiration from a pretty young woman. It is a known thing that middle-aged or elderly men often fancy themselves in love with young girls, who in their turn are flattered by their attentions,' she continued. 'No doubt there may have been something of the kind between you and Miss Bird,' she added disparagingly.

Oh, why doesn't she stop? thought Miss Morrow, feverishly topping and tailing gooseberries. She could see that Mr Cleveland was getting more and more angry at the way she was talking, and she was afraid that Miss Doggett might easily goad him into saying something which he would afterwards regret.

A doddering old man fancying himself in love with a pretty girl! thought Francis, who was now in a fury. So that was what he was. He remembered the happy times he had spent with Barbara, the intelligent conversations they had had, the harmonious love-making—here he exaggerated a little but nobody could blame him for that—the many ways in which they were in sympathy with each other. He knew only that he was angry with Margaret for her attitude of good-natured ridicule and with his aunt for her interference and for the fact that they were treating him at one moment like a child and at the next like an old man who was not quite right in the head.

'I love Miss Bird and she loves me!' he said hotly. 'It is just that, since you insist on knowing.' And then he went out of the room and dramatically slammed the door.

Why had he said Miss Bird? Why not Barbara? thought Miss Morrow, missing the real significance of his statement and concentrating only on trivialities. 'I love Miss Bird and she loves me!' . . . Miss Morrow felt her mouth curling at the corners. When she had controlled an impulse to giggle, she raised her head and saw that Miss Doggett looked grimly triumphant, while Mrs Cleveland was sitting still with an expression of amazement on her face. And, indeed, she was amazed. Francis speaking like that! She could hardly believe her ears. It was as if something entirely out of the course of nature had happened, as if a chair, a table, a cat or a dog had spoken with a human voice.

'Well, Margaret, I hardly know what to say now,' began Miss Doggett. 'What are you going to do?'

'Do?' echoed Mrs Cleveland vaguely. 'I don't know, I shall have to think about it. There's probably nothing in it,' she added, but her voice faltered a little.

'But, Margaret, if what Francis says is true, you will have to divorce him. You cannot possibly keep up this farce of marriage, this hollow, empty thing,' said Miss Doggett grandly. 'It is possible that there may be even more than we know about in this affair. I think it is very probable. Young women nowadays are not content with mere *declarations* of love.' She paused significantly. 'I don't know *what* you are going to do,' she went on in a wailing tone. 'You and Francis can hardly go on living together after this. And yet the scandal of a divorce will ruin him. And think of Anthea,' she added, piling it on. 'It may ruin her chances. I don't know *what* Lady Beddoes would say. I'm sure she is a very high-principled woman.'

At the mention of Anthea, Mrs Cleveland suddenly gave up behaving admirably and burst into tears. 'She mustn't hear of this,' she sobbed. 'What a good thing she's gone to the pictures. I'll go to my room and pretend I had a headache; then she needn't know.'

'Well, we shall see,' said Miss Doggett, who had hopefully taken her smelling salts out of her bag. 'Of course if there is to be a divorce you cannot very well keep it from her, but for the present it will certainly be better to say nothing about it. Come,

183

Margaret,' she said, taking her arm. 'I think you had better go to your room now.' Miss Morrow, left alone in the drawing-room among the gooseberries, felt more strongly than ever that she was not a woman of the world. She had thought that there was nothing in the affair, and now Mr Cleveland had declared before them all that he and the young woman were in love with each other. Even she could hardly fail to realise that this was something rather serious. She looked around her hopelessly, feeling useless and out of place in such a situation. Then she saw that the bowl of gooseberries was still unfinished, and it comforted her to know that there *was* something she could do.

When she had finished the topping and tailing she took the gooseberries into the kitchen, where Ellen, who had just come in from her evening off, was finishing the washing-up.

'I've brought the gooseberries,' said Miss Morrow, feeling that her presence required some explanation but not being able to think of a convincing one.

'Well, Miss Morrow, fancy you being here,' said Ellen, looking surprised.

'Oh, I've been helping with the gooseberries,' she said gaily. 'We've all been doing them. Many hands make light work, you know.'

'Too many cooks spoil the broth's more like it,' said Ellen uncompromisingly.

'Oh, well, that's another way of looking at it, isn't it,' said Miss Morrow, feeling rather snubbed. 'Good night.'

184

18

A LONDON VISIT

It was remarkable, Mrs Cleveland thought when she woke up next morning, how well she had slept. She had gone to bed expecting to lie awake half the night in tears and worry. But thanks to Miss Doggett's excellent bromide, she had gone off to sleep almost at once and had not even woken when Francis had looked in to attempt some sort of explanation.

So she had just gone off to sleep, he thought resentfully. She didn't care enough to stay awake and listen to what he had to say. He looked round the room and saw that she had even folded her clothes neatly on a chair by the bed. There was no sign that she had been any more agitated than she was on any other night, he thought, as he went sulkily to his own room, undressed and got into bed. And so it was he who had lain awake, not exactly worrying, but working himself up against what seemed to be his wife's apparent indifference towards the whole affair.

He came down to breakfast very late to find the table in a wild, desolate condition, as it is when people have already eaten. There were hollowed-out grapefruit skins, empty eggshells, one piece of toast in the rack and two cups full of dregs and coffee grounds.

So they'd had breakfast, he thought resentfully; they hadn't waited for him, he grumbled, forgetting that they never did. Quite a hearty breakfast they'd made, too; they had left him only one piece of toast. He got up angrily and pressed the bell very hard.

Ellen appeared in the doorway with fresh coffee and toast. 'I heard you come down, sir,' she said. 'Perhaps you'd like an egg?'

'I see they've had their breakfast.'

'The mistress and Miss Anthea have gone up to London,' said Ellen rather stiffly. 'They had to catch the ten-ten train.'

'To *London*?' said Francis, with as much amazement as if Ellen had said Buenos Aires or Baffinland.

'Yes, sir, the mistress wanted to do some shopping at the Sales.'

'*Shopping*? Well, *really* . . .'

'Did you say you'd have an egg, sir?' asked Ellen patiently.

'Oh, yes, I don't mind what I have,' said Francis crossly. Going to the Sales at a time like this, he said to himself indignantly. And then he noticed a letter in Margaret's handwriting by his plate. With an unconscious feeling of pleasure at the drama of the situation, he tore it open.

Dear Francis [it said], Anthea and I are going up to London for a day or two. There are several things I want to get at the Sales, it will be such a good opportunity to buy sheets, blankets and towels, as you know, and also to think over that little matter that cropped up last night.

We shall stay at Amy's, probably over the weekend, but shall be back on Monday or Tuesday. Don't worry about us. Margaret.

Disappointment and exasperation filled him as he read it. The greatest crisis of their lives—for so he had come to regard it—referred to as 'that

186

little matter that cropped up last night' and lumped together with the sheets, blankets and towels.

He crumpled up the letter in disgust and put it into his pocket. So that was all the thought Margaret had given to the events of last night. Oh, well, if she didn't care, neither did he. Two could play at that game, he thought, delighted with his wit.

He looked around for the *Daily Mirror*, which he always liked to read at the breakfast table, but they had taken it with them, and so he had to be content with *The Times*. He was soon in difficulties with its large pages and in the end had to read one small folded section. His grapefruit spurted up into his eyes, and he read over and over again:

The Earl and Countess of Gnome have returned to London from New York.

The Hon. Mrs Arnold Younghusband was among those present at the Memorial Service for Alicia, Lady Spoute.

Lady Beddoes has left 175 Chester Square for the Lido.

Beddoes, he thought. We know somebody called Beddoes, don't we? . . .

*   *   *

Of course, thought Anthea, leaning back in her corner, it didn't necessarily mean that Simon had gone too, though he *might* have done. If only he would write! She had only had a postcard from him since term ended, and that was weeks ago. She had written him three long letters, and he hadn't answered any of them. But perhaps he would be in London. She might even see him there. Hope springs eternal, especially in the breast of a young woman in love.

'What are you going to buy, dear?' asked Mrs Cleveland brightly. 'Have you made a list?'

'Oh, I'll see when we get there,' said Anthea absently. 'I'd rather like a tweed suit and a summer coat.'

Like a pair of old broody hens we are, thought Mrs Cleveland, when she realised that they had not spoken for half an hour. But then there was so much to think about. Her one idea was to go somewhere where she could think in peace. And where better than her sister Amy's house in Bayswater? Poor Amy was always so splendidly taken up with her own troubles that she never asked any questions. They need only be away a day or two, and, as they often went up to London for shopping, nobody would think it unusual. It was important to think things out sensibly. To face facts.

Francis and Barbara are in love with each other. She said the words over in her mind and would even have liked to say them aloud, as if by so doing she could better understand what they meant.

If Francis really loved this girl and she loved him, perhaps he would want to leave his home and set up another one somewhere else, she thought, unable to help feeling a little amused at the idea of it. If he could be bothered to, for Francis was so lazy that it seemed completely out of character to imagine him taking the trouble to deceive his wife and fall in love with another woman. Unless, of course, she had been mistaken in him all these years. Perhaps there had been *others*? . . . But no, now that she came to think of it, she was sure that there had been no others. Dear Francis, he had really been such a good husband. She began to look back on her married life, remembering not all the loving things he had said or written to her, not romantic moonlight evenings or spring days, as a young girl does when she has been jilted, but silly, homely things: Francis shuffling about his study in his bedroom slippers, taking Anthea for a walk in Port Meadow on a Sunday afternoon, and, only yesterday, standing in the doorway with a bowl of gooseberries. Remembering all this, she was somehow reassured. But, all the same, Francis and Barbara are in love with each other, she thought, bringing herself back to the point. Well, there was nothing she could do about it now, at this very minute, she thought with a sense of relief as the train drew in to Paddington.

'I'd better telephone Amy,' she said. 'Then we can leave our suitcases here and do some shopping before lunch.'

When they got to the shops, Anthea brightened up a little and was carrying quite a number of parcels by the time they had found their way, weary, hot and rather dishevelled, to a restaurant where hundreds of women in a similar state were wondering whether they ought to have the slimming salad lunch or the something more substantial which they felt they had earned after a hard morning's shopping.

'I love my shoes,' said Anthea. 'Now I must try and get a bag to go with them.'

'*Escalope de veau viennoise*,' said Mrs Cleveland in a dazed tone. 'Why, that's veal cutlet, isn't it? I don't think we want *soup*, do we?' she said urgently, as she saw a waitress approaching. 'We haven't quite made up our minds,' she said, looking round to see what everyone else was having.

All these women, do *they* have trouble with their husbands? she wondered. You, in your smart silly hat and silver-fox furs, you in your sensible navy felt and too-hot flannel costume, you with your calm face and dangling pince-nez . . . do *your* husbands have *lapses*, as Olive Fremantle calls them? And if so, what do you do about it? Perhaps you have lapses yourself, she thought, looking at the first woman's long scarlet nails and full, red, sticky mouth. Well, that might be one way out of it. But hardly for Margaret Cleveland. She belonged with the other two, especially with the one in the sensible hat and costume. *She* looked an excellent woman, full of good sense. Her opinion would be worth having.

At that moment she lifted up her left hand to tuck in a stray wisp of hair, and Mrs Cleveland saw that the hand was ringless. Then, presumably, she hadn't got a husband. She was a comfortable spinster with nobody but herself to consider. Living in a tidy house not far from London, making nice little supper dishes for one, a place for everything and everything in its place, no husband hanging resentfully round the sitting-room, no husband one moment topping and tailing gooseberries and the next declaring that he had fallen in love with a young woman. Mrs Cleveland sighed a sigh of envy. No husband.

The same could be said of her sister Amy, she realised later in the afternoon, as they sat drinking tea in the gloomy house in Bayswater, except that one didn't, for some reason, envy poor Amy. One

190

never had envied her. It was impossible to imagine her ever allowing herself to get into a position where she could be envied. One felt that she would not enjoy life at all if she were not continually enlisting sympathy for something or other.

'Oh, Margaret, such a *sickening* thing happened!' she said at tea. 'You know that little dressmaker who always does things for me? Well, I went there last week with my pattern and material and everything, and what do you think? The house seemed to be all shut up, so I asked next door and they told me that she *died* a month ago. Isn't it *sickening*?'

Mrs Cleveland murmured that it was indeed.

'Of course when Percy was alive I used to buy all my things at Marshall's, but now—well, there aren't so many pennies.'

She became rather coy and babyish, and Mrs Cleveland murmured with profound wisdom that one did indeed have to cut one's coat according to one's cloth.

'Well, tomorrow we'll have a lovely day shopping, won't we?' said Amy, brightening up. 'I do so enjoy these little jaunts. You ought to come up to town more often. Of course Anthea does come up, don't you, dear?' she said, turning round and fixing her prominent pale blue eyes on her niece. 'I've heard *all* about a certain young man who lives in Chester Square.'

Anthea smiled a sickly smile.

'Is he *very* handsome?' her aunt asked.

'Oh, yes,' said Mrs Cleveland vigorously, 'but of course he isn't the *only* one. Anthea has so many friends.'

'Oxford's full of young men,' said Anthea rather

shortly. 'I think I'll go for a walk in the Park,' she said, standing up.

Simon *might* be in town, she thought, even though he said that he never stayed in London for more than a week at a time. Lady Somebody might be giving a dance for her horrid débutante daughter, and Simon was very eligible. But it was nearly the end of July now. *The Times* and the *Telegraph* were full of announcements of people leaving for Scotland or the South of France or, more simply, 'abroad' or just 'the country'.

'Lady Beddoes has left 175 Chester Square for the Lido.' Poor Lady Beddoes. Was she enjoying herself in fashionable beachwear and red toenails? Whatever would she do with herself all day? Anthea wondered as she trudged through the Park in her not very comfortable high-heeled shoes.

It was such a long way to Simon's house. Anthea got lost in the vastness of Belgrave Square and took the wrong turning out of it, so that she found herself walking nearly into Knightsbridge. She was very tired and had a blister on one heel by the time she reached Chester Square.

Anthea stopped and patted her hair. She wasn't looking very nice but it didn't matter now. For when she reached the house she knew that nothing mattered; it was so shut up that it might just as well not have been there at all. She could hardly have had a greater shock if it had been in ruins. She had been so sure he would be there.

But inside the dust would be collecting on the marble bust of Pilsudski, the flowers in Lady Beddoes's little conservatory would be dying for want of water, Simon's desk would be littered with notes and invitations days and weeks old.

Anthea walked slowly away. She found it soothing to count the houses and stare into the windows. Sometimes she saw an empty room and the notice CARETAKER WITHIN, and once she looked down into a basement kitchen and saw a prim-looking maid smoking a cigarette and a manservant in shirtsleeves reading a paper. She walked on and on until she realised that she was tired and wanted nothing so much as to get onto the first bus that was going to Marble Arch.

When Anthea reached the tall, dark house in Bayswater Amy had got on to the servant problem. Mrs Cleveland was listening. Not knitting or doing anything, just sitting there with her hands folded, a picture of resignation in a navy foulard dress with a small white pattern.

19

AN EVENING ON THE RIVER

Francis Cleveland felt thoroughly at a loose end after his wife and daughter had gone. He pottered about the house and garden feeling vaguely resentful, as if he had been in some way ill-used. Margaret had just gone off in a huff without even listening to what he had to say about Barbara. If she wasn't careful the whole thing might become far more serious than she had bargained for. It would serve them right, he felt—Margaret, Aunt Maude and all those gossiping North Oxford women—if he ran off with Barbara. He would show them, he thought defiantly. They would soon realise that they had been mistaken, he laboured, although he had no very clear idea *how* they were going to be made to realise it.

After tea he walked up the Banbury Road on his way to see Barbara. Nobody who saw him, a tall, stooping man with a handsome but mild face, would have guessed at the violent, defiant thoughts that were jostling each other in his mind. Miss Nollard and Miss Foxe, who passed him in St Giles', even remarked to each other what a nice man he was and how pleasantly he smiled when he said 'Good evening'. Francis had imagined that his greeting was highly ironical in its honeyed affability and that it conveyed, very subtly of course, his contempt and dislike for all the female inhabitants of North Oxford. But we are often allowed to keep our illusions in small matters, and so he went on his way feeling very pleased with himself.

Barbara was living in lodgings in St John Street, and was supposed to be doing some work on her thesis. When Francis came into the room he found her sitting at a table writing. He bent and gave her a perfunctory, almost husbandly kiss, but as this was in Barbara's opinion the most bearable sort, she was perfectly satisfied and began to talk about the work she was doing.

'They've gone away. They went this morning,' said Francis, interrupting her rudely.

Barbara of course knew what he meant. 'They' always meant his family. She hesitated as if she did not quite know what was expected of her.

'Now we can really enjoy ourselves,' he said boldly. 'We can do whatever we like.'

'Oh, yes, that will be nice,' she said vaguely,

194

even a little apprehensively. 'I don't quite know what I'm going to do about my thesis,' she said quickly. 'I looked in Bodley this morning and found something about it in one of those American periodicals, but of course it hasn't been done at all thoroughly . . .'

There was a pause.

After a while Francis said, 'You haven't kissed me properly today. Come here.' He held out his arms to her.

'Oh, but I *have* kissed you,' she protested. 'I kissed you when you came in.'

Francis sighed. Barbara was in some ways a little unsatisfactory. These beautiful walks and understanding talks between intelligent people were all very well, but he was beginning to get just a little bored with them. It was a tiring business trailing around Oxford in the hot weather pretending to be more misunderstood and ill-used than one really was, he thought, with a sudden flash of honesty. Barbara was a sweet girl and he was very fond of her, but he could not help feeling that the affair was beginning to *drag* a little. Because, when one came to think of it, almost anyone could give sympathy and understanding—Miss Morrow, Miss Nollard and Miss Foxe, even Margaret. Indeed, sympathy and understanding were a great stand-by for a plain-looking woman who could never hope to be more to a man than a dear sister. But Barbara was young and pretty, and it was surely not surprising that he should expect a little more from her than from, say, Miss Morrow. Could it be, he wondered, that she was not quite what she seemed? Those dark glances, so full of passion, from those beautiful eyes: could it be that they were just her natural way of looking at everybody? There was nothing in the invaluable *Cambridge History of English Literature*—nothing, indeed, in the whole Bodleian, even—to provide the answer to this question.

'You're so provoking,' he said peevishly. 'I don't know what to make of you.'

'How do you mean?' she asked, gazing at him soulfully.

'You look so amorous and really you're just a cold fish,' he said shortly.

No woman, however much she values her virtue, likes to have it described in such unromantically blunt terms, and so it was only natural that Barbara should protest.

'Oh, but I'm not cold,' she assured him. 'It's only that I prefer a more romantic setting than this.'

Francis brightened up a little. 'Let's go on the river this evening,' he said. 'It should be romantic there. We'll go from Magdalen Bridge. I always think that's the nicest part.' And the farthest away from North Oxford, he added to himself.

'Oh, I'd love that,' said Barbara quite enthusiastically.

A beautiful evening on the river. Perhaps a bottle of wine, thought Francis boldly. Niersteiner . . . Simon Beddoes always took a bottle of Niersteiner on the river. Age could sometimes learn a thing or two from youth. Respectable Oxford dons were naturally a little rusty in some things. They had forgotten the details of these romantic episodes: what one ought to eat and drink; even, sometimes, what one ought to say. Well, that was natural. One couldn't imagine even brilliant men like Arnold Penge, Lancelot Doge or Arthur Fenning being much good at this sort of thing. Thinking of them, he had a sudden desire to go into Randolph and have a gossip with them. He felt he would like to boast and say, 'Ah, you'll never guess what I'm going to do this evening.' But of course one must be discreet. It would never do to give anything away.

Opposite Randolph he stopped and began to cross the road. There was a good deal of traffic in St Giles', and he stood on an island looking up at the façade of the college.

'Ah, Cleveland,' said a deep, rumbling voice. 'You are pondering on the vicissitudes of human life. I can see that.'

Francis turned and saw Dr Fremantle standing beside him.

'I wasn't really thinking about anything,' he said, as one usually does on such occasions.

'But you are gazing at our Victorian-Gothic façade,' said Dr Fremantle. 'And you are seeing the green creepers that now cover it, and you are thinking that they must soon turn red and brown until at last they die. Am I not right?'

'I'm afraid my thoughts were less exalted,' Francis admitted, as they walked across the road together.

'Ah.' Dr Fremantle put a wealth of expression into that single sound. 'I am apt to forget that the Fellows of Randolph are not all old men,' he said. 'Some of them are still able to enjoy the pleasures of this life instead of preparing for the next. I don't suppose there will be many pleasures there, or at least hardly comparable with those of this world. You are a lucky man, Cleveland. You don't have to waste your time thinking exalted thoughts.'

'Well, I should hardly have thought it was

a waste of time,' said Francis, feeling like an undergraduate.

'It is an occupation for old people,' said Dr Fremantle shortly, 'for Olive and me, together. Now you can see what sort of an occupation it is,' he added with a short bark of laughter. 'Are you going away?' he asked.

'Yes, eventually,' said Francis. 'The usual family holiday.'

'You look rather depressed,' said Dr Fremantle in a fatherly tone. 'Do you know what I should prescribe for you?'

'What?' asked Francis politely.

'A weekend in Paris,' declared Dr Fremantle. 'But you shouldn't go alone. Perhaps you have a friend who could go with you?'

'Edward Killigrew or Lancelot Doge?' suggested Francis vaguely.

'Well, yes, Edward Killigrew and mother,' said Dr Fremantle. 'That would be quite a family party. But it was hardly what I meant.'

'No, I guessed that,' said Francis knowingly. In another minute, he thought, noticing the twinkle in the old man's eye, we shall begin quoting Limericks to each other.

Paris . . . Francis thought as he walked home. The word had so many associations, and each time somebody said it one imagined something different. Dr Fremantle's jovial yet secret voice conjured up a picture of the Continent in the days of King Edward the Seventh: the Entente Cordiale, black silk stockings and garters and rather naughty jokes. Miss Doggett's shocked pronunciation of the name made it into a dark, wicked city where one might have an 'unpleasant experience' and where it was

198

essential to get the name of a good, respectable hotel from Cook's. Simon Beddoes's caressing voice gave the impression of a place where he knew a little hotel, where it was always spring and one was always on honeymoon, though not necessarily *monsieur et madame*, except in the hotel register. Paris, when Francis had said it, had hitherto been just the capital of France, where he and Margaret had once lost their luggage and passed an uncomfortable night on the way to somewhere else. But now he began to think of it differently. Barbara had said that she liked a romantic setting. What city in the world was more romantic than Paris, provided one didn't lose one's luggage?

When he reached his own gate he saw Miss Morrow scuttling away from it.

'Good evening,' he called out. 'What are you doing?'

'I don't know,' said Miss Morrow, who had not been able to think of any adequate reason why she should be hanging round the Clevelands' gate. She could not very well explain that Miss Doggett had told her to watch for Francis's return and to notice whether he brought Miss Bird with him.

'When are you going away?' he asked.

'Oh, soon, I hope,' she said. 'Oxford's so depressing now.'

'You ought to go to Paris,' said Francis surprisingly.

'Paris? What should I do in Paris?' said Miss Morrow.

'Oh, you might have some interesting experiences there,' he said vaguely.

Miss Morrow shook her head. 'No, I'm afraid nothing would happen to me,' she said regretfully.

'I shouldn't even have the sort of experience my cousin Bertha had.' She paused and then laughed suddenly. 'I must be off now,' she said. 'Good-bye!' She felt quite guilty at having nothing to report to Miss Doggett, almost as if it were *her* fault.

But later in the evening she *did* see a most extraordinary sight. She was going out about nine o'clock to post some letters, when she noticed Mr Cleveland hurrying out of his gate. That in itself was nothing extraordinary, and she would have thought nothing of it, had he not been carrying a bottle of wine. It struck her as so very odd that she could not resist waiting to see where he went. But after she had seen him get on a bus she was really none the wiser. He might be going anywhere or nowhere. All the same, the whole affair seemed a little suspicious—rather Crampton Hodnet, was how she put it to herself. Oh, yes, distinctly Crampton Hodnet. She supposed she ought really to tell Miss Doggett. But what good would that do? Unless one could do positive *good* by telling a thing, one ought to keep quiet, thought Miss Morrow stoutly. She would *not* tell Miss Doggett.

She went back to Leamington Lodge, thinking vaguely about Omar Khayyam. How very odd Mr Cleveland had looked carrying that bottle! She could hardly help laughing to herself.

How did one carry a bottle easily and nonchalantly, as if it were the most natural thing in the world to be carrying? Francis wondered. He felt so foolish with it in his hand, and yet it would have looked even more odd if he had tried to hide it under his coat. He was glad when he and Barbara and the bottle were all safely together in a punt, where it did not seem quite so much out of place.

It was an ideal evening for the river. There was a warm breeze that stirred the leaves above them, and as it grew darker an enormous, unnatural-looking moon came out. Faint music could be heard in the distance and occasionally voices: townspeople, Americans, foreigners, the usual vacation inhabitants of Oxford.

'Of course I'm not really much good at punting,' said Francis apologetically, 'but I dare say I can get it along.'

'I'm afraid I've never learnt properly,' admitted Barbara.

'Ah, you've always been taken on the river by some accomplished young man,' he said gallantly.

'Yes, I suppose I have, really,' agreed Barbara, lying back on the moss-green cushions. She liked this picture of herself surrounded by admirers. The cold-fish remark was still rankling a little. He would soon find out how wrong he had been, she thought boldly. 'How nice to have a bottle of wine,' she said. 'That's essential for a romantic river party.'

'Yes, I thought it would be a good idea,' said Francis.

'"The viol, the violet, and the vine",' quoted Barbara in a dreamy voice.

'This seems to be a nice place to tie up,' said Francis, pointing to a tree-shaded bank.

'Oh, yes. How do we fix it?'

'I'll stick the pole into the mud,' he said, 'and there's a rope at the other end that ought to be tied to something.'

Barbara got up and walked along the swaying floor of the punt. 'I'll do it,' she said. 'There's quite a convenient branch here if I can reach it.'

'Mind you don't fall in,' said Francis jokingly.

201

Barbara stretched out towards the branch with the rope in her hand ready to tie it, but at that moment the punt suddenly lurched away and there was a cry and a splash. She had fallen into the water.

'Barbara!' Francis dithered about, encumbered by the long, awkward pole. At last he flung it onto the bank and, without really thinking what he was doing, floundered into the water after her. He splashed round the punt and eventually found her. She was in no danger. She even appeared to be swimming. There had been no need for him to jump in at all, he thought with sudden annoyance, but the next moment this unworthy thought was chased from his mind as he put his arms around her and helped her back into the punt. Barbara, who was of course soaked to the skin, shivered convulsively and drew nearer to him.

He kissed her and she responded with more warmth than she had ever done before.

Dear Francis, she thought, jumping into the water to save me. Of course she hadn't really needed saving, but his action had somehow turned a ridiculous mishap into a romantic episode. There was something beautiful about that. She felt that they were very close to each other.

'Barbara,' he said in a rather odd, high voice, 'how would you like to go to Paris with me?'

'*Paris* . . .' She looked up at the dark tangle of branches above their heads. 'Oh, Francis, it would be *divine*.' Little shivers passed all over her. If they weren't careful they were both going to catch cold, she thought, but had no wish to spoil the romance of the moment by pointing out that they ought to hurry home and take hot baths. For it *was* a romantic moment. It seemed to Barbara the most romantic moment she had ever known in her whole life.

'We shall get pneumonia if we don't hurry home,' said Francis at last.

'Oh, look, the poor bottle of wine. We never had it,' said Barbara. It lay abandoned among the cushions, still unopened. Looking at it, Francis suddenly remembered that he had forgotten to bring a corkscrew . . .

As he let himself into the house, Ellen was just going up to bed.

'Good night, Ellen,' he said.

'Good night, sir.'

She glanced at him, but without interest. Evidently she saw nothing unusual in the fact that he was carrying a bottle of wine and had evidently fallen into the river. She had always thought him a bit touched anyway.

20

AN UNEXPECTED OUTCOME

Francis woke up with the feeling that it was a special day. This was, for him, a most unusual feeling. He couldn't remember having experienced it for years. All days were so much alike, or should be, giving the same lectures and tutorials, seeing the family or the undergraduate faces that had looked vaguely the same for the past twenty years, so much so that some dons could scarcely have told you what year or even what season it was, unless their wives had made them put on woollen underwear, when they would realise that it must be time for a certain set of lectures which were given only in the winter term.

But today was different. Why? he wondered. And then he remembered. He sat up in bed in a panic. He was going to Paris with Barbara. What on earth had made him think of doing such a thing? He sat up in his blue-striped poplin pyjamas and remembered. Dr Fremantle, the evening on the river, the bottle of wine . . . he saw that it was still there, unopened. It looked curiously out of place standing on the dressing-table in his respectable, almost monastic, bedroom.

He got up and went down to breakfast. There was nothing from Margaret. Well, he hadn't written either. He felt angry and defiant, and bitter against his family for their neglect. He was altogether in a good mood to appreciate the little note that Barbara had written him. He hadn't thought of doing anything like that. It was an omission, like the corkscrew.

Darling [it began], *I shall never forget last night. It was heavenly wasn't it? I never realised before how much I love you. It will be wonderful in Paris. Just you and me . . .*

He would certainly have to go to Paris now. It was all settled. He wasn't at all used to doing such things, but he would feel such a fool if he backed out. Darling Barbara, he thought, it would be wonderful in Paris with her. Youth and Beauty and Romance. The Right True End of Love . . . He went on stolidly eating his eggs and bacon, trying to recapture something of what he had felt last night. Of course it wasn't so easy at nine o'clock in

204

the morning. But at nine o'clock *tonight*, well, that would be different, he thought hopefully . . .

Of course, things weren't *quite* the same in the cold light of morning, thought Barbara, as she stood in Elliston's, fingering a pale blue chiffon nightgown. Of *course* she was going to enjoy it, it was going to be the most wonderful experience of her whole life. She had written to tell him so. This feeling that one would give anything to get out of it wasn't *real*, it was only what anyone might feel before setting out on such an adventure. She mustn't be a coward. She mustn't, above all, be a cold fish.

Paris, she thought. Paris with Francis, she emended, for when she said just Paris she remembered being led round the Latin Quarter on a hot August morning, poring over a Métro map to find the best way to get to L'Opéra from Cité Universitaire; the voice of a conscientious young American repeating over and over again 'I've *gotta* see the Mona Lisa'; a dreadful day at Versailles towards the end of the tour when the party was beginning to get quarrelsome and on edge. This was Paris as she remembered it. But Paris with Francis . . . she paused, unable to sort out the confusion that was in her mind at the thought of it. Oh, it would be wonderful, she told herself gaily. The beautiful city would become a thousand times more so when there was somebody one loved to share the beauty. They would be able to wander about Montmartre together, look at their favourite pictures in the Louvre, stand in the gardens of the Petit Trianon and remember Marie Antoinette, walk in the Champs Elysées and the Place Vendôme. But the Place Vendôme reminded her of the great couturiers who had their salons there, and that brought her back in a humble way to the blue chiffon nightgown. Because of course when one went away with somebody one loved there were nights as well as days; indeed, she believed that as far as some people were concerned the days could hardly be said to count at all. What a pity it was, she thought regretfully, that even Francis seemed not always to realise that there could be such a thing as platonic love and that the most beautiful relationship between a man and a woman was one in which they were in perfect *spiritual* harmony. Surely the poets had written about such a relationship? she thought hopefully, casting about in her mind for examples. But somehow she could think only of one quotation, the beginning of a poem by Abraham Cowley:

> *Indeed, I must confess,*
> *When Souls mix 'tis an happiness.*
> *But not complete till bodies too do join.*

Well, of course, she admitted reluctantly, one naturally wanted one's love to be complete, although it was her private opinion that hers could hardly be more complete than it already was. Everything would be different in Paris. Oxford was too full of unsuitable associations: a wife, a family, a house in the Banbury Road. She quickly put all such uncomfortable thoughts out of her mind. It was too late now to go remembering things like that.

'What time do we get to Dover?' she asked quite gaily when they were on the road later that day.

'I don't know exactly,' said Francis vaguely. 'We can get the night boat, though, I'm sure of that.

206

We'll have a lovely time,' he added in a soothing voice, which sounded as if he were trying to reassure himself as well as her.

He ought to have been feeling happy and carefree, but he had not realised till now how difficult it was going to be for a dull, virtuous, middle-aged don to change suddenly into a dashing lover. But he could hardly turn back now, and of course he really wanted to go, he told himself stoutly, and at least it would show *them*—which meant in his mind the female inhabitants of North Oxford—that he was something more than a doddering old man whose head had been turned by the admiration of a pretty young woman. But as they got nearer to Dover he began to think that that was just what he was, and that what he was doing now was only an additional proof of his dotage. It was an uncomfortable feeling, and he did his best to shake it off by making bright, unnatural conversation with Barbara, who responded in the same strain.

'A pity it isn't a nicer day,' he said, when the first drops of rain splashed against the windscreen.

'Oh, well, it doesn't really matter, does it?' she said. 'It's sure to be fine in Paris.'

'And even if it isn't,' he said, trying to say what was expected of him, 'it won't really matter. I mean, we shall be together,' he finished rather lamely.

'Do you know what time this boat actually goes?' she asked.

'I'm not *sure*,' he said, 'and it does seem to be farther to Dover than I thought.'

'Yes, we aren't nearly there yet,' said Barbara.

They drove along in silence.

'Well, here we are,' he said. 'This seems to be the

207

Druid Hotel. I'll get out and ask about the boats.'

It was raining heavily now. Barbara looked out and saw a square, yellowish building with a peeling stucco front and a general air of decay. Some servants hurried out to the car, old people, with shrivelled, birdlike faces and rusty black clothes too big for them.

After a few minutes Francis came back again. 'We've missed that boat,' he said. 'I think we'd better stay the night here. It will be more comfortable, really.'

'Oh,' said Barbara in a colourless tone which seemed to express nothing.

'You go into the lounge while I arrange about things,' he said.

'My friend Sarah Penrose lives near here—' Barbara began and stopped suddenly, for she had been going to say that she could spend the night with Sarah. But of course that would be quite impossible.

She stood in the lounge, nervously twisting her hands and looking around her with some agitation. She saw that the room was decorated with stiff palms in brass pots and that grouped in a corner, as if for artistic effect, were a number of old people reading the newspapers. They looked as if they had been left there many years ago and abandoned. Or perhaps they were people who at some time long past had intended to go abroad and had then either not wanted to or forgotten all about it, so that they had stayed here ever since, like fossils petrified in stone.

The place seemed to have a calming effect on her, and she sat down on the edge of a green-plush-covered chair. It was still raining outside, and she

208

was sure that if she were to touch the greenish wallpaper it would be damp or even mouldy. She had the idea that she was in a tank under the water or in a vault, and that if she spoke to one of the reading figures it would not answer her. She picked up a tattered copy of *Country Life*. It was dated 1932.

It gave her quite a shock when Francis came in. The occupants of the lounge looked up in surprise, as might corpses in a vault on hearing a live human voice.

'I've settled everything,' he said. 'Perhaps you'd like to come upstairs.'

She followed him meekly up the dim stairs and into a large, gloomy bedroom.

'Our weekend in Paris,' he said, with an attempt at gaiety, but his voice had a hollow ring.

Barbara felt she ought to make some sort of response, but somehow her voice would not come. She sat down on the enormous double bed with its hot crimson coverlet and looked about her.

'What a funny room,' she said at last.

'Yes, it's very gloomy and Victorian, but we don't mind that, do we?' he said rather uncertainly. 'I think I'll go and have a bath,' he added more briskly, 'and then we can have dinner. It's rather late, but they said they could give us a meal.'

He came to her and kissed her gently on the forehead.

I *can't*, she thought, sitting still and unresponsive. The kiss seemed to have woken her out of the dazed calmness which had come over her in the lounge, and all her panic came rushing back. Once more she could think of nothing but escape. I must get out of here, I must go to Sarah, she thought.

When he had gone along to the bathroom, she thought, I must leave a note. One had to remember things like that. It was usual on such occasions. Oh, if he comes back before I have finished! My pen. Oh, *where* did I put my pen? I must write in pencil. It doesn't matter as long as I let him know something.

She burst out of the room and ran down the stairs. But nobody followed her, nobody asked where she was going, nobody even noticed her. When she had reached the entrance hall with its stiff, unemotional palms she had calmed down enough to realise that she must try to look as if she were doing nothing unusual. By the time she was outside the hotel she felt almost light-hearted and was able to turn her mind to considering the best way of getting to Sarah Penrose.

I'm free, she thought; there won't be any going to Paris. There won't be any more love, or at least not *that* kind of love. I've run away from Francis. Not *run* away, I've left him, I've given him up. I've *renounced* him. There was nothing shameful about renunciation; on the contrary, it was noble. 'I must not think of thee . . .' There was that poem in the *Oxford Book of Victorian Verse* about it. Barbara had often read it, but never before had she really understood what it *meant*.

She was sure she would never marry now, and there came into her mind the comforting picture of herself, a beautiful, cultured woman with sad eyes—she thought vaguely of Tennyson and the Pre-Raphaelites. She should have quoted Christina Rossetti in her note to Francis, she thought regretfully.

210

Better by far you should forget and smile
Than you should remember and be sad.

To smile, but never laugh—Barbara was not fond of laughing anyhow.

By the time she reached Sarah's friendly red-brick house she was feeling very nearly happy.

She might have been surprised and even disappointed if she could have seen Francis sitting calmly in the lounge of the Druid Hotel, making conversation with the old people.

'What's happened to your daughter?' asked an old lady. 'Has she gone to bed? I didn't know young people ever went to bed early.'

'My daughter?' For a moment Francis was puzzled. And then he understood. 'Oh, she's got a friend who lives near here,' he said. 'They were at Oxford together.'

'Oxford? Do you know Oxford?' said one of the old clergymen, pricking up his ears. 'I was at Oxford. I was up at Randolph in eighty-five.'

'Did you know Dr Fremantle?' asked Francis politely. 'The present Master?'

'Fremantle?' mumbled the old man. 'Let me see . . . Oh, yes, there was a Fremantle up, but he was junior to me. A very gay young man. I remember . . .' And he went off into a confused reminiscence of something to do with a 'lady of the town, a rather notorious person'.

But Francis was not listening. He was thinking of old Herbert Fremantle: a very gay young man. Somehow the idea of it filled him with an overwhelming sadness. It was as if he himself had suddenly become an old man with nothing to do but think exalted thoughts, with an occasional backward glance at a youth that was long past. For he realised now that he had tried to do something that was impossible. What had made him embark on this ridiculous escapade? He hesitated. What was Love, anyway? he asked himself, looking around at the old people. ''Tis not hereafter.' This place where he was now might very well be hereafter, and love, if it existed at all, would be nothing more than 'calm of mind all passion spent'.

He sank into a kind of apathy, and the conversation lapsed. For a time there was complete silence, and then from somewhere, quite near, he couldn't exactly make out where, came the sound of somebody playing the piano. There was a jangle of chords, and he recognised the waltz melody from Offenbach's overture *Orpheus in the Underworld*. It went on and on, sometimes hurrying and yet never seeming to get any nearer to the end. It became part of the surroundings, with the rain, the green wallpaper, the palms, and the heavy breathing of a deaf old lady who had fallen asleep.

After a while the old people roused themselves and went upstairs to sleep again. Francis followed them without a murmur. Indeed, he now felt himself to be one of them.

Barbara's note was still in the pocket of his dressing-gown. Better not leave it there, he decided, coming back to reality for a moment. He lit a match and destroyed it and then got ready for bed. He felt melancholy now but not unhappy. After all, everything had happened for the best. Things generally did. Margaret always said so, and wives were usually right.

Aunts were right too, he thought, as he lay in bed looking round the overfurnished Victorian room.

212

It was somehow like going to bed in Aunt Maude's drawing-room, he felt. Well, they were all right and he was wrong. He would be back in Oxford tomorrow. He wouldn't let them know he was coming early. He would give them a surprise. Life was very uneventful there and it would be nice for them to have a surprise, was his last thought before he put out the light and went to sleep.

21

THE ROAD HOME

The next day it was raining heavily, as it often does in the middle of an English summer. The trees with their thick, dark foliage were dripping. It ought really to have been a beautiful day, Francis felt, as if to reward him for his virtue. He had been going to Paris with a young woman and he had not gone. Surely that was virtue? But then he remembered one of Mr Wardell's sermons. He could see the vicar leaning eagerly over the edge of the pulpit, his red face beaming, saying, 'And aren't we *all*, each *one* of us, apt to think of goodness as something *negative*, something *not* done, rather than something *done*?'

Still, he had not gone to Paris with Barbara. The fact remained. He could hardly remember now what had put the idea into his head. Barbara . . . an attractive girl with dark, passionate eyes, but a cold fish, oh, definitely a cold fish. He smiled, feeling rather pleased with himself, as if he had coined a particularly apt expression.

If only Margaret had been a little more reasonable, all this would never have happened. It hardly occurred to him how lucky he was to have a wife who, besides being a wife, could also be held responsible for everything that had happened to him! Of course all those gossiping North Oxford women were to blame too. Aunt Maude, Mrs Fremantle, old Mrs Killigrew, Edward Killigrew. You could lump him in with the women and never notice the difference. He'd never have had the spirit to do what I've done, thought Francis, chuckling to himself. Mother wouldn't let him.

At that moment the car began to make snorting sounds, as if echoing the chuckle, and suddenly it stopped altogether.

Well, this is a nice thing, thought Francis mildly.

He got out, lifted up the bonnet and peered inside. He knew nothing whatever about the workings of a car. Very gingerly he put out a finger and touched something. Nothing happened. He touched something else. There was oil on his finger but still nothing happened. He pressed the self-starter vigorously and then swung the handle in front. But it was no use.

He began to feel very angry. It wasn't fair. His virtue surely deserved a better reward than this. He was miles from a garage and no car had passed him for at least ten minutes. He prowled round the car, prodding the tyres, as if expecting to find the trouble there. Didn't people sometimes get under cars? The only thing to do was to stand in the road and hope that a car would soon come past. So he planted himself in the middle of the road, ready at any minute to adopt a striking attitude which would force a passer-by to stop.

It was thus that Mr Latimer, bouncing along in his high, old-fashioned two-seater, saw him, a tall, bedraggled and ridiculous figure with both arms upraised, shouting, 'Stop! Please stop!'

'Well, *well*,' said Mr Latimer, drawing up with a jerk. 'What on earth are *you* doing here?'

'What are *you*, if it comes to that?' said Francis crossly.

'I'm coming back from my holiday. Oh, I had a *marvellous* time!' Mr Latimer spoke with such unusual enthusiasm that Francis stared at him in surprise. He noticed that he was wearing a light grey flannel suit and a collar and tie. Had he given up being a clergyman? Francis wondered. Was that why he seemed so elated?

'Now, what's the trouble?' said Mr Latimer, getting out of his car.

Once again the bonnet was lifted and peered under, parts of the engine were poked and prodded, but with no more result than before. Mr Latimer then stood back and began to talk rather technically, using long and important-sounding words. Mr Cleveland joined in. Neither would admit ignorance, although each knew that the other knew nothing whatever about the workings of a car.

'Well,' said Francis at last, 'the only thing to do is to leave it and tell them at the garage. We're quite near Oxford.'

They squashed together into Mr Latimer's car and went bouncing off. It was still raining heavily, and the hood leaked, so that the water fell in a steady trickle onto Francis's shoulder.

Mr Latimer kept up a flow of happy chatter as they drove along. He showed no curiosity about Francis, and did not ever ask where he had been or whether anything interesting had happened in Oxford during his absence. He was full of his holiday in France and the wonderful time he had had—the glorious weather, the beauty of Paris, the delicious food, the historical interest of the cathedrals and churches he and his friend Mr James had seen. He was particularly enthusiastic about these last.

Francis shivered and listened politely. Fancy Latimer being so excited about cathedrals and churches, he thought. But it was not long before he began to understand the reason for this unusual enthusiasm. It appeared that as Mr Latimer and Mr James were looking round a certain cathedral, they had got into conversation with a party of English people. Among them had been a spinster lady with her niece, a beautiful girl of nineteen.

'She's just left her finishing school in Switzerland,' said Mr Latimer, his rapturous tones making poetry of this prosaic statement. 'Her name is Pamela.'

Francis made a donnish little joke about *Pamela, or Virtue Rewarded.* But there was no answering laugh.

'She's awfully pretty, but intelligent too, if you see what I mean,' said Mr Latimer earnestly.

Francis murmured that he did see. It would be a good way of describing Barbara, he thought sardonically.

'I expect I'm boring you terribly with all this,' said Mr Latimer boyishly, 'but I suppose you haven't forgotten what it's like to be young,' he added, in a tone that showed that he supposed no such thing. 'Of course, books are more in your line,' he went on generously. 'The Bodleian and all that.'

Francis hunched his shoulders and shivered. He was afraid he was catching cold. He could think now of nothing nicer than to be in bed, with Margaret fussing over him.

'Well, here's the garage,' said Mr Latimer. 'I'll just hop out and tell them, shall I? How many miles would you say it was?'

When they had given their directions they drove on and were soon in the Banbury Road.

22

THE PRODIGAL RETURNS

'Gone away, Ellen?' said Mrs Cleveland, trying not to appear surprised. One must keep up appearances, even when one came home ready to forgive all and found that there was nobody there to forgive. 'Oh, yes, I remember now,' she went on. 'Mr Cleveland said he might go away if the weather was nice.'

'It's been raining all the time here,' said Ellen flatly. 'Oh, and Miss Doggett and Miss Morrow are in the drawing-room,' she added, with the air of somebody producing a pleasant surprise.

'Oh.' Mrs Cleveland sighed and took off her hat.

'I'm going upstairs to unpack,' said Anthea.

Mrs Cleveland stood for a moment in front of the drawing-room door, plucking up courage to go in. She felt that it needed a great deal of courage to face Miss Doggett when one had had a tiring train journey and was longing for tea.

'Well, Aunt Maude,' she said as brightly as she could, 'we're back.'

Miss Doggett and Miss Morrow were sitting side by side on the sofa. Miss Doggett was wearing a terrifying new hat trimmed with a whole covey of cyclamen-coloured birds, but Miss Morrow was her usual drably comforting self.

'Did you have a nice time?' asked Miss Morrow. 'I'm longing to see all the things you've bought.'

'I got a jumper suit and a hat and some things for the house,' said Mrs Cleveland, relieved to be talking about ordinary things. 'I'll show you,' she added, moving towards the door.

'Margaret, I think this is hardly the time,' said Miss Doggett bluntly. 'I want to know what you are going to do about Francis.'

'Do?' Mrs Cleveland sank down into an armchair. The room looked dusty. One couldn't leave servants alone for a day. Or husbands, she thought heavily. What had Francis been up to now?

'Francis has gone away,' said Miss Doggett clearly, as if repeating a lesson.

Mrs Cleveland felt stupid and helpless. She almost said, How nice!

'Miss Bird has left her lodgings, her landlady told me yesterday.' Miss Doggett paused to let the full import of her words sink in. 'It is obvious that they have gone together,' she added, in case Margaret should be *very* dense.

'But *where*?' asked Mrs Cleveland hopelessly.

'We do not know that, but we shall know in time.' Miss Doggett pursed her lips and the cyclamen birds nodded. 'No doubt he will send you a hotel bill or something of the sort.'

'I've just remembered,' ventured Miss Morrow

218

timidly. 'I was talking to Mr Cleveland one evening and he said something about Paris.' That was the Crampton Hodnet evening, she thought.

'*Paris?*' Miss Doggett shot out the name in a thrilling melodramatic whisper. She turned to her companion. 'Miss Morrow, why did you not tell us this before?'

'I don't know.' Miss Morrow fumbled with her handkerchief. 'I didn't think it was important.'

'Well, *really*, Miss Morrow, it is hardly your business to decide whether a thing is important or not,' stormed Miss Doggett. 'You should certainly have told me. I should have thought you would have realised that when a man says he is going to *Paris* . . .' She waved her hands in a vigorous gesture. 'We can only wait now. Margaret, you have all my sympathy. I am afraid this is going to make a difference to many things. It is not at all likely that Lady Beddoes will allow her son to marry the daughter of divorced parents.' She shook her head gloomily.

At this mention of her daughter, Mrs Cleveland's face clouded over. She was worried about Anthea. She had not seemed at all her usual self in London. She had been depressed about something, very *low*, as Amy would say.

She looked out of the window and saw the postman coming up the drive.

'I expect there will be a letter from Francis,' she said with dignity. 'And then you will see that you are quite wrong.'

'I only hope so,' said Miss Doggett without much conviction.

'Oh, *Mummy!*' Anthea burst into the room. 'A letter from Simon!'

Mrs Cleveland at once forgot all about Francis and Paris and the hotel bill when she saw that her daughter was in tears. 'Darling, what's the matter?' she cried. 'Is something wrong?'

'He's fallen in love with somebody *else*,' wailed Anthea, flinging herself into a chair and brandishing the letter in her hand.

Her mother and Miss Doggett were at once fussing round her, leaving Miss Morrow to reflect on the lack of restraint displayed by young people nowadays. If *I* were jilted, she thought, trying to imagine herself in such a situation, I should keep it to myself. I should never let anyone know that I minded. But then she looked at Anthea's dishevelled golden hair and nervously moving hands and realised that of course she was only twenty. Oh, what a blessing it was to be thirty-six, thought Miss Morrow fervently. Youth took itself so seriously and was therefore the more easily hurt, but, on the other hand, it had certain obvious advantages. There could be *others*, many others, when one lived in Oxford and was as pretty as Anthea.

'Oh, dear, oh, *dear*.' Miss Doggett wrung her hands. Even the cyclamen birds seemed to droop. That Anthea's hopes should be shattered in this way was something that had never occurred to her.

'I think you'd better go upstairs, dear,' said Mrs Cleveland. 'Would you like to go to bed?' she asked uncertainly. 'We'll have tea. I think we all need it.'

'She ought to lie down,' suggested Miss Doggett. 'The shock has been very great, but it will be much worse when she realises it fully.'

'Oh, I don't mind what I do,' sobbed Anthea, allowing herself to be led out of the room by her mother and great-aunt.

Cruel Simon, thought Miss Morrow, seeing the letter lying on the sofa. What had he said? There could surely be no harm in reading it.

She picked up the letter. It was quite short, written on a single sheet of foreign-looking notepaper.

Dear Anthea,

I expect you have been wondering why I hav'ent answered your letters. The truth is that I have been meaning to write for some time but hav'ent had a moment till now. I think you will agree that it has been evident for some time that we were growing rather weary of each other's company and that it would be no use our continuing to meet under such circumstances. As a matter of fact I have met somebody else out here, and it is not unlikely that we shall become engaged in the near future. You must meet her sometime, I'm sure you would be great friends. I do hope this won't be too great a shock to you, dear. You know I would hate to hurt you, but I think you will agree that I have done the kindest thing in telling you the truth. I shall always be awfully glad to see you in Chester Square whenever you happen to be in town. We have had some good times together, hav'ent we?

Yours –
Simon

Miss Morrow could hardly help laughing when she had finished reading. The sprawling, childish writing and curious parliamentary phraseology seemed to her infinitely pathetic. 'It has been evident for some time . . . it is not unlikely

221

that . . .' Miss Morrow jumped forward thirty years and saw Simon as the Secretary of State for Something, answering questions in the House. But then, she thought, with cynicism unsuitable in one who was not a woman of the world, he would avoid the truth at all costs. And he would probably have a secretary who knew where to put the apostrophe in 'haven't'.

She put the letter back on the sofa and looked out of the window. It was a pity, she thought, that romantic love didn't last. 'The Blessed that immortal be, from change in love alone are free.' And not even Belgravia and North Oxford, however blessed they might be in most things, could expect quite as much as that.

She stood at the window for some time, watching the people hurrying by in the rain—Miss Nollard and Miss Foxe, evidently going out to tea, old Lady Halkin's companion hurrying home with a white cardboard box of cakes. And then she saw a familiar, high, old-fashioned two-seater drawing up at the gate. Mr Latimer and Mr Cleveland got out.

Oh, dear, oh, dear, everything's happening all at once, thought Miss Morrow hopelessly. First Anthea and now *him* coming back.

'Where's Margaret?' demanded Mr Cleveland accusingly.

'She's upstairs,' said Miss Morrow.

He rushed out of the room, leaving Miss Morrow still at the window and Mr Latimer hovering in the doorway.

'Have you had a nice holiday?' Miss Morrow asked.

'Oh, *marvellous*!' Once Mr Latimer was started he babbled on happily, as he had to Mr Cleveland,

222

about the weather, Paris, the food. But after the cathedrals he stopped expectantly.

'It must have been very interesting,' murmured Miss Morrow. 'I'm glad you had nice weather. It's been rather wet here most of the time, and of course there's been this trouble hanging over us.'

'Yes, yes, of course.' Mr Latimer brushed aside the trouble with no more concern than if it had been a fly settling on his forehead. 'Miss Morrow,' he declared, with more diffidence than usual, 'something very important has happened to me, and I want you to be the first to know of it.'

Miss Morrow looked startled. Surely he wasn't going to propose to her again? she wondered for one wild moment. But no, it could hardly be that. From the way he put it, it sounded as if it was something that had happened in France. She remembered that he had spoken much of churches and cathedrals; indeed, most of his holiday seemed to have been spent in one or another. Could it be that he had *gone over to Rome*? she wondered, suddenly enlightened. A change of this kind was usually regarded as something very important. She believed his friend Mr James was very High, and now that she came to notice it she saw that he was not wearing a clerical collar, though of course he had told her that he never did on holiday. One got to know people better without it. They talked to one more freely. The absence of a clerical collar added to the joviality of the party. People did not always realise, as Dr Fremantle did, that a man's a man however he wears his collar.

'Something important?' she said. 'But why should *I* be the first to know?'

'You are my friend,' said Mr Latimer simply,

'and you will understand better than anybody else. Actually I've told Mr Cleveland and I shall tell Miss Doggett, of course, as it will make a difference to the future.'

Certainly, thought Miss Morrow. A Roman Catholic priest could hardly live with two women. 'What is it?' she asked again.

A coy but not unattractive smile lighted up Mr Latimer's handsome face. 'I have fallen in love,' he said, with impressive simplicity.

'Oh, I see.' Miss Morrow had difficulty in keeping her disappointment out of her voice. She had somehow expected something less ordinary. And yet one must be reasonable and remember that falling in love is never ordinary to the people who indulge in it. Indeed, it is perhaps the only thing that is being done all over the world every day that is still unique.

'How splendid,' she said, filling her voice with enthusiasm. 'Do tell me about it—if you'd like to, that is.'

Mr Latimer needed no encouragement. Out it all came—the cathedral, the English tourists, Pamela and her aunt, pretty and intelligent, if you see what I mean . . . Oh, it had been a wonderful holiday!

'I knew it would happen to you some day,' said Miss Morrow, feeling rather elderly. 'And of course she returns your love?'

Mr Latimer looked rather shocked. 'Oh, yes, of course,' he said. 'We're unofficially engaged in a way.'

Miss Morrow nodded. A great unrequited passion was hardly in Mr Latimer's line, she realised, the sort of love that lingers on through many years, dying sometimes and then coming back

224

like a twinge of rheumatism in the winter, so that you feel it in your knee when you are nearing the top of a long flight of stairs. 'Unofficially engaged in a way' was perhaps after all more suitable.

'Well, well, what a lot of things seem to have happened this afternoon.' She sighed. She started to ask Mr Latimer about how he had met Mr Cleveland and to tell him about Anthea and the letter from Simon, but he was so obviously not taking in a word she said that she gave it up and began to wonder how he would ever be able to write his Sunday sermons. Then she started to wonder what was going on elsewhere in the house. Poor Mrs Cleveland would have her hands full now, with her husband and her daughter to deal with, she thought.

At that moment Ellen came into the room bringing tea, and Miss Morrow ventured upstairs to tell the others it was ready. Halfway up she met Mr Cleveland coming down. He looked rather disgruntled.

'Anyone would think the world had come to an end,' he muttered. 'She hasn't even noticed I've come back.'

Miss Morrow effaced herself into the shadows by the Gothic umbrella stand, which had been a wedding present from Miss Doggett. 'Tea's ready,' she said in a neutral tone.

'Tea!' he called loudly.

Miss Doggett and Mrs Cleveland hurried into the room.

'Anthea doesn't feel like coming down,' said Mrs Cleveland to nobody in particular. 'I'll just take her a cup of tea.'

'Oh, dear, this *is* a tragedy. Poor Anthea, I've

225

never seen anybody so broken,' wailed Miss Doggett. 'He seemed so devoted. I really cannot understand it.'

'She says she might fancy a piece of walnut cake,' said Mrs Cleveland, coming back with a plate.

'Will somebody tell me exactly what has happened?' asked Francis mildly. 'I'm quite in the dark. Is Simon dead or something?'

'Worse,' said Miss Doggett, shaking the cyclamen birds vigorously. 'It would almost have been better if he had been.'

'A fate worse than death?' said Francis frivolously. 'I thought that was usually reserved for young girls.'

'Like my cousin Bertha in Paris,' said Miss Morrow, unable to stop herself.

Francis suddenly looked very embarrassed and began offering cake to everybody, although they all had something on their plates.

'A brilliant match,' Miss Doggett intoned. 'It would have been such a splendid thing for Anthea.'

'Well, to tell you the truth,' said Mrs Cleveland, coming back into the room, 'I don't think it would have been a very good thing. They were both so young, and Anthea will meet lots of other people. But poor child, she has cried so much. It's terrible not being able to do anything for her.'

'Yes,' said Miss Morrow, 'and it's such cold comfort to say that Time is a Great Healer.'

'There are some sorrows that Time can never heal,' said Miss Doggett. 'And to think,' she added in the same breath, 'that she might have had a house in Chester Square!'

Poor Miss Doggett, thought Miss Morrow, watching her. She feels it as much as Anthea does.

The shock of Simon's letter had put the other affair completely out of her mind. Indeed, nobody was taking any notice of Francis Cleveland, not even his wife, who seemed much more concerned over the weakness of the tea and whether Anthea could have managed a bigger piece of cake.

'She always has such a good appetite,' she said. 'I do hope she won't fret too much. It's lucky we're going to the sea soon. A holiday is just what she needs.'

'Yes, a holiday can make a great difference,' said Mr Latimer from his corner. 'I had a *marvellous* time in France.'

'I'm so glad,' said Mrs Cleveland politely. 'Did you meet some interesting people?'

'Oh, yes, as a matter of fact I did . . .'

And so for the third time that afternoon he told his story. It seemed to gain a little in the telling, Miss Morrow thought. This time they were actually *engaged*, there was nothing unofficial about it.

'Well, *well*!' Miss Doggett seemed unable to decide what attitude to adopt towards this unexpected news. 'What did you say her name was?'

'Pamela,' said Mr Latimer rapturously, taking a chocolate biscuit. 'Pamela Pimlico.'

'Not a relation of Lord Pimlico?' said Miss Doggett hopefully. 'It's an uncommon name.'

'As a matter of fact she's his youngest daughter,' said Mr Latimer modestly.

'Well, this is splendid. I believe she is a *charming* girl.' Miss Doggett was all smiles. The cyclamen birds bobbed about so vigorously that nobody would have been surprised to see them leave the hat and fly away.

'Oh, look,' said Miss Morrow, 'here come the vicar and Mrs Wardell. Are you going to tell them the news?'

'Why, of course,' said Miss Doggett, who had at once taken charge of everything. 'Agnes, what *do* you think, Mr Latimer is engaged to one of Lord Pimlico's girls. Isn't it splendid?'

'Have you got the ring yet?'

'Well, no, not yet,' Mr Latimer admitted, 'but I've been thinking about it.'

Diamonds and platinum, thought Miss Morrow, it was inevitable. A platinum ring set with a moderate-sized solitaire diamond. Miss Morrow was sure that in the matter of engagement rings he would have conventional taste, and as he was only a curate, the size of the diamond could hardly be more than moderate, if that. It might even be *very* small, like the head of a pin, the sort of ring the poorer undergraduates gave their girl-friends. But it would be a diamond.

'I'd thought of getting a solitaire diamond set in platinum,' said Mr Latimer, fulfilling Miss Morrow's expectations. 'I think she'd like that.'

'If I were ever engaged I should like a large, semi-precious stone, like an amethyst or a topaz,' said Miss Morrow.

Miss Doggett seemed to think this very amusing. 'Well, Miss Morrow, we must let Mr Killigrew know that. I'm sure he would oblige.'

'Do you know,' said Mrs Wardell, suddenly gripping Mr Latimer's arm, 'I'd got *quite* the wrong idea. I actually thought there was something between you and Miss Morrow!'

Miss Morrow joined as heartily as anyone in the laughter which followed this amazing admission.

228

Everyone seemed to think it was very funny, although Mr Latimer's laughter sounded a little forced.

'Agnes gets such odd ideas,' said Mr Wardell proudly. 'Indeed, I think we all do at times,' he added in a more serious tone, shooting a glance at Mr Cleveland as if to make sure that his eyes had not deceived him. 'We sometimes get hold of the wrong end of the stick. Indeed, we may even imagine that we have got hold of a stick which turns out not to be a stick at all.'

'Oh, Ben, you *are* getting involved,' said his wife. 'I'm sure nobody knows what you're talking about.'

The babble of conversation went on and grew so lively that Mrs Cleveland began to wonder whether her uninvited guests would ever go. It seemed so ridiculous to think that at an important time like this one's house should be full of people who refused to go. She felt she would like to stand up and clap her hands and say 'Shoo!' as if they were all a lot of chickens. But being a polite woman she urged them to eat more bread and butter and more cake, and even made pleasant conversation, when she wasn't peering into the teapot or ringing for more hot water.

Francis watched her dispassionately. He supposed it was too much to expect her to notice him, even when they had so much to talk about and he had come back at what he imagined was an unexpected time. He had a headache from shaking about in that wretched little car, and he felt so *hot*, with cold shivers running down his back at the same time. Perhaps there were some aspirins in the medicine cupboard. He crept unnoticed from the room and went upstairs. And when everybody had at last gone, Mrs Cleveland found him sitting on his bed, looking bedraggled and pathetic.

'Why, Francis dear, I don't believe you're well,' she said, hurrying towards him and catching hold of his hand. 'You look quite funny.'

'I feel hot and shivery and I've got a headache,' he said gratefully. 'I think I've caught a chill.'

'I'll take your temperature,' she said. 'I expect you ought to be in bed.'

'Listen,' he said, when she returned with the thermometer, 'I didn't go to Paris.'

'I know you didn't, dear,' she said soothingly, popping the thermometer into his mouth.

Muttering sounds came from him; he was trying to say something.

'Hush, Francis, you'll break it,' she said. 'You can tell me when it's over.'

There was a silence, during which Mrs Cleveland looked round the room and noticed that the mantelpiece needed dusting. And why, she wondered, was there an unopened bottle of wine on the dressing-table? Whatever had Francis been doing with himself during her absence?

'Now, we'll see.' She took the thermometer out of his mouth and examined it. 'Oh, dear, it's up a little,' she said. 'You must go straight to bed. I'll get you a hot water bottle.'

'Wait, Margaret, you must listen,' he said petulantly. 'I didn't go to Paris. I only went as far as Dover.'

It sounded rather silly like that, he thought weakly.

'I didn't go to Paris. I only went to Dover,' he repeated, but she had gone out of the room, and when she came back she seemed so concerned

230

about whether the bottle might be too hot, whether they had any quinine in the house, and even whether he might not be going to get pneumonia, that the fact of where he had been and where he had not been slid naturally into the background. There was nothing Mrs Cleveland liked better than looking after an invalid.

23

OLD FRIENDS AND NEW

Anthea was in her bedroom, applying a deep fuchsia-coloured varnish to her nails. It was the beginning of term again, and Simon's friend Christopher, who was still up, had asked her to lunch. It was important that she should look nice. She had been reading an article in *Woman and Beauty* which said that you shouldn't let yourself go just because your young man had fallen in love with somebody else. You should go out and get some new clothes, a new hairstyle, a new lipstick, even a new young man. You would soon begin to feel better. Indeed, after the first shock had worn off and her wounded vanity had recovered a little, Anthea seemed to be no different from her usual self, except that she now had an excuse to buy a great many new clothes and to appear with her lips and nails painted in rather bold and alarming colours.

It was a lovely October day, and Oxford was full of hopeful young freshmen, smoking new-looking pipes, fighting their way through Woolworth's and emerging triumphant with kettles and lampshades. Groups of chattering young women, some plain and spectacled, others with some degree of beauty and elegance, crowded into Blackwell's to buy second-hand copies of the Pass Moderations set books. The entrance to the front quadrangle of Randolph was blocked by a group of rich young men newly arrived from town. Suède shoes, pin-striped flannels, teddy-bear coats and check caps—Anthea knew the uniform so well. Any one of them might have been Simon. They stood aside for her to pass and their blank faces lighted up for a moment as they watched her making for Christopher's staircase.

'I've never been in this part of Randolph before,' said Anthea, making conversation.

'These are my new rooms,' said Christopher. 'Rather nicer than my others, don't you think?'

Anthea, who had noticed very little difference, made some polite comment. Have I got to eat my lunch with this enormous photograph of Simon facing me? she wondered. It was one she particularly disliked. His charming, usually rather childish face had assumed for the occasion an expression which had in it something of Napoleon and something of Sir Oswald Mosley and almost nothing of Simon Beddoes.

Christopher saw her looking and cursed his tactlessness. He ought to have put it away. Simon would never have made a faux pas like that. That was why he had always got everything he wanted.

'You look marvellous,' he began and was just going to pay her a pretty compliment when his elderly scout came creaking into the room with lunch.

'I hope you'll like what I've ordered,' he said anxiously. It occurred to him that as she must have had so many meals in Randolph it would perhaps have been better to take her to the George. This luncheon party wasn't going to be a success, he thought unhappily.

But somehow it was. It seemed that Anthea liked chicken better than anything else in the world, that she adored Liebfraumilch above all wines, that the chocolate mousse was the most marvellous she had ever tasted. And when the old, creaking and, one felt, rather disapproving scout had cleared away the things, it seemed perfectly right and natural that Christopher should kiss her.

'Did you know that *I* loved you too?' he said earnestly. 'But Simon always had everything.'

Anthea felt she wanted to giggle. He kissed just like Simon. He might have *been* Simon, except that he was slightly taller and had fair hair. She felt curiously comforted as she laid her head against his rough tweed shoulder.

'You've always got me, darling,' he said.

Yes, thought Anthea philosophically, and if I hadn't got you I'd have Freddie or Patrick or somebody else. Everything went on just the same in Oxford from year to year. It was only the people who might be different. The pattern never varied.

When she got home just before teatime she found her father talking about a class of eight young women he had promised to take for Donne and Dryden.

'It's nice that term has begun,' said Mrs Cleveland. 'The long vac always seems so *very* long, doesn't it?'

After two months, it was difficult to realise that

233

there had ever been such a person as Barbara Bird. Even Edward Killigrew seemed to have forgotten all about it and was now full of a new and very exciting scandal about an old clergyman who had been reading in the library during the long vacation.

Mrs Cleveland was sometimes inclined to congratulate herself on her handling of what might have been a very awkward situation. She had managed things very cunningly, she thought. And then she would remember that really she could hardly be said to have managed things at all.

This year, she thought, there will be *eight* young women to deal with, but everyone knew that eight were less dangerous than one.

'Who shall we have to tea on Sunday?' she asked. 'We must get going straight away.'

Anthea groaned. 'Oh, dear, on it goes! All these hopeful young men coming up every year, and I suppose it will never change. There will always be North Oxford tea parties as long as there's any University left.'

'I shall get some large, *solid* cakes,' said Mrs Cleveland thoughtfully. 'After all, people don't really notice what they eat.'

'No, they come to see us,' said Anthea quite happily. 'I shall wear my new red dress.'

The life of Oxford went on in so much the same way that she would hardly be surprised to see Simon coming to tea on Sunday as he had come on that first Sunday of term a year ago. And if he did not come, surely there would be somebody among their guests who looked and talked like him and who would fall in love with her. It was a melancholy thought, she decided, glad that one can never live the past over again.

'Let's have Christopher,' she suggested rather self-consciously. 'He said he was free this Sunday.'

Mrs Cleveland smiled but made no comment. 'And we'd better ask the good old steadies like Henry and Jock and Edgar Cherry, and perhaps Michael and Gabriel. Or will Aunt Maude be wanting them? I always feel that they're more hers than ours.'

'Michael and Gabriel of course,' said Miss Doggett. 'They would be so disappointed not to be asked.'

'And you said something about Canon Teep's nephew,' said Miss Morrow, who was making a neat list.

'Oh, yes, and we might ask Mr Bompas too. I've always been meaning to ask him about his aunt. *And*'—Miss Doggett paused impressively— 'Viscount St Pancras. I have discovered that I was at school with a relative of his. He is coming up to Randolph this term. I believe he did *brilliantly* at Eton. They have a delightful town residence in Belgrave Square. I thought he might be a nice friend for Anthea,' said Miss Doggett, putting her intentions rather mildly.

Of course it had been a terrible tragedy for Anthea, losing Simon—as far as Miss Doggett was concerned he might just as well have been dead and buried—but perhaps God *was* all-wise after all, she thought reverently. One knew that He moved in a mysterious way His wonders to perform. Might it not be that what had happened was part of some Divine Plan to set Anthea free for even Higher Things than the son of a sometime British Ambassador in Warsaw? Chester Square was very desirable, but *Belgrave* Square . . . Miss Doggett's imagination stopped short, as it might have done in trying to form a picture of Heaven.

'It is a good thing that Anthea likes young men,' she said aloud, 'because he is only eighteen.' *Oswald William Robert FitzAuber, Viscount St Pancras. b. 1919.* That had been a little disappointing, Miss Doggett felt, regretting that undergraduates had to get younger every year. Still, it could not be helped, and where there was life there was hope, so to speak.

Miss Morrow tried to look intelligent, but she found it all too confusing. 'We shall miss Mr Latimer when he's married,' she remarked.

'Yes, indeed we shall.' Miss Doggett sighed heavily. 'I dare say he will get a living soon.'

Crampton Hodnet would be nice, thought Miss Morrow. Such a pretty village.

'And that will mean another curate,' said Miss Doggett, as if this consoling truth had just dawned on her.

'Why, yes,' said Miss Morrow brightly, 'so it will.'

Miss Doggett would get another Mr Latimer, and Anthea would get another Simon. There was really nothing in this world that could not be replaced. If I were suddenly *taken*, Miss Morrow thought, a substitute could easily be found. A dim, obedient woman, who would wind Miss Doggett's wool and put the buns into the Balmoral tin, as I shall be putting them on Saturday.

The days of the week slipped by, and at last it was Sunday. Viscount St Pancras had written to say that he would be delighted to come to tea, and so Maggie had been told to make some rather more elaborate cakes than were usually given to the undergraduates.

After lunch Miss Doggett went up for her rest as usual and, as Mr Latimer was staying with Pamela's people, who, to Miss Morrow's secret disappointment, did not live in Pimlico at all but in Kensington, Miss Morrow was by herself.

She sat gazing meditatively at the vase of coloured teasels which filled the fireless dining-room grate. Yesterday had been warm, but today was cold and raining. And yet it was somehow right that it should be so, she felt. It had been just like this at the beginning of the last academic year, which had brought so many new people into their lives: Mr Latimer, Simon Beddoes, Barbara Bird ... They had come and some of them had gone as if they had never been.

Miss Morrow began to hum aimlessly without knowing what she hummed, but after a while she recognised the tune as that of a hymn which used to fascinate her as a child.

> Within the churchyard, side by side,
> Are many long low graves:
> And some have stones set over them
> On some the green grass waves ...

Well, we all came to it sooner or later, whether in Bayswater or Belgravia, in North Oxford or Crampton Hodnet. She looked at the drooping branches of the monkey-puzzle. It will be here when we are all gone, she thought.

And then she remembered that there was really no need to sit in a North Oxford dining-room at ten past three on a wet Sunday afternoon thinking about death and graves unless one wanted to. A simple movement could fill the room with rich, unsuitable music from Radio Luxembourg. She switched on the wireless, and the sound of it poured out into the room. Except for a slight scratchiness of the records it might have been the very same music that she had listened to this time a year ago, for modern dance tunes sounded very much alike to Miss Morrow's unworldly ear.

After twenty minutes of music Miss Morrow went upstairs to change her dress, and shortly afterwards the rustle of mackintoshes was heard in the hall.

In they came, a great herd of them all at once, Michael and Gabriel, Mr Bompas, Willie Teep, Miss Jennings and Miss Matador from Somerville, and, at the end, a thin, nervous young man with spectacles, who did not look as if he would be at all equal to the rich cakes which had been made in his honour—Viscount St Pancras.

'Oh, Miss Doggett, isn't it *frightful*, we're in our third year,' said Michael and Gabriel, rushing to greet her. 'Change and decay in all around we see, but not *here.*'

'No, I do not think you will find any change and decay in Leamington Lodge,' said Miss Doggett, smiling.

And Miss Morrow was inclined to agree with her.

238